BLIND EYE

BLIND EYE

Marilyn Todd

Severn House Large Print
London & New York

This first large print edition published 2009
in Great Britain and the USA by
SEVERN HOUSE PUBLISHERS LTD of
9-15 High Street, Sutton, Surrey, SM1 1DF.
First world regular print edition published 2007 by
Severn House Publishers Ltd., London and New York.

British Library Cataloguing in Publication Data

Todd, Marilyn
  Blind eye. - Large print ed.
  1. Secret service - Greece - Sparta (Extinct city) -
  Fiction 2. Traitors - Greece - Sparta (Extinct city) -
  Fiction 3. Detective and mystery stories 4. Large type
  books
  I. Title
  823.9'14[F]

  ISBN-13: 978-0-7278-7758-1

Printed and bound in Great Britain by
MPG Books Ltd, Bodmin, Cornwall.

One

The young stallion tottered to his feet and stretched the long night from his legs. The rest of the herd was still asleep, but the yearling sensed a new beginning in this warm Sicilian spring. And as the first of Apollo's rays burst over the cave-riddled hills that formed a backdrop to the pastures, he snickered.

Until yesterday, each day in his short life had been the same. He rose, he ate, he frolicked, and from time to time he slaked his thirst in the waters of the River Kedos from which the great plain took its name. But yesterday was different. Yesterday, he'd glimpsed the future—

He baulked, of course, when they first put the bridle to his mouth. This was an outrage! Monstrous! And for as long as it took for the shadow of the umbrella pine to pass across the bank of yellow spurge, he'd kicked and bucked and raged. Then he noticed how the older horses had also had blankets thrown across their backs, and that they carried men upon them. Curious, he watched horse and rider trot, then canter, then finally gallop over the wide open grasslands, and these riders weren't like the herdsmen he was used to. They were covered head to foot in metal, the same colour as the sea shimmering behind him in the breaking dawn. Silver. Shining. Polished. And as hooves and breastplates echoed like thunderclaps, the yearling found their thrill contagious.

Today, the sense of new beginnings was even stronger. It didn't come through the dew that glistened on the pasture, or the crackle of the sleeping herdsmen's fire. There was no rustle in the junipers, no change in the soft breeze, but it was there. Pulsing. Throbbing. Pushing through the soil and surging through the clouds. And, as the soft mist that hung over the plain began to clear, his young keen ears picked up a sound.

A soft hiss, with a strangely musical twang, ending in a thwack.

Another new experience. Something else that excited him. Then one of the mares began to scream. Rolling, writhing, she shrieked and kicked, and suddenly the whole field was thrashing in a sea of red. Panicked and confused, he raced to his mother, but his mother didn't move. The yearling nudged her with his nose. Inhaled the same scent that he recalled from his birth. Blood, which ought to have been comforting, but now brought only terror, and as he fought to nuzzle her awake, a burning pain slammed into him. He saw a feathered stick embedded in his neck. Felt something sticky trickle down his throat.

Huddled tight against his mother's flank, the stallion watched his bright new future leach into the meadow.

Two

Four hundred miles away, on the other side of the ocean, a very different day was dawning. Thrusting her feet into a pair of pale blue kidskin sandals, the High Priestess of the river god Eurotas marched across the courtyard, oblivious to the fig trees that scrambled against its white-washed walls and the pomegranates that provided welcome shade.

'You can put this morning's ritual log back on the pile,' she told the Guardian of the Sacred Flame. 'I'm consigning this instead.'

She tossed a roll of crumpled vellum to the tripod, but not before the Guardian's eagle eye had glimpsed the royal seal.

'An offering which not only burns faster than our sacred oak,' he observed dryly, 'but one which I suspect will burn rather hot.'

'Then we must pray that royal wax cools quickly, Perses.' Iliona gave the scroll a good, hard prod with the fire iron. 'And if you could collect the ash at your earliest convenience, I'd be grateful. The King specifically requested a prompt reply.'

'I don't suppose I could talk you into laying on a ceremonial olive branch instead?'

'No, my dear friend, you cannot.' It was not for

the King to tell the High Priestess how to spend her temple's income, much less dictate what manner of worshippers Eurotas should be attracting. 'I won't have my shrine turned into a political arena,' she added crisply.

Peace had opened up the world. A thousand city states were forced to put aside their differences to fight the Persian armies, and in doing so discovered strength in unification. As a result, giant strides in science and technology were being made, trade was booming, and a fresh new style of thinking had been inspired.

Only philosophy was proving a double-edged sword...

For those who'd grown fat on this rising tide of progress, worship had become a platform for power, their lavish donations giving them free rein to impose policies that suited their own interests. But for every triumph, there were a thousand losers. Inevitably, they were the poor and the enslaved.

'The King might not value barley cakes in the same light as silver or gold,' Iliona said. 'But it's not right to oust these people, simply because he fancies a new showcase for his treasures or needs rich men's backing for his plans. They have nowhere else to turn.' Someone needed to make them feel there was at least *some* purpose in their lives.

Perses watched the edges of the scroll blacken and curl. 'You do realize that the King wants to appoint his sister as High Priestess?'

'Then he should have given her the job three

years ago, instead of offering it to me.'

'Unfortunately, he has the backing of the Council of Elders, and gestures such as these are being perceived as inflammatory.' One hand tapped the smoking tripod while the other indicated the pillars, posts and lintels that had been garlanded with gorse.

'It's the spring equinox, Perses. A triumph of equality, a celebration of balance. We must honour the gods with our rejoicing.' Iliona spread her arms in a theatrical gesture. 'Eurotas is one of the few rivers in Greece to flow all the year round. The people of Sparta are truly blessed.'

One eyebrow lifted mournfully. 'Save your eulogizing for the crowds tonight. As far as the King's concerned, your feasting the rabble in a shrine turned yellow with furze is extravagant to the point of recklessness.'

'Bending to pressure can only weaken Eurotas's standing,' she tossed back. 'The King knows my views about demonstrating strength through belief in my convictions.'

'If he didn't before, I'm sure burning royal reprimands and sending back the ashes will make it clear,' Perses murmured.

Iliona watched basket bearers glide over marble floors on silent feet while handmaidens fluttered back and forth, singing paeans to the dawn. On the far side of the courtyard, the waters in the bowl of divination were being purified by white-robed acolytes. Cats too fat to catch the temple mice suckled kittens in the shade.

'You just concentrate on keeping the Eternal Flame from going out and consigning Sparta to oblivion,' Iliona said. 'Leave me to worry about the King.'

'With a wife who nags, a mother-in-law who shares my roof, six small children and a dog who shares my bed, oblivion cannot come too quickly, I assure you.'

'Liar! You love them all. But there's one more favour, I'm afraid.' She pulled at her earlobe. 'The thing is, Perses, I need a scapegoat.'

A worried look crept into his face. 'For the King?'

Iliona laughed. 'To dress up in goatskins and have me drive you out of the precinct, you idiot.'

The goat represented winter, and his banishment on the night of the equinox put a symbolic end to the ills he had inflicted.

'Again?' The Guardian groaned. 'Couldn't you find someone else to be the butt of public humiliation this year, my lady?'

'Easily. But who else would give the children piggy-back rides, then roar like a lion, snarl like a wolf and play pin-the-tail-on-the-scapegoat as well?'

'Madam.' He inclined his head gravely. 'You give me no choice but to accept.'

Since they both knew this to be true, Iliona said nothing, while out along the river, herons stalked the first fish of the morning and the low of oxen played bass to the skylark's soprano. Across in the Great Hall, the first of the petitioners had already arrived, and she sighed as the

10

cloak-maker knelt in obeisance. Poor sod. So preoccupied with the future that the present completely passed him by. Yet it was not to the Hall of Prophecy that the High Priestess's pale blue kidskin sandals took her. Casting a watchful glance over her shoulder, she slipped out of the courtyard and tapped one-two, one-two-three on the door of the temple physician. After a moment, the bar on the inside lifted softly.

Checking again that nobody saw her, the High Priestess slipped inside.

Three

'Is it true?'

The boy struggled up from the treatment couch. His head was pushed back down by a young woman with hair blacker than a raven's wing, who continued to bathe his lash wounds without looking up.

'Is it true?' the boy persisted through a mouthful of blanket. 'That soldiers are already searching the temple for me?'

Iliona thought, news travels fast. She'd only just seen the cloak-maker herself. 'There's only one visitor,' she assured him, 'and he's after salvation, not you. You're quite safe.'

'For now,' the girl muttered, blotting his back with a clean strip of linen.

'The doctor's right.' Twelve years old and he didn't even wince when she drizzled vinegar into the wheals. 'Sooner or later, the *Krypteia* will catch up with me.'

'Don't you believe it,' Iliona told him. She'd cheated the bastards before, she would do it again. With luck, it would give them insomnia into the bargain. 'Jocasta?'

'The cuts aren't deep, but his skin's shredded like flax and he's lost a lot of blood.' Expert hands applied a poultice of vervain and hyssop. 'Nothing a fortnight's rest won't put right, though.'

'Two weeks?' The boy's voice rose several octaves. 'Two hours is bad enough!'

Iliona watched the poultice bound in place with a bandage and thought, according to the season, she'd watch barley being scythed or beans being sown, and sometimes the Reaping Hymn would carry on the breeze, other times it might be the bleating of goats, or simply the croaking of frogs in the night. Never once, though, in all her thirty-four years, had she heard the tread of Sparta's secret police – but they were here. The *Krypteia* was everywhere. Unseen, yet all-seeing. Unmoving, while observing every movement. Her hands clenched into fists. What depths of inhumanity did these men plumb, to allow a child to be whipped to ribbons?

'I'm grateful for the physicking, but you shouldn't have brought me here,' the boy said.

'Then you shouldn't have passed out under my

12

window,' Iliona smiled back. Above the river, a ragged vee of migrating cranes trumpeted and honked against the backdrop of a cloudless azure sky. 'What's your name?'

'It don't matter. I'll be out of here in a minute.'

'True,' Jocasta said. 'But you'll need to build your strength up first.'

He let her spoon soup down a throat that had no idea that henbane had been added, and as it drugged him into sleepy obedience, the flight of the cranes became mirrored in the deep, dark, swirling pool over which the temple stood sentinel. In the old days, when a king died, his corpse used to be sacrificed to the demon who was supposed to live in the lake. Today, of course, only traitors were thrown in. The trouble was, Iliona thought, they were thrown in alive.

'I'll drop by later,' she whispered. 'In the meantime, keep the door locked and open it only on our agreed signal.'

Risking her own life was one thing. Risking Jocasta's was a different matter entirely.

Across in the Great Hall, the swathes of gorse reflected double in the marble, bringing sunshine to even the darkest corner. Musicians added to the gaiety with reed pipes, drums and lyres, while fountains babbled and scented incense wafted up in spirals from copper braziers on the walls. At the sound of the High Priestess's footsteps, the cloak-maker jumped up, purified his fingers in the lustral bowl, then delved into his satchel to bring out so many coloured ribbons that the almond trees around the precinct would probably bow with the weight where he'd hung them.

'Great Lady of the Lake who counts the grains of sand on the shore and measures the seas in the ocean, I beseech your help.'

What was it this time, she wondered. His bunions? Had his chickens stopped laying? Or was it another dream about owls that he wanted interpreting?

'You hear the voice of the voiceless and see through the eyes of the blind.' Shaking hands unwrapped a shoulder of mutton with which he hoped to appease the bloodlust of the demon. 'You walk the wind and look down on the actions of mortals.'

Did she indeed?

'My wife ails badly, my lady. I fear she is dying.'

'Tell me the symptoms.'

Not that she needed to hear them. The last of the wine that had been fermenting for the past six months in vats had just been strained into amphorae for ageing, an annual process which culminated in the Pitcher Festival. Strangely enough, the cloak-maker's wife fell unaccountably ill the day afterwards, complaining of pain behind the eyes, a furred tongue, a stomach that refused food and...

'...a head that pounds louder than the blacksmith's anvil.'

Iliona swallowed her smile. 'Then we must call upon the gods to manifest a miracle. Come.'

Along the fields that bordered the river, a

14

platoon of labourers armed with mattocks and hoes waged war on their enemy, the caterpillars determined to decimate vegetables that had been cosseted through autumn gales and winter rains and destroy the tender shoots of the new season's grain. None of these workers suffered from hangovers, she noticed, but then they were *helots*. Serfs, slaves, call them what you will, they still were barred from Spartan festivities.

'Take a seat in the plane grove,' she instructed the cloak-maker. 'Close your eyes, and when I tell you to open them, I want you to recount to me all the sounds you have heard.'

It didn't make a scrap of difference that his problems could be solved here and now, on the spot. Supplicants needed to feel they were under divine protection, but the trouble was, they also believed the Olympians were too busy with heroes and kings to bother with ordinary folk. A river god, now, that was different. Eurotas wouldn't have the same calls on his time as Zeus or Poseidon, just as he'd be more sympathetic to the marshy swamps that congested their lungs and understand about the wolves that snaffled their lambs. But at the end of the day, a god was still a god and even though his temple towered ten times above their heads and the approach to it was almost regal in its splendour, they would not come if Eurotas was accessible. Iliona's solution was her claim to prophecy.

Never underestimate the power of illusion.

So she left the cloak-maker in the sacred grove, where white doves cooed and bronze chimes pealed, and after a suitable interval in which she'd checked that the sacrificial altar had been decked properly with turf and that the beacon fires would burn long into the night, she went through the motion of interpreting the sounds.

'At the place where two winds blow and the tortoise marries the mare, that is where you will find the cure for your wife.'

'My lady.' The cloak-maker was close to tears as he kissed the gold hem of the oracle's robe. 'How can I ever thank you? At a place where...?'

'Two winds blow.' In other words, the cross-roads.

'Where the tortoise marries the hare?'

'Mare,' she corrected patiently. 'I am seeing visions of a mare.'

A runner had placed a phial containing one of Jocasta's potions inside a rusty army helmet – the helmet being the tortoise, the plume being the mare – and what did riddles matter, providing people went home happy?

The day passed as it usually passed. More petitioners came, more riddles were set, more dreams interpreted in a way that would set their minds at rest. Libations were poured, the bowl filled three times before the fourth was poured out, because the ritual made all the difference to these people. There were letters to dictate and accounts to keep tally of, yet with every task that she supervised, Iliona was constantly on the alert.

Was that one of the temple cats? Or something

16

more sinister shifting through the shadows?

Was it the wind that rippled through the reed beds? Or a darker force on the move?

She couldn't walk the winds, of course, or look down on the actions of mortals. But as she checked the treasury records against the reserves, she was well aware that sacred ground offered no protection for the boy and that her reputation counted for nothing with the *Krypteia*. Smashing pottery offerings that required ritual breakage, she pictured mountains that dazzled with snow in the winter. Heat hazes that melted the summer horizons. Herbs that grew wild in the hills. How, in the name of all the gods, could a land of such beauty give rise to so heinous a monster...?

By mid-afternoon, it had become a challenge just to mount the temple steps. Pilgrims flooding in for the equinox were making sacrifice here, pouring libations there, chanting, weeping and beating their breasts, because they hadn't trekked all this way to play down their piety. Thankfully, though, not a single sound penetrated the sacred inner chamber, and, closing the door, Iliona felt the pressures of management slip from her shoulders. In the eyes of the faithful, this high, quiet, windowless chamber was the home of the god, and she lifted her eyes to where his colossal statue stared into eternity from a throne of ivory and gold. At his feet, a gold basin filled with water reflected the dust motes that danced in the rays of the flickering lamps, floral oils wafted up to the ceiling. This might well be

17

Eurotas's private paradise, she reflected. Equally, though, it was hers.

'My lady.'

She spun round. From treasury to treatment room, dormitories to kitchens, Iliona knew this chamber more intimately than any on the complex. Knew the way its cedar door creaked no matter how often the pivots were greased. Knew which flagstone dipped. Which wick was prone to smoking. How could she have missed, in the stillness and silence, the sound of masculine breathing? How could she not have picked up the scent of leather mixed with woodsmoke above the oils in the braziers?

She cleared her throat. 'Entry to this shrine is forbidden to those who do not serve Eurotas.'

'I serve the State,' he said, stepping out of the shadows. 'And since the Eurotas runs right down the middle, I'd say that qualifies, wouldn't you?'

'Serve the State how exactly?'

She might be wrong. Croesus, let me be wrong. Let him be nothing but a thief who slipped past the guards and is looking to bluff his way out.

'Apologies.' He threw his leg astride one of the griffins that flanked the throne. 'I rather assumed you'd know me.' His head dipped. 'My name's Lysander. Commander of the *Krypteia*.'

Every bone in her body locked solid. 'Tell me.' His voice was low and full of gravel. 'What's your opinion about last week's slaughter of the cavalry horses in Sicily?'

The question was so unexpected that relief made her knees weak. Of course! If he knew the boy was here, the army would have come marching in, the temple closed, she'd be manacled ankle and wrist.

'My opinion's no different to any other Spartan's,' she said, clasping her hands behind her back so he wouldn't see them shaking. 'The whole nasty business was staged start to finish.'

And how arrogant to imagine she was important enough to concern the Head of the *Krypteia* at the very moment when her country was fighting for its political survival! At first, she reflected, everything had gone smoothly. After the unification, it had been agreed that Athens would protect the seas with her formidable navy, while Sparta undertook to secure the interior. But even the greatest powers need support, and over the years, Syracuse, Corinth and Arcadia had grown to become Sparta's closest allies.

Until a deadly rain of arrows immobilized Syracuse's cavalry.

'Staged very well, as it happens.' Lysander adjusted to a more comfortable position on his metal mount. 'Syracuse immediately drew the obvious conclusion: that we wiped out their defence force as a prelude to taking over.'

Proof came in the silver found on the archers, killed when they tried to flee the island. The coins were found to be stamped with the *lambda*, the eighth letter of the alphabet that was the definitive symbol of Sparta and which every warrior presented face-on to the enemy in battle. And which, oddly enough, was staring at her right now from the breast of Lysander's tunic.

This chamber might be the god's private heaven, she reflected, but no paradise was complete without the obligatory serpent.

'On the strength of that, our merchants and envoys were dismissed on the spot,' he said. 'Giving us no opportunity to prove our innocence.'

One of the *Krypteia*'s key functions, of course, was that it served as Sparta's nemesis, ruthless and relentless, rooting out traitors and avenging the nation's wrongs. Years might pass and then, one moonless night, a body would be discovered outside a tavern in Athens, or floating face down in the Straits of Corinth.

Iliona squared her shoulders. 'Unfortunate though the situation is, this temple does not concern itself with politics.'

'Oh?' He stroked the bronze wings of the griffin with an equally bronzed hand. 'I was under the impression that your own appointment was political.'

'If you're referring to the fact that the King is my second cousin, that's irrelevant. We've never been on the best of terms.'

'Which probably explains why he's looking for an excuse, indeed any excuse I'm told, to appoint his sister in your place.' Measureless eyes bored into hers, and she saw that they were grey. Grey as a mountain wolf's pelt. 'But then, you. You, my lady, count the grains of sand on the shore and measure the seas in the ocean. You hear the voice of the voiceless and see through the eyes of the blind.'

'Are you calling me a fraud?'

'Absolutely, categorically not.' His smile was colder than Mount Parnon on the night of the midwinter solstice. 'Though it's interesting that those who consult you are, for the most part, *helots* and *perioikoi*. The lowest, if you like, of the low.'

'Without *helots* working our fields, there'd be no harvest. And as for the shopkeepers and craftsmen who form the middle caste, they're the backbone of Sparta's economy, and besides.' She stared him out with dogged intensity. 'You, more than most, ought to realize that the harsher one's life, the more important one's future.'

When you have nothing, comfort and hope become priceless.

'Are we talking about their future,' he asked, 'or the King's? Is it really coincidence, for example, that he installs his cousin as High Priestess in one of the country's prime religious sites?'

'Second cousin.'

'Of course. Second cousin. And I'm sure that when it comes to shaping the future of the subjugated masses, the King has their very best interests at heart.'

He slid off the griffin, and as he patted its beak, she studied the features reflected back in the bowl. He wore his hair long, as befitted a warrior, and, since military training commenced at

21

the age of seven, it was hardly surprising that his physique manifested the grace and athleticism that daily instruction was bound to imbue, or that his arms and thighs displayed the scars of more than one battle. How old was he, though? Forty? The lines round his eyes gave nothing away, and now she thought about it, the face in the water was as expressionless as that of the statue.

The serpent in paradise began to uncoil.

'You went to all the trouble of sneaking in here just to accuse me of holding on to my job by acting the King's puppet and brainwashing people you hold in contempt?'

With one foot, he hooked over a stool and rested his weight on it. 'Do you know the legend of Alphaeus and Arethusa?'

'Vaguely.' It was one of the more obscure myths, and in any case it centred round Arcadia, Sparta's northern and impoverished neighbour.

'Then let me tell you the story.'

Arethusa, he related, was an Arcadian wood nymph, who liked to bathe in the waters of the River Alphaeus. One day, the river god saw her and, overcome with lust, he tried to seduce her. She fought him off, but he chased her and chased her, right as far as the ocean, but even here Arethusa wouldn't give up. She kept on swimming, all the way to Sicily, where she begged the gods to change her into a freshwater fountain, so she could rest.

'We men,' Lysander clucked his tongue, 'when we set our minds on something, what persistent creatures we are.' He rested his elbow on his knee and cupped his chin in his hand. 'I've always found persistence pays off in the end, though. Once Arethusa saw the lengths her suitor was prepared to go to, following her halfway across the world, she surrendered, and even today, the people of Syracuse believe the joining of their waters is responsible for the well that bubbles up in the city. They even made Arethusa their patron.'

'I assume it's no coincidence that Arcadia is another of Sparta's closest allies?'

'According to legend, if you toss an object into the river in Arcadia, it will wash up in Syracuse.'

'Naturally you believe that.'

Lysander took his foot off the stool and smiled the sort of smile a wolf might produce when it spotted a lone lamb on a hillside.

'Let's take a walk,' he said.

From the window of the treatment room, Jocasta watched them cross the courtyard and pass beneath the gate. In her hands, yellow-brown seeds of fenugreek were pounded with methodical precision, since the temple janitor's neck had erupted in another painful boil.

Her mind wasn't on the janitor.

Unlike Iliona, Jocasta had recognized Lysander straight away. He wasn't an aristocrat, like the High Priestess. He was a freeborn citizen who'd worked his way up through the ranks of the most formidable fighting force the world had ever seen, and the training of the Spartan warrior was legendary. During their twenty years'

23

conscription, they were pushed to their physical and mental limits, forced to endure unimaginable pain, freezing temperatures, searing heat, hunger and thirst, as well as a whole host of other deprivations in which survival missions played a crucial part. Having then qualified as seasoned camouflage and endurance experts, they were enlisted into the *Krypteia*, where for two years they honed their skills by spying on *helots*. No. Not just spying, Jocasta corrected. They were also tasked with killing them.

To sneak up, swiftly, silently and totally at random, if so much as a sniff of rebellion had been mooted by any member of the enslaved labour force, no matter that it had not been uttered by the actual victim.

Repellent though the system was, she had to admit it was effective. Slaves outnumbered citizens twenty to one, and these slaves chafed at the yoke. But thanks to the *Krypteia*, no *helot*, whether in the fields or the kitchens, washing clothes or collecting firewood, could ever be certain they weren't being watched. For all they knew, a member of Lysander's hated death squad might be listening in on their conversation. Stealing up on them this very minute to slit their throats in punishment for someone else's talk of mutiny, and Jocasta ought to know.

Jocasta was a *helot*.

Behind her on the pallet, a twelve-year-old with lash wounds on his back slept a deep and dreamless sleep.

Four

Crickets rasped in the afternoon heat as Lysander led the way down to the river. Blissfully unaware of the demon's reputation, butterflies sunned their wings on heliotrope, bees buzzed round the horehound and swallows performed parabolas in search of flies. Had it been anyone else, Iliona thought, she would have taken him into her house, offered him wine, cheese and fruit, and probably put him up for the night. With Lysander, she'd rather invite a nest of vipers into her home. In any case, he didn't seem to expect hospitality. Briefly, it crossed her mind that it might be because he'd never been offered it.

'Come the full moon,' he said, gathering a handful of pebbles, 'the High Priestess of Alphaeus's shrine meets with the High Priestess of Arethusa's, as indeed they do every spring, for the Festival of the Fountains.'

Iliona watched him skip stones across the deep, dark swirling waters that, during the winter snowmelts, were perfectly capable of sucking a man in and not spitting him out for three days.

'Last year, it was the turn of the Syracusian priestess to visit Arcadia. This year, Arcadia goes to Syracuse.' Grey eyes slanted her a sideways glance. 'I suppose you know the High Priestess of Alphaeus fell victim to pneumonia around the winter solstice?'

'Damp valleys have their price.'

'Which is why Sparta sent condolences to her successor. A charming creature with blonde hair, oval face and blue eyes. In fact...' he let the pebbles ripple through his fingers, 'one might even say the Lady Chloris is not unlike you in her appearance.'

Iliona watched a moorhen paddle between the reed beds and saw that the shadows had started to lengthen. 'If you're asking me to go to Syracuse in her place, the answer's no.'

'The climate's good, the food's better and Sicily boasts miles of sun-drenched beaches backed by waving pines and rocky coves.'

'It also boasts a mountain that belches fire, an entrance to the Underworld and is home to one-eyed giant cannibals known as the Cyclops.'

'None of which you believe, but in any case, I'm sure you wouldn't care how many invisible chariots come charging out of Hades, providing it clears your country's name.'

'My decision has nothing to do with patriotism, Lysander. I'm a priestess. I serve Eurotas first, middle and last, and that is the end of the matter.'

'Hm.' He rubbed his jaw. On the far bank, the first of the field hands began to trek home after their labours, mattocks and hoes slung over their shoulders, their bodies turned to copper by the sun. 'Patriotism.' He plucked a long blade of grass and chewed on the juicy end. 'An interesting word, wouldn't you say? It has so many different connotations.'

'It does not,' she replied evenly. 'Neither does the word neutrality, if that makes things clearer, since all temples are, by definition, impartial. Must I remind you that this is one of the few rivers in Greece that doesn't dry up in the summer? My job is to keep it that way.'

'Yes, of course. You serve Sparta through your allegiance to the river god, who gives us fresh water, fertile soil and bountiful crops in return.'

He nodded slowly, steepling his fingers, while high in their roosts, rooks cawed out their territories, and warblers sang in the willows.

'It's one of life's paradoxes,' he said at length, 'that in order to maintain peace, Spartans have had to turn themselves into the toughest of warriors, with boys entrusted to the army from the age of seven, obliging us to be father, mother and confidant during their formative years, then companion, tutor and brother as they grow older.'

Iliona ran her fingers down the pleats of her robe and noticed that her palms were starting to sweat.

'That training is harsh,' Lysander admitted. 'Even at that age, the boys are kept hungry and cold, in order that they might learn to live off the land and not be seen, much less caught. I grant you some take to this life better than others, and before you say it, yes, me perhaps better than most. But recruits are free to leave any time.'

Quite possibly, she thought, but unless they complete their full twenty years, they're stripped of their citizenship, their lands taken from them and their family suffer the shame. Branded tremblers – in other words, cowards – they became social pariahs, but even assuming their shoulders were broad enough to bear such a load, they were still faced with the task of earning a living. And how could they do that, when the only trade the army had taught them was dying?

'The hour is late and you have my answer. I won't travel to Syracuse or impersonate the Priestess of Alphaeus, so if you'll excuse me—'

'It's a sad fact that we lose half a dozen men to ravines and bad weather every year, and that their bodies are not always found. What, I suppose the deserters argue, is the loss of one or two more?'

Shadows deepened and the birds ceased to sing. A frog plopped into the water.

'You can't take a whole cross-section of humanity, push them to their limits, then expect every last one to conform,' Iliona said tartly. 'We're talking about human beings, not pots in a kiln to be churned out one after the other.'

Measureless eyes stared back at her. 'What about those who discover poetry, philosophy, the arts, through our teachings? You forget, my lady, that most soldiers are not noble born like yourself, where manners and music are drunk in with your mother's milk.'

He was fishing.

'And you forget that, as aristocrats, we also drink in the obligations of commitment and responsibility. Just as all minds cannot be indoctrinated into thinking as a group rather than as individuals, Lysander, not all souls can survive the public humiliation that resignation would entail.'

'Funnily enough, the army understands that very well, and providing the matter's addressed correctly, we have ways of dealing with it.' He stroked his jaw. 'Sustaining this superior military force requires a massive administration and unimaginable support and, contrary to popular belief, we're not unsympathetic to those who don't make the grade as warriors. But I suppose you're right. A certain amount of desertion is inevitable. By the way...' His voice was smooth as honey. 'I don't suppose you've seen a twelve-year-old boy round here?'

Still fishing.

'As it happens, the janitor's son turned that age last week.' Lambs bleated in the distance, and a horse in the stables whinnied.

'I was thinking more of a boy with lash marks on his body.'

Not body, Iliona thought. Back. The lash marks were on his *back*, proof that, when he'd run the gauntlet of whips, he'd hunched himself into a ball. The scent of herbs drifted on the air, oregano, lavender and mint.

'It's all part of the initiation process,' Lysander said equably. 'Once a year, the *Krypteia* piles an altar with cheeses and tasks the boys with

29

capturing them.'

'An altar that's ringed by guards armed with whips,' she corrected. All she had to do was hold her nerve for a little bit longer. 'Who defend the cheeses with no quarter given.'

'None whatsoever, that's the point.' He turned to face hills tinged blood red in the setting sun. 'We don't breed warriors to be brave and reckless, that only results in an unnecessary waste of life.' He looped his thumbs in his belt and rocked gently on his heels. 'Sparta trains her men to be steadfast and disciplined, and the cheese fight is simply one method of teaching them, at a very early stage, that there's more than one way to catch a coney.'

'For pity's sake, they're twelve!'

'The defence force is barely two years older,' he countered. 'In fact, most participants relish the challenge and it's no coincidence that, eight years out of ten, the younger team wins. It's all part of the patriotism you referred to earlier. The opposite of which, if my memory serves me correctly,' his smile was tight, 'is called treason.'

Iliona watched the last vestiges of daylight fade over the pool into which the bodies of traitors were thrown, trussed but very much kicking.

'I will be packed in the morning,' she said.

Beside her, the man with the gravel voice nodded.

Five

High above Syracuse, the chisels, hammers, barrows and rollers that powered the vast stone quarries slowly fell into silence. The men who worked them filtered away. Dust settled. Shadows fell. The creatures of the night reclaimed the hills.

Shuffling beneath the jagged man-made cliffs, a giant figure scratched at his stubble. The itch of it was driving him crazy, but he knew of a pool, higher up still, with enough reflection to guide a blade. With luck, the moon would provide sufficient light.

Leaving the quarries to the scavenging jackals, he stumbled up the path towards the City of the Dead, his senses guided by the sound of rushing water. The river was a relatively recent discovery, made when tomb-makers, gouging out another routine sepulchre, found themselves knocking into thin air instead. The cavern was promptly turned into a grotto, in which part of the stream was diverted to create a pool of crystal-clear water. Offerings were left beside this pool. Mammals came at night to drink from it. Small birds bathed in it. But this was probably the first time it had been used to shave whiskers.

Theo rolled the blade between his fingers and

wished the moon would rise. Out in the bay, ships bobbed on waters turned oily by the gloom. Below, lamplights twinkled in a kaleido-scope of yellow. And as he patrolled the long lines of columns and statues, he thought how nice it would be to wander round a market with-out people screaming their heads off. To be able to sit in a tavern with a pitcher of wine, without having stones thrown at you. But since this was impossible, he continued to prowl the silent metropolis, stopping from time to time to stroke the soft grey heads of the poppies that unfurled among the fissures in the rock, but always, always, scratching at his stubble. Impatient eyes scanned the eastern sky. Where the hell was that bloody moon?

At first, he hardly noticed the sound. Among the soft rasp of the cicadas, it could be mistaken for just another melodic chirrup. Then, as the singing grew louder, he realized the voice was a woman's. Melting into the shadows, he became one with the statues that marked the tombs.

'From the Great Burning Mountain
To the plains that spit mud
To the hills that fall into the sea.'

Her voice floated softer than gossamer on the warm evening air.

'Oh, isle of the gods,
Sweet isle of the Sicels,
I devote my whole being to thee.'

He smelled her before he could see her. Skin that had been perfumed with the oil of sweet lilies. And as she turned the corner, he saw that her hair hung down her back the colour of corn silk, and that her step was bouncy and light.

'From the Great Burning Mountain
To the pastures and streams
Where the oxen of the sun god would graze.'

He watched her arrange a posy of flowers on one of the rocks.

'Oh, isle of the gods,
Sweet isle of the Sicels,
Let it be here where I end my days.'

The locals held that evil spirits stalked these sepulchres at night. That's why most of them gave the City of the Dead a wide berth once dusk fell. Yet here she was, this beautiful creature with soft skin and soft hair. All alone, and singing so sweetly...

Hands bigger than a cheese paddle balled into fists. Closing his eyes, he smelled lilies. White lilies. Virginal, silky and soft—

A pair of lovers, meeting at the grotto at midnight, were too preoccupied to notice the blood that had pooled on the stone.

In the pines, an owl hooted twice.

Six

'Welcome aboard the *Tyche*, milady.'

The boatswain guided Iliona up the gangplank, where linen drapes formed a makeshift cabin at the stern. Behind them, the market town that also served as Sparta's port and arsenal bustled into life as stallholders laid out everything from hides to lyres to preserved figs under awnings. Iliona knew she'd never take normality for granted again.

'I hope you find your quarters comfy.'

That, she thought, rather depended on one's definition of the word. After all, what were swansdown cushions and a thickly padded mattress, compared to bedding down in a nest full of scorpions?

'Thank you, the arrangements are charming.'

Because all things were relative, she supposed, and spying for her country was better than shaking hands with the demon.

And if only, she thought, *it was that simple...*

Down on the quayside, a redhead of nineteen, maybe twenty, had a sailor pinned to the wall by his throat and was squeezing parts of him that apparently didn't enjoy being squeezed.

'Put your hand up my skirt again, you bloody pervert, and I'll cut your filthy throat.'

It was a growing problem, foreigners coming into port and mistaking girls in traditional dress for whores. A record, though, that Spartan women had become pretty adept at setting straight. In this modern, changing world they didn't see any need to give up the elegance and comfort of wearing gowns slit to their hips. In fact, Iliona thought, admiring the way the redhead forced an apology from her gibbering abuser, female liberation was a direct consequence of Sparta's warrior society. With their menfolk stuck away in barracks, women here enjoyed more autonomy and freedom than any of their Greek counterparts. Downtrodden they were not.

'Here you go, ma'am.'

'Thank you.' She had no reason to doubt the artless smile of the wide-eyed youth, who returned the bracelet that had obviously slipped off in the crush.

'Oh, and this,' he said.

She actually *felt* her jaw drop. That pearl choker had belonged to her mother, and the only time Iliona took it off was before bed. That clasp could not possibly have worked loose of its own accord—

'I'm Phillip,' he said with a grin. 'Lysander thinks my talents might come in useful on this mission, and isn't it wonderful?' He let out a low chuckle. 'To be a thief and a spy and be paid for it, too!'

She studied this boy, with the looks of an angel and the innocence of a puppy, who could steal the curls from Poseidon's beard. 'Don't you have any conscience?'

'I look upon it more as finding things before people have actually lost them.'

'How on earth do you sleep at night?'

'How on earth do you?'

'Me?'

'Your miracles are nowt but smoke and mirrors, either. It's why Lysander picked you – the quickness of the hand deceives the eye and all that, right? *Hey! Manetho!*' He waved to a big bear of a man lumbering up the gangplank. 'Good to see you again, mate!'

'Likewise, little flea.' The newcomer ruffled his sandy mop. 'What have you been doing since Corinth?'

'Everything possible to stay on the right side of the law, because old habits die hard, me old chum. Certain objects can't help sticking to my hands.' He shot a sideways wink at Iliona. 'Like this bronze buckle...'

'You.' Manetho growled, as he tightened the belt he hadn't even realized had slipped. 'Some day, those light fingers of yours will get you into a whole load of trouble, boy. And if they don't, then your chatterbox mouth surely will.'

Phillip laughed. 'Given that Cretan archers are the best in the world, ma'am, often offering themselves up as mercenaries, Lysander reckons it's fair to assume that the horse-killers came from there. But he needs proof, he says, before opening up a diplomatic nightmare, and though you mightn't think it to look at this ugly lug,

Manetho's the finest tracker Sparta's ever seen.' He blew out his cheeks in admiration. 'Stalks stags, then wrestles them to the ground by their antlers.'

The colour that suffused Manetho's grizzled face suggested this was no idle boast, and as tracker and thief wandered off to reminisce about Corinth and no doubt other missions, Iliona thought about a different diplomatic nightmare that might be opening up.

In theory, Sparta's democracy was structured in such a way that no single individual could take control. In practice, of course, the kings, the elders, even the inspectors were so obsessed with their own re-election that political and economic policies fell by the wayside. As a result, they welcomed anything that diverted public attention away from their own short-comings ... and no prizes for guessing how well treason drew the crowds. Worse, the poison would very quickly spread to Iliona's friends and family – including second cousins. And given that the King had appointed Iliona himself, it would be argued that he supported desertion, in direct contravention of his own army's policy. Now how corrosive was that, when Sparta's sole power was its military? Iliona ticked the points off on her fingers. The High Priestess of Eurotas executed for treason. Her family tainted. The kingship threatened. Sparta weakened in the eyes of its people. Lysander had undoubtedly won this particular battle. But the war was a long way from won.

'My, my, my! Lady Iliona, what an *honour*.'

A little cherub of a man with a halo of curls encircling his bald patch fluttered at her elbow. He blinked incessantly.

'You won't remember me, but your physician fixed a potion for my mother's stomach ulcer. Calendula infused with marshmallow root, and great Ganymede, that ulcer hasn't flared up since. I cannot thank you enough.'

'I'm betting Silas can't just recall what was in that potion,' a gravel voice rumbled and instantly the soft scents of leather and woodsmoke drove out the prickle of sawn timbers down on the dockside. 'I'll bet he knows the date, the hour, the price and the quantity.'

The little head bobbed. 'The date? *Certainly*, my lord Lysander. Three days after the autumn equinox, four seasons past, and it was shortly after midday.' His cheeks bunched in embarrassment. 'The shadows were short,' he said, shrugging.

'Is that all you can remember about your visit to my temple?' Iliona laughed.

'Well, no, actually it isn't.' His rosebud lips pursed, as though ashamed of his prolific memory. 'My mother was prescribed two gourds of the remedy, a viscous brown liquid to be taken three times a day, and the price was three obols, though, uh—' another apologetic shrug – 'we left another three-obol piece on the altar as we were leaving.'

Small, cuddly and looking for all the world like everyone's favourite uncle, who would suspect Silas of being a spy?

'How many of us are there on this mission?' she asked, as the little man bundled off to stow his luggage.

Grey eyes fixed on the pennants overhead. 'Surely you weren't expecting Alphaeus's priestess to travel without a generous entourage?'

'I'll let you into a secret, Lysander. I have no expectations whatsoever about this trip.'

'Really.' The anchor stones were hauled up to the chant of the Heaving Song. 'Well, I don't know about you, but it seemed a reasonable assumption to me that, barely a few weeks into her new post, the Lady Chloris would want to make a good impression.'

'Lucky me. I'm not only a fraud, I have an ego as well.'

'Dedication,' he corrected with what might have been a chuckle, or then again might have been a cough from the marble dust. 'You have *dedication*, my lady. And if it sets your mind at rest, all Sparta requires of you is to carry out the various rituals that the real priestess would undertake, without arousing suspicion.'

'Yes, who could possibly be suspicious of someone who's never visited Alphaeus's shrine in her life and wouldn't recognize his statue if she cracked her shin on it? Especially someone who's never heard the words of his hymn, much less led the sacrifice. I'm assuming by the way that, being Arcadia and the land of Pan, it's a goat we'll be dedicating?'

'I have absolutely no idea, but I'm sure you'll

39

carry it off with conviction.'

Your miracles are nowt but smoke and mirrors, either. It's why Lysander picked you. He must have had the temple under surveillance for some considerable time, she realized. Turning a blind eye to her activities, until the time was ripe to call in his debt.

'Without this festival for cover,' he was saying, 'we would never have had the opportunity to clear our name.'

'So why do I have a feeling that, if things turn sour, you and your agents will vanish into the night, leaving me high and dry?'

'I'm hoping it won't come to that.'

'That's a real weight off my mind.'

'Hm.' With the gentlest of jerks, the *Tyche* put to sea. 'I could have phrased that a little better, I suppose, but what you have to remember is the speed with which events have overtaken us.'

The fact that Syracuse's defence force was incapacitated the instant the seas opened up again after the winter smacked of seriously meticulous planning.

'Who do you think's behind the sabotage?' she asked.

'Athens.'

'Nonsense.' Thanks to the current brokerage of power between Athens and Sparta, Greece was enjoying a peace she'd never experienced in the course of her entire history. 'Why would they want to jeopardize all that?'

Impassive features concentrated on the mast. The cedar was rich with pitch and papyrus, and, at the top, a lookout kept watch from a large wicker basket.

'Perhaps peace means different things to different people.'

'How can it?' Forget granaries full to bursting point and the export not simply of surplus produce, but of luxuries such as marble, ivory carvings and racehorses. 'Surely,' she argued, 'it's better to have graveyards filling up with the bones of old men, instead of the cream of their youth.'

'Exactly the attitude an ambitious nation preys on, I would suspect, if they want to tip the balance of world power in their own favour.'

While Athenian artists painted heroes on vases and Athenian sculptors reproduced legends in stone, he added, Athenian politicians rallied other equally ruthless city states. Calling themselves the Delian League, they annexed the likes of Euboea, Naxos and Scyros, all of whom welcomed the security of warships patrolling their shores, since piracy had brought so many to their knees. Until, one day, little Naxos noticed that the profits from her marble quarries were heading straight into Athens' coffers. As was the wealth from the mineral deposits on Euboea, and so on, and so on, and so on.

'Nevertheless,' he said, folding his arms, while Iliona seemed to need both hands to grip the rail. 'It was only after they took the Levantine trade routes, controlling all the shipping that passed through, that the rest of the Greek world woke up to what was happening.'

'But they petitioned our help,' she pointed out, as the ship passed beneath cliffs that loomed a tad too close for comfort. 'We blocked any further encroachments by forming a Confederacy of our own.'

'With Syracuse, Corinth and Arcadia at the forefront.'

Ah...

'Athens was never going to settle for stalemate,' he said. 'Not content with half the power, Athens wants the lot – but you know.' Lysander slanted her a sideways grin. 'As far as Sparta's concerned, this is just another cheese fight. How are the boy's wounds healing, by the way?'

'I've no idea. He ran off in the night.'

'Did he really?'

'If he hadn't, wouldn't Jocasta still be tending to him?'

She indicated the physician, stashing instruments beneath the whale, her yellow robe billowing as the *Tyche* see-sawed through the shifting currents. Because not even the *Krypteia*, she thought, could be suspicious of some old rug that the temple very kindly donated to a poverty-stricken widow up in the hills.

'You shouldn't have brought her along.'

'I didn't realize I needed your permission.'

'She's a *helot*.' His grey eyes didn't flicker. 'Turn your back on her, even for a moment, and there'll be a blade between your ribs, I guarantee it.'

Iliona stared up at the cruel, black, jagged cliffs and thought, the serpent that started off in paradise wasn't merely on the move. It was growing stronger every minute.

Once free of the coast, the sea became smoother than an Etruscan dancer's kilt. Across the gulf, the isle of Cranae shimmered in the heat. It was on that lump of rock, Jocasta mused, that Paris and Helen consummated their relationship. Whether in the form of rape, as the Spartans claimed, or the all-consuming passion that the rest of us believed, it was still there that the tinder had been lit for a war that launched a thousand ships and lasted eight long brutal years. Watching seabirds wheel and dive, it crossed Jocasta's mind that this might well be the last time she ever saw it.

But. She let out a sigh. What must be, must be.

'...gargle with this...'

For big, strong sailors, they had an awful lot of petty ailments.

'...two drops in your ear every morning, and again at night...'

Another hypochondriac trotted off happy, but as she massaged weather-beaten chests with oil of myrrh to clear their niggling coughs and prescribed endless fennel seed infusions for persistent constipation, dark eyes followed the *Krypteia*'s Commander as he moved around the deck. How many of her people had he killed with his bare hands? How many soldiers had he trained to steal from people who had bugger-all to start with – just to prove that they could do it?

'...dewcup poultice should reduce the inflammation...'

Helots weren't slaves in the conventional sense. A whole nation had been put to bondage for a start, and they were the property of the State, rather than individuals. She watched him consulting with the helmsman, joking with the quartermaster, and thought, you can despise us, you can chain us, you can yoke us to your ploughs, but we *will* rise again.

'...bathe the infected area twice a day with this...'

Freedom is our birthright, Messenia is our home. Jocasta applied three drops of basil oil to the wasp sting on someone's belly and doubled the strength of chamomile and cloves for someone else's toothache. We will reclaim both, and when we do – oh, when we do – the scream of the vixen, our emblem, will be heard the length of your land. Your streets will run with blood. And that's a promise.

'...this decoction of celery seeds ought to fix it...'

She brushed a lock of hair from her face with the back of her hand, and considered the popular belief that Sparta put their warriors through hell and back to make them strong for the good of world peace. Bollocks. This ruthlessness was born out of fear, fear of the enemy within. An enemy, moreover, that they themselves had created, nursed and nurtured, and which now outnumbered them more than twenty to one. With odds like that, they had every reason to be

44

frightened, because ten generations of bondage hadn't weakened the *helot* spirit. It had made them more determined, and for Jocasta, as with all *helots*, freedom was only a matter of time.

And that time was coming—

'Tell me, I've always been curious,' a cultured voice murmured, slipping into the cushion opposite. 'What's the difference between a decoction and an infusion?'

The way his dark hair fell over one eye gave the impression of sharp and shifty, while his wide, toothsome smile conveyed just the opposite. To achieve such ambiguity, Jocasta decided, he must have practised very hard.

'Infusions are steeped. Decoctions are either simmered or boiled.'

'Ah.' He nodded. 'The temperature of the water. Thank you for clearing that up.'

She wasn't remotely surprised that her aristocratic visitor made no move to leave.

'Is there anything else I can clear up for you?' She rattled a box of pills marked 'Penile Warts'.

The smile broadened as he indicated the figurehead towering above the stern. 'Thank you, but I have no more need of doctoring than our gilded protectress. I'm Talos, by the way.'

'How eccentric of your parents to name their son after a mythical monster.'

'Actually they named me ... well, who cares? The point is, Talos was a giant made out of bronze. It was his job to hurl rocks at ships to prevent them from landing, so that the terrible secret of the Minotaur would remain hidden on

45

Crete. Somehow the name seemed to suit me.'

'As I recall, the original Talos had but the one single vein. When it got pierced, the hot metal that was his lifeblood drained out and he died.'

'So?'

'So even your namesake needed a doctor.' Her lip twisted. 'Albeit in the form of a bronze-smith.'

His laugh was the only genuine thing about him, she thought. 'That was a very polite way of telling me I'm an arrogant son-of-a-bitch. Most people don't wrap it up quite so nicely.'

'What is it you want of me, Talos? Only there's a long line of men shuffling impatiently behind you, and only two hours of light left in the sky.'

'Have you considered the possibility that my motive might be the same as theirs?' One eye glinted roguishly beneath the floppy fringe. 'That I, too, wish to take pleasure in the company of a pretty woman?'

So their queuing had nothing to do with medicine after all. 'No.'

'They think pretty girls on board are as lucky as black cats and amber touchstones, and I work for Lysander, remember. We spies need every bit of luck we can get.'

'Here.' Jocasta slapped a pot of ointment in his hand. 'Massage this into your inflamed ego and find someone else's time to waste. *Next!*'

She watched him cross the deck, chuckling as he tossed the pot from hand to hand and back again. Was the gesture coincidence? Dispensing a routine tincture of rue, she glanced at the

46

figurehead, after whom this ship was named. Tyche was the goddess of fortune who juggled the Ball of Chance, and her rules were simple. When it's up in the air, then you win. When it falls back in her hand, sorry, you lose.

'Where is it, Bronze Man?' Jocasta whispered. 'Where's your ball of chance at the moment?'

The sense of doom that weighed on her heart sat at odds with the calm cobalt sea.

Theo knelt in the grove of evergreen oaks and buried his head in his hands. Memories flitted like moths past his eyes.

He was seven years old, saying goodbye to his friends and leaving the mountains behind. There were ships. A long voyage. Then a new home, in a new land, with forests and caves to explore... So vivid were the images of childhood that he could almost smell the rich, red earth after the rain, the perfume of the walnuts in blossom, the tang of the mushrooms in the woods.

Time rolled forward, like leaves in the wind. He was ten, now, beginning an apprenticeship that would take twelve years to master. There were toasts to the future. Pride as his father bestowed on him the brand of the smith. Pride in the work they turned out.

The leaves spun again.

Now he was reliving his father's slow death. Burying his mother's bones. But at the back of it, always, was the smell of the forge, and the sparks of hammer on anvil. Together they spelled out contentment and comfort, for though

Theo knew himself to be a freak, he had never felt lonely. Not, oh god, not until now.

He stared at his blood-splattered pantaloons. At the stains that wouldn't wash out. Closing his eyes, he saw the girl, kneeling with her back to him as she arranged flowers and laid out her cakes.

He couldn't go home, they would kill him for sure.

He had nowhere to go, and nowhere to turn...

An ache worse than fever wrenched at his gut, and as flycatchers trilled high in the treetops, tears splashed down the side of his cheek.

But all he could smell was the oil of white lilies, with which the girl had perfumed her skin.

And the stench of blood on his clothes.

Seven

The *Tyche* bellied out her mainsail and leaned into the wind, her tiller creaking, her tackles clacking, her pennants clattering like hens. The water was so clear that Iliona could see the broad wings of a ray gliding effortlessly alongside. She leaned over the rail for a better view.

'I hope you're not planning to jump before we reach our destination,' a voice rumbled in her ear.

'I hope I'm not pushed before I get home,' she

retorted. 'Assuming you even bother to put me on board for the return journey.'

'Hm.' His hair was tied at the nape to stop it blowing in his face. Naturally, the thong was of leather. 'You don't have a very high opinion of men, do you?'

'Unless the rules changed overnight, the priestess of Eurotas is not obliged to be celibate.'

'True, but you haven't remarried after your divorce and you're not romantically attached to anyone at the moment.'

'Maybe I'm discreet.'

'Maybe you've erected a wall.'

'Maybe it's none of your business.'

He laughed. 'Maybe you're right.'

For several minutes they stood watching the bow rise and fall beneath the shadow of the great sail. High above their heads, sailors shinned up the ropes like monkeys, while, over in the galley, sardines sizzled over charcoal.

He needed to win, she thought. It was vital he won every point, and since his calculations were based on intelligence and logic, detachment gave him a competitive edge. And that, as it happened, was his weakness. She watched his shirt billowing in the wind. Followed the way his lips pursed in determination. Lysander might not give a damn about *helots* and *perioikoi* – the lowest of the low, he had called them. But by setting riddles and interpreting dreams, at least people had something to cling to. Call it smoke and mirrors if you like, but what he didn't realize was that it went beyond self-preservation.

If the High Priestess was thrown to the demon over which their temple stood sentinel, then the whole fabric of their lives would unravel. If the oracles were exposed as a sham, they'd lose the protection of the river god in whose power they trusted, so all they'd have left was the demon. And vengeance was not a good god.

At high noon the Old Man of the Sea
Emerges from the salt and makes for shelter
on the strand.
Then his briney sons, the flippered seals,
Heave themselves from the surf to sleep
beside him on the sand.

The song was Homer's, but Homer had never put so much passion into his poetry. Goose pimples rippled her arm. The youth was called Drakon. He was part of Lysander's team, but with wavy fair hair that fell to his shoulders and a lyre that danced to his touch, he was Apollo in all but the name.

'It unsettles you, then, that a dedicated killing machine is capable of such tenderness.' Lysander rubbed his hand over his jaw. 'I wonder what you imagined we did, when we weren't slitting throats or smothering babies.'

'If it's sport you're after, I suggest you bait a bear, because I'm not in the mood for fencing.' She might as well make her position clear. 'I'm along because I have no choice, but Athens' perfidy isn't my fight, and as far as I'm concerned, if men make war, then men can bloody well

50

make the peace. So far, you seem to be doing a pretty lousy job.'

'I was right.' Expressionless eyes watched the crew hauling on the stays. 'You really don't like men.'

'That's not true.'

Yet a quarter of a century on and she could still hear her father bragging how, day by day, little by little, he was working to make a new Sparta. Being only a child, she assumed he meant politics – until he called her in to his chamber and showed her how to pour liquid from a tiny blue phial into the King's wine. Five times his big hand had covered her small one as they poured, father and daughter, laughing and conspiring together. On the sixth day, the obol dropped.

Day by day, she realized, the King had been ranting a little more wildly.

Little by little, he'd been behaving more oddly.

And the worst part was, while the poison had been slowly eroding his wits, her father remained the best friend the King ever had...

A galley slave handed Iliona a trencher of sardines. She passed the plate to Lysander. Rebel if you must, she'd thought at the time, and her opinion hadn't changed since. But do it on the battlefield or through hand-to-hand fighting. No child should ever be conspiracy to cold-blooded murder—

'On the subject of making things clear,' he said, spearing a morsel of fish on the end of his dagger. 'I want you to know that, as far as the King, the Council, even my own agents are concerned, you volunteered for this task out of patriotic duty and I don't see it in anyone's interests to disillusion them. And afterwards, as far as I'm concerned, providing you play your part, the slate is clean.'

'Clean?'

'You can personally burn the file in your own sacred tripod, if you like.' He popped the morsel in his mouth. 'I hear you have a particular penchant for ashes.'

'You wanted to see me, sir?'

Iliona was surprised to recognize the redhead she'd seen on the quay, pinning the sailor to the wall by his throat. All credit to him for trying his luck, though. This girl stood every bit as tall as Lysander and her thighs looked like they could crush melons.

'Yes, Roxana, I did.' Lysander wiped his mouth with the back of his hand and dipped his head to Iliona. 'I'd be very grateful if, between now and docking, you could find some time to instruct our young team member here in the gentle art of pouring libations and all the other paraphernalia she'll need, if she's to pass herself off as your assistant.'

Assistant, Iliona wondered. Or guard?

'I've been studying the attendants at different shrines in the run-up to this mission,' Roxana told her. 'I've practised holding lustral bowls and handling sacrificial knives, oh and I've spent several hours familiarizing myself with various relics as well.'

'Lucky you.' Iliona wondered if the girl ever

smiled. 'But you needn't worry,' she said sweetly. 'I'm told the trick isn't so much accuracy, more the conviction one carries it off with.'

Lysander was too busy extricating fish bones from his mouth to notice.

'I won't let you down, my lady.' Roxana turned to her commanding officer and all but saluted. 'Sparta will not be disgraced, sir.'

'Indeed it won't,' he agreed, dismissing her with a nod.

The girl reminded Iliona of a lioness. They shared the same aura of watchfulness and stealth. And about the same sense of humour.

'As the goddess Artemis dedicated her virginity to the moon,' he said, 'so Roxana has dedicated hers to the State, whether,' a muscle twitched at the side of his mouth, 'the State wants it or not.'

He tossed the remnants of his supper over the side and proceeded to pick his way across the coiled anchor cables.

'Incidentally,' Iliona called after him, 'what will the real High Priestess of Alphaeus be doing, while all this is going on?'

'Enjoying a lengthy bout of Spartan hospitality.' Lysander rested a leisurely hip against the whale. 'Luckily for the Lady Chloris, the King's feasts are legendary, his musicians are gifted, and his palace, as you well know, lacks for nothing by way of luxury.'

'In other words, you want to keep an eye on her.'

The wolf smiled. 'In my business, no party

ever trusts the other, but even so.' He winked. 'It would be foolish to make an enemy of one's allies. Don't you think?'

Iliona sighed. So much for fish bones, then.

The moon rose over the pass that separated Arcadia from her neighbour Sparta, and the Lady Chloris tucked into a chunk of the lamb that was roasting on the spit. All her life she'd striven to advance her cause – marrying for political ends, bearing children for political ends, forever flattering, pushing, wheedling her way upwards – and now, by Zeus, she had done it.

Admittedly, there had been a tricky moment back on the eve of the winter solstice, when it looked like the Council might appoint that little cow of her cousin. But a quarter-talent of silver in the right pocket and Chloris was appointed to a post than which, royalty apart, there was no higher honour in the land, at least not for a woman. And since Arcadia was a poor, rough country full of poor and even rougher people, spending the summer as the King of Sparta's guest was not exactly a hardship.

Wiping a dribble of grease from her chin, Chloris envisaged other trips. Delphi, a leisurely tour of Ionia, even Egypt, assuming she could engineer the funding, since she wasn't one of those sanctimonious types who felt their entire time should be spent at the temple. That's what it employed all those lackeys for, and now that she'd been promoted above the threshold of female repression that prevailed so strongly in her country, there was no end to the opportunities for her. She clicked her fingers for more lamb to be sliced off the spit.

'Call that a slice?' she sniffed in disdain. 'Well, you can top this goblet up, while you're about it. And no half-measures, like last time!'

Anyway, administration didn't place laurel wreaths on a person's head or anoint their feet with myrrh. It was all about prestige. Slipping under her blanket of lynx fur – nights in the hills were bloody cold this time of year – Chloris wondered how much this little undertaking would win her. A lot, that much was sure. Without her co-operation, Sparta couldn't hope to enter Syracuse, and such was the need for secrecy, even her own people believed she'd made the trip herself.

Plumping a pillow that she would really *have* to draw someone's attention to in the morning, Chloris wondered what it would be worth, both personally and to Arcadia. According to Lysander, the terms of recompense were to be thrashed out during her stay.

'You will not be disappointed on either count,' he assured her and damn right. She understood *why* they daren't entrust a non-Spartan with something this important. It was now up to them to understand how *much* this lack of trust was worth. A wolf howled. Chloris shot up in her pallet. Oh, for pity's sake! Nothing was going to tear her to pieces while she was under the protection of the finest armed guard in the world!

All the same, she wriggled closer to the fire.

Yes, and in those negotiations, she must stress Arcadia's importance as a staging post between Sparta and Corinth. A *bridge*. She must remember to call it a bridge, because when the time came to return home, she could weave a river into her triumphal speech, an obvious cue for her own role – *ugh*! What on *earth* was that black thing crawling over her face? She squashed the bug between her fingernails and flipped over on to her side. Thank goodness, she'd be sleeping in the palace tomorrow night. One more day of camps and cramps and smelly mules and she'd be ill, she knew it. She simply wasn't *born* for this sort of life, and she had it all planned: Delphi next year, Syracuse the year after that, and quite frankly, if she couldn't fit in Carthage at the same time, she wasn't the woman she thought she was.

This time when she heard a grunt from where the pack-mules were hitched, Chloris didn't blink an eye. For heaven's sake, these men went into battle wearing dog tags, because they expected to die for the cause. What was to feel insecure about? Bloody mountains, she thought, pulling her furs round her neck. Full of spooks and shadows, though of course if Lysander's strong arms had happened to be wrapped around her at the moment, she probably wouldn't be worrying so much. She turned over on her other side. Considering he'd engineered this secretive little exchange, she was rather hoping he'd have accompanied her.

'My mother always said, take one tall, dark, silent type three times a day and you'll never need a doctor,' she'd quipped archly.

'Your mother's a very sensible woman,' he'd murmured in reply. 'Regrettably, my presence is required in Syracuse, though you have my oath that the guards I send will ably fill your prescription.'

'There's nothing to say we can't commence the medication here and now,' she'd suggested, but Lysander made some feeble excuse about another appointment, and it stood to reason, she supposed. These Spartan warriors spent so much time away from women, they were bound to favour their own sex in bed, but what a shame. She wouldn't have minded a fling or two with him.

From the far side of camp, there came a scuffle.

'Good heavens, *now* what?'

As she raised herself up on one elbow to tell them, *do* try to keep it down, a hand clamped across her mouth. She tried to scream, but her head jerked up, and from somewhere Chloris heard the unmistakable rattle that a throat makes when its windpipe has been severed.

Too late, she realized it was her own.

As the *Tyche* danced across the seas, her linen sail buffeting and her ribs dipped low, the traitor watched at the constellation of the Lion twinkling brightly in the sky.

And smiled.

Eight

'Hello, I'm Alys. May we come in?'

A pixie face rimmed by a froth of blonde curls peered round Iliona's door. Outside in the corridor, the usual domestic bustle of sweeping, dusting, beating tapestries had the added piquancy of panic, with slaves rushing to make up beds and fetch in food for guests who'd arrived two days ahead of schedule.

'We?'

All Iliona could see was one small child with two red, and distinctly uneven, spots blazing out from either cheek, a great smear of wine lees across its mouth, and more soot round its eyes than one stick of charcoal could decently furnish.

'Me and Zygia.' She indicated an empty space to her left. 'Zygia is my best ever friend.'

'Well, then, you'd better make yourselves at home.'

Slopping across in sandals that were a million sizes too big and a dress that pooled round her ankles, Alys hefted her imaginary companion on to the bed. 'You wait here,' she told the air, with a firm wag of her finger. 'But you'd better behave yourself this time.'

'Doesn't she always?'

'Huh!' The pixie helped herself to dates from the dish and crammed them into her mouth. 'I'm *always* in trouble because of her, and I shall probably get a spanking later, even though Zygia said it was all right to borrow grandmother's frock.' She wiped her sticky fingers down grandmother's exquisite pleats. 'If the sandals end up scuffed, I'll get another one, but you can't help it, can you, when they don't fit?'

'At least your grandmother won't suspect you've been at her make-up.'

Big, blue eyes rolled. 'Don't you believe it. Niobe has eyes in the back of her head, at least that's what everyone says, only don't tell her I said so, or I'll be put to bed without any supper – what's that, Zigs?' Small hands formed a cup through which she whispered in her friend's imaginary ear. 'Zygia asks why didn't you swim here under the ocean, like Alphaeus?'

'Oh, I would have done,' Iliona replied solemnly, 'but since I was with colleagues from the temple, it didn't seem fair to take the shortcut while they had to go by boat.'

'See,' Alys hissed. 'Told you there'd be a reason.' More cupped hands, more whispering. 'Zygia wants to know if we can take a look at your ceremonial robes, please?'

'You could, but the trunks haven't been delivered yet.' Like dogs, children had no sense of time. Iliona had only just arrived herself. 'But if you want to come back tomorrow...?'

Further conferring in hushed undertones.

'Zygia says she'd like that very much. She says she gets bored, stuck in the women's quarters all day.'

Yes, of course. This wasn't Sparta, where women were equal. In Syracuse, like the rest of Greece, they were firmly under the male thumb. Even Niobe, High Priestess to the city's patron deity, lived separately from the men in her own palace.

Iliona knelt down to pixie level. 'I expect Zygia gets lonely, too.'

The painted face froze, pain clouded Alys's eyes. Then she reached for the last three dates and stuffed them into bulging cheeks.

'Nope.' She put her hands on her hips, the way she'd seen exasperated adults do. 'We haven't got *time* to be lonely,' she trilled. 'There's weaving in the morning, spinning in the afternoon – it's all go here, you know.'

'I'm sure it is, but ... aren't there any other children for you to play with?'

'Not *re*ally.' The little nose wrinkled. 'The girls are either too old or they're babies, and I don't understand why it's fine for *boys* to climb trees and swing from ropes, but I get a jolly good hiding.'

'Call me odd, but I've never found hidings either jolly or good.'

'I wish you lived here, then Zygia and me would *never* get bored – uh-oh!' Alys dived under the bed at a speed a green lizard would be proud of. 'Those are grandmother's footsteps!'

She wasn't wrong.

'My dear, how wonderful to meet you.'

A woman wearing more gold than Iliona had ever seen in one place swept into the room. 'I'm Niobe, and I'm so sorry temple duties kept me from meeting your ship.'

'Please don't apologize. We're early.'

Lysander had wanted as much time in Syracuse as he could engineer. And wasn't it interesting that, the instant the ropes went round the mooring blocks, he'd donned a slave's tunic and disappeared into the crowd?

The wolf merging with the pack.

'Personally I'm delighted the headwinds were in your favour, my dear.' Niobe took both of Iliona's hands. 'Instead of having to grit your teeth through some dreary old reception ceremony, you can have fun at the Stag Festival tonight instead, and please say you're not too tired to attend. It really is one of our most exciting carnivals.'

'Tired?' Iliona laughed. 'After five days at sea, you can't imagine the energy I have to burn.'

Much of it mental energy, of course. Too many questions, too few answers, and no one to talk things through with.

'Good, because it was my intention to welcome you to Syracuse by giving you a tour of the city. Will an hour's time be rushing you?'

'I'll be ready and waiting.'

As her grandmother's footsteps receded, Alys wriggled out from under the bed. 'You're so lucky, going to the festival, going round the town. I never get to go *any*where.' Reddened lips

61

puckered in resignation. 'Still, at least I won't have to worry about getting on the wrong side of Artemis. She's a very scary goddess, and you want to be careful.'

'Do I?'

'Oh, yes.' Blue eyes widened to saucers. 'There's this story, you know – rather like Arethusa, but without the happy ending – about this handsome prince who stumbled upon Artemis when she was bathing. She was so cross that he'd seen her naked that she turned him into a stag, and guess what happened? He got torn to pieces by his very own hounds!'

For a child who claimed to be worried, Alys lapped up grisly tales.

'Another time she sent a boar that was bigger than an elephant, and it rooted up crops and vineyards and ... and well, *every*thing in its path. And you know why?'

'Why?'

'Because people hadn't been *nice* to her, which is what I mean. You don't want to upset Artemis, she's a *bitch*.' She heaped the dress over her arms, tiny toes slithering this way and that through the thongs of Niobe's sandals. 'When I come back tomorrow, will you tell me if the Cyclops was at the festival tonight?'

'There's no such thing as a Cyclops, Alys.'

'Yes, there is.'

'No, darling, it's only a story.'

'Well, it isn't so, too so, because I've *seen* him. He was as tall as a house, wide as a ship, and I knew it was him, because of the eye in his forehead.' Her hands spanned a circle the size of a melon. 'It was *h-u-g-e*.'

'That big, eh?' Iliona sucked in her cheeks. 'And what colour was it?'

'Blue, silly!' Her nose wrinkled. 'Grandmother said I'd imagined the whole thing, but you ask Zygia, she saw him, too, and I wanted to go back and have a look, but by the time I turned the corner, the Cyclops had gone. Did I tell you his eye was *this* big?' The circle doubled. 'So if he's there tonight, you *will* tell me?'

'Trust me, no detail will be spared.'

'Promise?'

'On my oath.'

'Good.' The pixie lifted her imaginary friend off the bed, skipped to the doorway, then stopped. 'But don't forget. Artemis has a bow that rains arrows of death on anybody who upsets her.'

'I'll be as nice as pie.'

'Yes, I know, but suppose you're standing near someone who *isn't*? And suppose she's a really bad shot?'

Of all the theological debates that had ever raged, Iliona doubted that one had ever been mooted. It was several minutes before the stitch in her side finally subsided.

From its place tucked away in the depths of her remedy chest Jocasta fished out a tiny leather scroll, on which certain symptoms had been detailed. Stomach pains, vomiting, muscle cramps and diarrhoea – the usual indications of severe gastric upset. The type that happens all the time.

Next, from further down still, below flasks of lubricants, phials of potions and drugs in horn containers, she extracted a small boxwood container, no different from twenty others in the chest, and placed it on her lap.

Healers heal. Saving lives is what physicians do. But it never hurts to be prudent, Jocasta thought, running her fingers over the top. And the advantage of this particular procedure was that there was no liquid to be drunk, no food to be ingested, that could ever point the finger of suspicion. Death from natural causes, blame the oysters.

Out across the bay, the sun slanting through the clouds turned the sea to molten copper. Like hounds on the scent of wild boar, tugs tracked through the maze of merchantmen that lay at anchor because they were too big to moor at any of the limestone blocks and towed the smaller ships to berth. Lighters flittered back and forth like fireflies, loading and discharging at frenetic speed.

Jocasta lifted the lid of the boxwood container.

Like the lyre strumming softly in the courtyard down below, the application of death was a gentle process. In fact, it involved nothing more than sculpting a small scarlet seed with a distinctive black spot, like an eye, to a sharp needle point.

The victim wouldn't even feel the scratch.

With great care, she removed the papyrus leaf in which her five precious seeds were wrapped.

The boxwood kept them cool and dark. The papyrus prevented rot and drying out.

But so deadly were these seeds, so delicate, that Jocasta checked them regularly. The last time had been on board ship, just as the *Tyche* brailed her sails to come in under oars, and she was probably worrying for nothing. None of the other medicines had been damaged in the crush of disembarking. All the same, though—

She unfolded the papyrus.

The seeds, of course, were in perfect condition. The problem was, there were only four.

Nine

Somehow, Iliona had expected the streets to be quieter in the afternoon, now that the market had packed up. But if this was quiet, heaven help a busy spell.

'Syracuse started off as just this little island,' Niobe explained, as their chariot weaved through bales of linen rolled out on the flagstones and dodged wheels of yellow cheeses. 'Nowadays, thanks to two excellent natural harbours, hills that simply drip with fruit trees, and being surrounded by impossibly fertile plains, we seem to have spread over half of Sicily.' She waved a hand encased in rings and bracelets in the vague direction of the mainland. 'Not,' she added, 'that you'd think it, with all this bloody traffic. I mean, honestly.' She rolled heavily, if expertly, kohled eyes. 'Have you ever seen so much congestion in your life?'

Iliona hadn't. On her left, red-slippered Cypriots rubbed shoulders with turban-clad Babylonians. On her right, Nubians covered in ritual scars held up animal skins. Antelope, lion and leopard. Merchants called to one another in more languages than there were months of the year. In fact, she thought, the whole city was just one relentless tide of commerce. As the horses clip-clopped across the bridge, she was starting to get a better feel of what lay at stake with that act of sabotage. Syracuse was definitely a prize worth winning.

'What's that up there?' she asked, squinting towards what seemed to be white cliffs in the hills.

'The quarries. Monstrous workings, but purely for domestic building, I'm afraid. The stone's far too soft to export – so we've resigned ourselves to selling timber, grain and olive oil at perfectly obscene profits instead!'

'And beyond them?' There seemed to be some landscaping up among the trees.

'Now that, my dear, that's the City of the Dead. You couldn't ask for a more delightful spot to lay your ancestors, especially now the grotto's finished, and the views, I have to say, are absolutely stunning. But definitely one to be avoided after dark.'

'Ghosts don't frighten me.'

'Who said anything about ghosts?' Niobe lean-ed with the chariot as it swerved to avoid a group of sailors careering out of a tavern, whores on either arm. 'There's something far more sinister stalking those tombs, believe me. A giant crea-ture, with a single eye in the middle of his forehead.'

'A Cyclops?' Iliona laughed. 'You've been spending too much time with Alys!'

Far more likely moonlight playing tricks on the statues that marked the graves, but to her surprise, Niobe did not return her smile.

'There are dark forces at work,' she said grim-ly. 'Don't say you haven't been warned. Now then, this is the agora. Isn't it *splendid*?'

No one could argue that point. Temples, civic buildings, sculptures and basilicas fringed the square. Beyond them, in a maze of twisty alleys, the clack of potters' wheels competed with the bustle of the shops, while the cries of peddlers and money lenders were drowned by the tap-tap-tap of cobblers bent over their lasts. Thankfully, there were libraries, bath houses and gymnasia close by to offer refuge from the bustle.

'You can't see it from here, but the Great Temple of Zeus lies just beyond the river. The rest is purely residential, including the Heights, which is where my brother lives – which reminds me!' Niobe snapped her fingers. 'Pull over,' she told the charioteer. 'Sorry about this, my dear, but I'd just like to inspect that pack of hunting dogs, do you mind?'

'You *hunt*?'

'Not likely!' When she shuddered, the jangle of bracelets was deafening. 'But they're just the ticket to take my brother's mind off his bladder stones, poor man. People have no *idea* what a martyr he is to them.' Having pronounced Molossons better than Gaulish hounds any day and then given the seller her brother's address, she climbed back in the basket and dusted her hands. 'There, now, that'll put a bounce in his step at the forthcoming hunt.'

'Isn't spring the wrong time of year for hunting?'

Niobe shot her a cold look. 'It depends what you're after,' she said.

And it stood to reason that the High Priestess of this city's patron goddess couldn't have achieved her position by being naïve. For all her display of bonhomie and warmth, there would be a very different animal lurking beneath, and Iliona wondered what on earth made Lysander think he could fool this woman at the Festival of the Fountains.

Once back across the bridge, the driver took a different route, through streets which increasingly had an air of gentility. Mouth-watering aromas wafted out from communal ovens on which gorgons had been painted to prevent the curious from opening them and ruining the bread. Priests from the Temple of Apollo inspected sacrificial entrails. Priests from the Temple of Athene chanted prayers.

'How can you be sure it's Sparta behind the slaughter of your horses?' Iliona asked.

68

'My dear.' Niobe drew a deep breath. 'I under-stand, truly I do, the loyalty you Arcadians feel towards your neighbours.' She gave Iliona's arm a sympathetic squeeze. 'But who else has a motive?'

'Athens?'

Her laughter carried above the clatter of the iron tyres and the clip-clop of the hooves. 'You sweet child! I'd be tempted to give Sparta the benefit of the doubt, if only for your sake. But I'm afraid what we found on the archers left us in no doubt.'

'You mean the silver?'

'It was stamped with the *lambda*,' she said bitterly. 'And they weren't carrying it for ballast. Oh, for heaven's sake, driver, what's the hold-up this time?'

'Wagon up ahead's broke its axle, marm. Road's completely blocked.'

'Well,' she tutted to Iliona, 'you did say you had energy to burn,' and it was a testament to the woman's bone structure that she couldn't only walk under the weight of all that gold, but set a cracking pace along the waterfront.

'So you're expecting invasion any day?' Iliona persisted.

The sounds of hammering echoed right across the island, since the arsenal was based down on the point. Catapults seemed to be the order of the day.

'Half our warships are on standby,' Niobe said, as if Iliona hadn't noticed how the *Tyche* had had to weave through them in the harbour. 'The rest

69

are on patrol, but I don't mind admitting the loss of our cavalry is a blow.'

'Why not call on Athens for support?'

'Because our voices would be hoarse,' she snapped. 'After all the help we've given them, brokering trade with Africa and supplying them with gold, what do they say?' She let out a loud, inelegant snort. 'They won't risk full-scale war with Sparta.'

Quite. But suppose there was a way to take control without resorting to confrontation? Iliona watched the waves slapping gently against the rocks. Until thirteen years ago, Greece had been the generic name for hundreds of scattered city states, constantly at war with one another over territory and trade, and whose only common denominator was language and religion. A discord the Persians had been quick to exploit, conquering them almost as fast as it took their horses to ride across them. It was inevitable, she supposed, that the larger states would prosper in the aftermath of peace, with Syracuse a prime example.

But forget Syracuse for a moment.

Corinth had traditionally been a major power, renowned for progressive thinking – witness, for example, the dragway she built across the Isthmus, effectively connecting the Gulf of Corinth to the sea. Though the tolls were steep, they were more than worth the time and risk of sailing round the Peloponnese. And when you added on the profits from her shipbuilding yards, not to mention Games that rivalled Olympia, it was easy to see why Corinth had become the third most powerful nation in the world.

Which was what bothered Iliona.

Ten years ago, when Athens first sought to create an empire through the back door, Corinth threw in with Sparta to maintain the equilibrium of power. The Spartan Confederacy was born. But if Athens could prove this was no more than a disguise for Sparta's own expansion plans, Corinth would transfer her political allegiance, other states would follow and Sparta would be isolated from the rest of Greece without a weapon being fired. Athens would have her empire within the year.

'But if Sparta thinks they can just walk in and take over, they're in for a shock,' Niobe was saying. 'Syracuse has turned itself from a far-flung outpost into a lively, cosmopolitan and, dare I say it, sophisticated community, and our influence stretches right around the world.' She broke off to dodge an Etruscan merchant balancing a basket of delicate, black ceramics. 'We've deposed tyrants, fought off the Carthaginians and put down more slave rebellions than I can count, and the bastards have got to land first, remember.' She wagged a firm finger. 'And of course we've already shipped in horses to replace the butchered herd.'

Fighting talk, Iliona thought sadly. Those horses would take weeks to train, and Sicily was a hundred and sixty miles across, one hundred miles wide. Were Sparta so inclined, she could land her troops virtually anywhere on this island

and Syracuse would be none the wiser – but in the end, it was irrelevant that there would be no follow-up invasion. The seeds of betrayal had been sown, that was all that mattered. Now, it was simply a question of time before Corinth tore up the treaty and the Confederacy toppled. Time which was fast running out...

'And here we are, at last!' Niobe pulled up so sharply that Iliona almost cannoned into the balustrade. 'The reason you travelled all this way.'

'It's beautiful,' she gasped.

Not only the shrine, with its gabled roof and gaily painted columns, where fragrant incense spiralled and the reflections of the sacristans were mirrored in the copper double-doors. But eight, maybe ten feet below the marble colonnade, was where the Spring of Arethusa welled up, rimmed by banks of wild papyrus and dappled by the shade of weeping willows.

'It takes everyone's breath away,' Niobe admitted with a chuckle. 'Even mine sometimes.'

'I had no idea the fountain was so close to the sea.'

Twenty paces from salt water, yet this was fit to drink.

'That's not the best of it.'

Niobe linked her arm with Iliona's and led her along the portico, where water from Arethusa's spring had been siphoned into a channel designed to cascade in a series of gentle steps into the harbour.

'See there?' She pointed to a slight disturbance

in the waters. 'On a calm day like today, it's barely a ripple and when the wind blows, you can't even see it. But that's Alphaeus, my dear. That's where your river god comes up.'

A freshwater spring actually welling up in the sea? And another just a few feet away, on the land? No wonder this spot was so holy.

'I hope you enjoyed our little tour,' Niobe said. 'And I apologize for not showing you the spring straight off, but I always like to leave the best till last.'

As she marched off to prepare for her role at the Stag Festival, Iliona studied the phenomenon of this unique double spring. As the river god crossed the ocean to join with his nymph, so Arethusa plunged into his arms to complete the circle, the legend said. Which was why, if you threw something into the Alphaeus, it was supposed to wash up in Syracuse – though there was no suggestion that it worked in reverse, that if you tossed something in here, it would wash up in Arcadia. Because how could it? Water bubbles up, but rivers don't run backwards, and that was the key to it all.

Rivers don't run backwards. Leopard spots don't fade.

For five days, while dolphins danced alongside the ship and Drakon paid tribute to Homer, Iliona had asked herself why, when he'd had her under surveillance for so long, had the *Krypteia* resorted to blackmail? Why go to so much trouble, when time was of the essence, when he must have known she'd leap at the chance to serve her

73

country? And why play it down? Why pretend this was *just another cheese fight*, to quote his own words, when in fact the future of not only Sparta, but the whole of Greece hung in the balance?

As far as the king, the Council, even my own agents are concerned, you volunteered out of patriotic duty and afterwards, as far as I'm concerned, the slate is clean.

The hell it was. In the eyes of the *Krypteia*, this was a case of once a traitor, always a traitor. Once this job was over, Lysander intended to denounce her.

Regardless of the outcome.

Iliona watched the feathered heads of the papyrus nodding above the pool. In the willows, finches sang. It was a funny thing, she thought. Lysander saw lack of compassion as his strength. She saw it as his weakness.

She wondered which of the two of them was right.

As the ground beneath his feet deepened to the black of night, Theo crawled out of the cave that had become his refuge and his home.

The itch was back.

And demanding to be scratched.

Ten

'Roxana.'

'My lady?'

Being the goddess of the hunt, it was only natural that Artemis's festival should be held in the woods, where her striding image towered over the clearing, quiver on back, bow of solid silver clasped in her hand. And as an outwardly confident Iliona clapped to the rhythm of the drums, the inside worried that, as guests of honour, eight Spartan spies would need to tread very carefully tonight...

'Why don't you attach yourself to one of the attendants at the Shrine of Arethusa?' she suggested. 'Explain to them that this is your first visit, you're petrified you'll make a mistake, and ask them to go through the rituals with you.'

'Lysander told me to stay by your side.'

Iliona bet he did. 'And I'm telling you that Artemis is both patron and protectress of the Kedos Plain, where the cavalry horses were being pastured when they were killed. Any slip-ups from us and the political consequences won't just be explosive, Roxana. They'll be irrevocable.'

Never mind eight summary executions.

'I appreciate the severity of the situation, my

lady.' The redhead drew herself up to her full, strapping height. 'But I refuse to disobey an order.'

'So you'd rather break the oath you swore, when you promised Lysander that Sparta would not be disgraced?'

Roxana's cheeks flamed scarlet. 'Of course. I will see to it at once,' she said, but her voice was stiff. If there was one thing Iliona couldn't afford to do, it was alienate anybody on this mission.

'Thank you,' she whispered. 'Oh, and Roxana.' She smiled. 'I'm sure I'll be perfectly safe without your protection for an hour.'

The amazon made a rapid assessment of the delegation standing at her back, then nodded. Iliona saw no reason to disclose her plans for shaking off the rest of the team, and as she began to count, she decided that whatever other horrors Syracuse might be facing, incurring Artemis's wrath wasn't one of them. From the music made for her with tambour and pipes to the great vats of wine drunk in her honour, there was enough respect being paid to keep giant boars from laying waste for millennia.

One hundred and ninety eight, one hundred and ninety nine...

She turned round to find that Jocasta had already left the group. And, to her surprise, Talos had also slipped away.

'Drakon?' Another ingenuous smile. 'I remember how well you sang the Hymn of Artemis on board the *Tyche*, and I was thinking. What better way to pay tribute to our hosts tonight, than to stage a personal rendition?'

Drakon's lyre practically leapt into his hand. 'It would be an honour, my lady, and a pleasure.'

'As for the rest of us,' she said, as he bounded off, 'the best way for us to repay Syracuse's hospitality is to throw ourselves into the festivities, don't you think? I'd hate to see the food on those trestle tables going to waste.'

'You won't need to tell Manetho twice,' Phillip laughed, nudging his tracker friend in the ribs. 'His favourite food is seconds. Even the nags in the stables fear for their nosebags when this man's in town.'

'This from the thief who'd steal the belch from a drunk,' Manetho growled back.

'Ah, but I'd sell it on for a profit, mate, that's the difference.'

'If you ate more, little flea, you wouldn't rattle so loudly.' He grabbed Phillip's arm. 'Let's see if we can't muffle some of that clattering.'

The sun's disc had dipped below the horizon long before they'd set off. Now its heat trapped the fragrant resins of the pinewood. Fats and juices from the roasting spits hissed and sputtered over the flames. Naturally, the meat turning was venison.

Suddenly a foot dangled from one of the overhead branches, and she started. 'Good grief, there are men perched up there,' she exclaimed.

'Oh, yes.' She forgot how much Silas blinked when he spoke. 'They're the recital slaves.' His apple cheeks bunched in embarrassment, as though he were ashamed of his prodigious

77

memory. 'Highly trained and highly sought after, in one, two, even three years from now, they will still be able to entertain their master's clients and guests with a verbatim account of tonight's hymns and speeches.'

'How demeaning.'

The little man smiled. 'Believe me, Lady Iliona, there are worse ways to be enslaved.'

'I'm sorry.' She should have realized that was how he'd started out.

'Don't be. If it wasn't for my training, Lysander wouldn't have needed my services and I'd still be in Argos. Although I have to confess, my master was none too keen to sell. I cost Sparta a full talent of silver, in the end.'

'One talent for another? I'd call that a bargain.'

'The fact remains, I am still a slave.' Silas bumbled off in the direction of the food. 'But then,' he sighed, 'who isn't? One way or another?'

Pacing the tombs, his giant feet feeling no stones through his thick, wooden clogs, Theo thought, he didn't want to, oh dear god how he didn't. But he just couldn't help it. He had to. He *had* to...

The marble statues, so perfect, so elegant, seemed to mock him as he lumbered among them. On the air, he could smell hyssop and thyme, and could see the bonfires down in the woods. Maybe no one would come tonight?

Would that make him feel better?

Or worse...?

At the grotto, he forced himself to look in the

78

pool. The face hadn't changed. It was still ugly. Mutilated. Theo punched a fist at the freak in the water. The face vanished, but he felt no relief.

As the agony twisted, he gripped the blade in his hand.

Barely two minutes passed before he heard footsteps. And caught a faint whiff of perfume.

For the Stag Festival, a dozen bonfires had been lit round the clearing, transforming night into day. Men with antlers strapped to their heads linked arms with girls wearing chaplets of scented spring blossoms. Lavender, arabis and pinks. Together the couples whirled round each of the fires in turn, singing and laughing, clapping and stomping, and as the festivities wore on, the vats echoed as the level of wine inside dropped, and the dancing grew more cavalier.

'Amulets, my lovely?' A shrivelled old woman, her face whitened with gypsum in a throwback to the days when female celebrants covered their bodies with clay and wore white in honour of Artemis's virginity, rattled her tray in front of Iliona. 'Guardian bees, for the goddess's protection?'

'Allow me,' a gravel voice said, and a figure dropped down from the branches.

'Oh, thank you, sir.' The beggar bit the coin to make sure. 'Thank you very much, sir. May the gods bless you, sir, and your wife, and your children.'

'From warrior to recital slave.' Iliona stared at

the carving in the palm of her hand and wondered how much of a sting this bee packed. 'How adaptable you people are.'

But even in his anonymous tunic and with his hair tied back in a queue, there was a stillness about Lysander that set him apart. The stillness that was unique to all men who walk the line of danger.

'We could not have employed this subterfuge without you,' he said.

Maybe.

'Eight devout Arcadians clustered round the shrine of a wood nymph aren't likely to accomplish very much,' she pointed out.

'Don't you believe it.' He took the wine cup from her hand and lifted it in a toast. 'To us, by the way. You and I.'

'I have no truck with blackmailers, Lysander. There is no "us".'

'Hm.' His mouth twisted from one side to the other. 'Then let's drink to you.'

As the silence between them stretched to infinity, the moon rose through the pines.

'You'll be surprised what a small group like ours can achieve,' he said at last. 'Each member of the team has been chosen for their specialist skills. Yours we've discussed, of course, and tomorrow Manetho heads for the caves, in search of traces of the archers who holed up there.' He took a sip from the wine cup. 'Silas is along to memorize conversations and testimonies, then repeat them in evidence if needs be. Roxana's job is to ensure no harm comes to you – though

I fear she's already in trouble for deserting her post – while Drakon's voice will earn him a seat beside the fire of any tavern. Where better to pick up gossip and clues?'

Iliona wondered how she was supposed to explain away the absence of one of her group, when Niobe was nobody's fool.

'What will Phillip be picking up?' she asked.

'As many incriminating documents as he can lay his hands on, once we've identified which of the scores of merchants, ambassadors, tacticians and bankers are actually behind the conspiracy.'

He didn't seriously expect her to believe this could be accomplished in a matter of days? 'And Talos?'

'Hm.' Lysander rolled the dark, Tuscan wine around on his tongue. 'Let's just say Talos employs specialist skills that will come in useful, should the cheese fight get dirty.'

In her mind she pictured a boy, whipped half to death and so traumatized by the event that he deserted. 'How much dirtier can it get?'

He upended the goblet. 'You have no idea,' he rasped, returning it to her hand. 'None at all.' And with that he was gone, melting into the crowd, a shapeshifter in all but the name.

Beneath the colossal wooden statue, quite a crowd had gathered to hear the Hymn of Artemis. The goddess's free hand rested on the neck of her totem, the stag, whose antlers were wreathed in pure gold and whose hooves were sheathed in bronze. Illuminated by flames burning in tripods that flickered as high as a man, it

81

looked for all the world as though it was prancing.

> *'And the daughter of Zeus bade the mighty*
> *Cyclops*
> *"Lay aside the task you're working on at*
> *your smithy."'*

Drakon's hair shone gold in the firelight and his fingers caressed the strings of his lyre as though they were lovers. The purity of his voice carried into the canopy.

> *'"Fashion me a bow, instead, a fine silver*
> *bow,*
> *And a quiver full of long silver arrows."'*

The Cyclops protested that he was unable to help, since he was working on a commission for Poseidon. A trough for the sea god's white horses. Artemis cajoled,

> *'"Fashion me a bow, a fine silver bow,*
> *And you may feast on the stag I bring*
> *down."'*

Spellbound, the crowd held their breath as the Cyclops capitulated.

> *'In her tunic of saffron, Apollo's twin sister*
> *Tried out her new silver bow.*
> *The first shot killed a stag beneath a lightning-struck tree,*

And the Cyclops dined like a king.'

'Speaking personally,' a cultured voice murmured in Iliona's ear, 'I've had it to here with arrows.' Talos peered at her through his floppy fringe. 'Horses. Archers. All of them sacrificed on an altar of greed.'

'Then you're in for a long night. The festival culminates with a volley fired into the dawn.'

Talos frowned. 'Surely the arrows are fired *away* from the light? It makes no sense otherwise. Why kill the dawn?'

'When you're a new country with a new future, symbolism comes second to theatre.' Iliona spread her hands. 'Imagine the effect a hundred hissing arrows makes against a pink sky, compared to hitting a mass of dark trees.'

'My lady.' He performed a theatrical bow. 'I see why the Temple of Eurotas is so popular.'

'Like the priests of Artemis, Talos, I simply make sure people get the best that they can.'

What specialist skills? she wondered. And why the secrecy?

'Not eating the venison, Bronze Man?'

Jocasta's face was unusually flushed, and there was an unaccustomed spark in her eye. Iliona did not think it was due to the goblet in the physician's hand.

'No, my tastes veer more towards the spicy.' Talos shot the newcomer a triangular smile, causing one eye to disappear behind his lopsided fringe. 'With just a little bit of a bite.'

'If that's aimed at flattery, you've picked the

wrong target, and if it was meant as an insult, you're wasting your breath.'

The triangle deepened, causing deep crevices to form at the side of his mouth. 'Would you believe me when I tell you it was neither?'

'No.'

He took a slow draught of his wine then lifted his head to the stars. 'They say Spartan warriors are tough, but god help the man who wins Jocasta's heart, for he will be battle hardened indeed.'

'Open wide and say *aah*.'

With a chuckle, Talos obliged.

'Just as I thought,' she pronounced. 'Not bronze all the way through. That tongue is definitely silver.'

'As my heart is gold.'

'And your neck solid brass.'

'Then I'd better leave before the heat of your overwhelming passion for me melts it.' Talos dipped his head in farewell. 'Ladies.'

As the hymn died away, a roll of drumbeats echoed round the clearing. In long white robes that swished in the silence, the High Priest of Artemis approached the statue, invoking the goddess in a low, sombre tone.

'...*O powerful daughter of almighty Zeus...*'

'You could at least have tried to be civil,' Iliona hissed.

'...*Queen of the Silver Arrows...*'

'Why?' Dark eyes scowled at the place where Talos had disappeared into the crowd. 'If these bastards are intending to kill me, I want them to

84

know who and what they're dealing with.'

'*Great Mistress of the Hunt...*'

'Jocasta, if these bastards are intending to kill you, they'll kill you and it won't matter a toss who or what they've dealt with.'

'I hate it when you pull your punches.'

'If I didn't speak my mind, Jocasta, we wouldn't be friends.'

'Who the hell said we were friends?'

Beneath the statue, the priest released a clutch of sacred quails, which ran flapping and squawking into the woods. Oblivious to the revellers' laughter, Iliona's mind peeled back time...

There was no moon that night. It had been hidden by clouds, low, grey and damp, and she'd been fast asleep when Jocasta knocked on her door. Knowing superstition and health ran hand in hand with the poor, she'd appointed Jocasta, feeling a fellow *helot* would be more able to relate to their physical, spiritual and emotional problems than any conventional doctor. Consequently, she hadn't thought twice at the knock.

'I have one of your warriors locked in my bedroom.' There had been no emotion in the physician's voice. None at all. 'You must come.'

Why me? she'd wondered. Why not wake the janitor or raise the temple guard? Questions that flashed through her mind in exactly the amount of time it took to read the lack of compromise in Jocasta's eyes, and in that moment, something was born. Now whether that something was friendship, who could say? But when she'd entered the room, she found the boy on his knees, rocking back and forth, shaking uncontrollably.

'Poppy juice,' he sobbed. 'You've got to give me poppy juice.'

'Are you an addict?' she'd probed. Beside her, the physician stood stiller than death.

'I don't need very much.' It was as though the boy hadn't heard her. 'Just enough to steady my hands, so I can tie a rope round a tree.'

His words could have been a blow, they hit her so hard. Coming from a family of aristocrats, war was a way of life – a code of conduct if you like – and Iliona had grown up with death and glory as the norm. But in that instant she saw there was no glory in death and nothing honourable about cold-blooded murder. In that second, she saw war through the eyes of recruits. Feeling how they would have felt, when sent out to kill *helots*. Driving a blade into an innocent, unarmed man's belly. Feeling his guts spill hot on their hands...

As the last quail ran off clucking into the woods, Iliona ground her heel into the bed of soft pine needles and turned her face to Jocasta. 'Then if we're not friends, why do you help the deserters?' she asked. 'And don't give me that crap about it being a physician's job to save lives.'

Dark eyes flashed in the firelight. 'Every deserter I help means one fewer soldier,' she snapped. 'One less threat to my people.'

Iliona watched her stalk off and thought, is that right? Then why don't you let these boys take their own life, Jocasta? Let them hang themselves, like the first one had wanted. Because that way you could *really* be sure—

Another roll of drumbeats, and the crowd parted, strewing palm leaves into the open corridor in which a procession of youths and virgins advanced barefoot, their heads garlanded with flowers. With torches held high and flutes tracking their progress, they laid stag-shaped cakes flavoured with honey and sesame at Artemis's sandalled feet.

'It would be so simple,' Roxana whispered in Iliona's ear, 'to slip a dagger between their ribs.'

She hoped the girl didn't notice her jump. 'I thought you were boning up on the rituals?'

'They've explained the basics and agreed to give me a demonstration in the morning. My task reverts to protecting you again, my lady.'

Guard. She meant guard. 'Whose ribs?' Iliona asked, and as a slave moved over to refill her wine cup, she took care to drink from the opposite rim from where Lysander had sipped.

'Haven't you noticed how many Attican brogues there are here?'

How could she miss them? Having blasted a hole in the Confederacy wall, Athens needed to consolidate their victory and gain more ground – but in a way that would not arouse suspicion. Syracuse would be extremely sensitive to the fact that every time Athens had stepped in to assist a weaker state in the past, that state had ended up enslaved. Therefore, it was important to maintain a pretence of neutrality, drifting round like wisps of white smoke, socializing and conducting business, just as they had before the horses were slaughtered. Everyone's friend. And everything in good time.

'Athens has a strong representation in every city state,' Iliona said. 'It doesn't follow that every Athenian is politically motivated, and I've heard nothing contentious in any of tonight's talk.' In fact, conversation tended to revolve around progress on the new Parthenon and how the Persians (everyone's enemy) had appointed a new satrap in Bactria. 'They're just having a good time, like everyone else.'

'Who cares?' The freckles on her nose stood out in anger. 'We could despatch every last one before anyone noticed.'

'I'm pretty sure it would draw someone's attention. Then it wouldn't only be the Athenians who'd be dead.'

Roxana's lip curled. 'Death is no more than a gateway to a better life.'

'Only the young can be so utterly certain of the unknown,' Iliona laughed, 'but I rather think you're missing the point. Martyrdom won't advance Sparta's cause.'

In fact, killing Athenian merchants and emissaries while posing as Arcadians would be the final nail in the coffin.

'That's what Lysander said, but it still bloody grates, knowing the Hand of Athens moves among us, watching, listening, biding his time, while we dance to his tune like fucking puppets.' Catlike eyes shone green in the torchlight. 'We could fumigate the whole filthy nest with one

88

strike.'

'Including the innocent.'

'War's war, casualties are inevitable. It's the innocent who suffer the most.'

'You seem very flippant about death.'

'Not at all.' Roxana's eyes narrowed. 'I'm sure Lysander told you, we aren't taught to take life recklessly, but these are hardly the weak and the vulnerable. Ask any Athenian, do you want total dominion, and you know damn well what they'll say.'

Guilty simply by association? And how sad that a girl of nineteen never smiled, never laughed, was earnest to the point of obsessive. Iliona wondered what demons drove Roxana so hard that she'd dedicated her life to the *Krypteia*, her virginity to the State and her sense of reason to misguided ideals.

'What saddens me, Roxana, is that you were taught to kill in the first place.'

'Not at all. My brother makes for an excellent teacher.'

There was a sinking in the pit of Iliona's stomach. 'Your brother?'

'Lysander sets the highest of standards,' Roxana said proudly. 'How else could he command the *Krypteia*?'

As the sky in the east lightened to grey and the first birds took to the wing, a dozen archers lined up in the clearing and lifted their bows to the dawn. Drumbeats rolled to heighten the tension. Trumpets blared. Then a pennant was waved, the clearing fell silent. As one, the archers let loose.

The sound was like a deep exhalation of breath that had been pent-up inside for too long. In perfect synchronization, the arrows soared over the pines, and even though the sound of their fall would be cushioned by the soft woodland floor, it was drowned by more blaring of trumpets and wild whoops of joy. To the joyous jingle of flutes and tambours, the crowd began to disperse, twirling and swirling in rhythmic unison as they headed home to their beds.

As guests of honour, the Arcadian delegation was among the last to leave. When the first scream came, nobody paid any attention. A sea-bird wheeling and shrieking over the sea. Then a second scream split the grey of the dawn, and suddenly legs were racing through the woods to its source.

The cries came from a child of no more than seven, who had lost her way in the crush and stumbled upon horror. Jocasta ran to the girl, calming hysteria with meaningless words and covering her eyes as she led her back to her frantic parents.

Iliona sank to her knees.

She had seen death before. The poor and the elderly were especially vulnerable. Infant mortality remained disconcertingly high and wounds sustained in battle often claimed victims months, if not years, later. Sometimes death crept up slowly. Other times it was swift. She'd seen lockjaw arch a man's back like a bow, and watched helplessly as ulcerated lungs infected people's bones.

But she had never, ever, seen death in this form—

The corpse was unrecognizable beneath the mass of arrows, but there was no disguising those long, flowing, golden locks. As the first blackbird started to trill, Iliona saw a terrible irony in watching Apollo's rays break over the horizon while the Apollo in this glade would sing no more.

'Oh, Drakon, Drakon, you poor sweet boy.'

Staring at the twisted, bloody pulp, his lyre smashed in splinters underneath him, Iliona could only pray that Roxana was right about that gateway to a better life.

God knows, this one had been too short.

The Serpent's forked tongue flickered in pleasure. The first apple in the orchard had fallen.

The worms of Paradise were starting to crawl.

Eleven

'What you need to remember, my dear, is that this tragedy could have been so much worse.'

Her face shaded by the cypress that ringed the Shrine of Arethusa, Iliona turned to face Niobe. Behind them, attendants in long trailing robes of white filed out through the bronze-clad doors, heads veiled and chanting softly.

'Really?'

The volley hadn't killed him outright. The arrows' force had been spent by the time they reached the glade, but their very weight and number was enough to bring him down. And it hadn't needed Manetho's skills to see the trail of blood that led across the grass and realize how desperately this fit, dynamic warrior had tried to drag himself for help, using his beloved lyre as a crutch. Iliona wondered why dying was never easy for the young.

'Not as far as Drakon is concerned,' Niobe was quick to make clear. 'I was referring to the repercussions that his death *could* have had. For instance,' she added swiftly, 'it could easily have been argued that the death of one of Alphaeus's servants was an omen. A sign that the gods are in opposition to our mutual celebration of the Festival of the Fountains, even to the extent that Artemis herself directed her enmity against it.'

'Yet you don't think this will happen?'

Artemis has a bow that rains arrows of death on anybody who upsets her...

'I made damned sure it won't,' Niobe retorted. 'Arethusa symbolizes everything that's good and pure about this city, and I will not have her image tainted by talk of evil portents.' She laid a reassuring hand on Iliona's shoulder. 'I made it clear to the City Elders that Drakon was simply in the wrong place at the wrong time, the poor boy. No stranger could possibly be aware of our curious custom of firing arrows into the dawn, I

92

told them, how could they? Only Syracusians do it back to front, as it were, and I have insisted that guards be posted out there in the future, to prevent any further accidents of this nature.'

You don't want to upset Artemis, she's a bitch...

Iliona pushed Alys's little painted face out of her mind and concentrated on the acolytes who swung silver censers with grim solemnity, purifying the air with their incense. But sweet as the music was from the flautists who banished the spirits of hell on pipes of sacred alder, it was a very different song that replayed inside her head.

Fashion me a bow, a fine silver bow,
And a quiver full of long silver arrows...

And as the sun slowly rose over the roof tiles, dark thoughts writhed like maggots.

You count the grains of sand on the shore and measure the seas in the ocean.

Nonsense. How could she – how could anyone? – have foreseen that Drakon was singing his own death beneath the goddess's feet?

You hear the voice of the voiceless and see through the eyes of the blind.

There was no possible means of preventing this tragedy. But there they were again, those little maggots. Gnawing. Nibbling. Scratching away...

She watched holy water being sprinkled over the embroidered cloth that covered Drakon's corpse. Listened to the wailing women as they

93

spattered their breasts with ash and tore at their hair. Waited while torch-bearers lined up beside the bier to light the golden-haired bard into the darkness. None of it altered the fact that it was she who had asked (no, let's get this right, had insisted) that Drakon entertain the assembly with his rendition. With a clang, the doors closed behind him. Once inside, his body would be taken down to the temple mortuary, where it would be washed and then anointed with oils, before being laid out in ceremonial robes until the time of his funeral. For Drakon, a new adventure was beginning. But for Iliona? The attendants dispersed. Niobe melted away. All that was left were a few droplets of water splattered over the flagstones. Even these were drying to nothing.

Taking a seat beside the sacred spring, Iliona tried to find peace among the ducks that wove in and out of the lacy papyrus, and the sparrows that splashed in the shallows. Instead, she found herself reliving the moment when a grown man's hand had covered her own, as father and daughter laughingly emptied a tiny blue phial into a goblet of wine...

'That's the way, Iliona. Drip-drip-drip. Clever girl!'

The memory shocked her. She couldn't imagine where it had sprung from, or why it had chosen this moment, but what surprised her most was the vividness of it. That, in the space of an eye blink, she was once again instrumental in administering the poison that quite literally drove the King mad. Twisting his mind to the point that he'd heard voices inside his head, ordering him to kill strangers in the street. And the worst part was that her father hadn't simply stood by while women and children were hacked down at random, he fed the King another venomous brew afterwards, to help calm his nerves. Eventually the voices told him to slash himself to ribbons on the steps of the temple. Had a more public case of suicide ever been witnessed?

One could argue, she supposed, that her father had done Sparta a favour. The King had been weak, and in ensuring a new king was crowned, Sparta had grown stronger, richer, infinitely more respected. Through her father's actions, strange but true, peace was assured. But what price glory...? Her own father, who didn't just get away with murder, Iliona thought bitterly. He was branded a hero for not giving up on his friend!

In that instant, that eye blink, she realized that it was treachery the maggots had been gorging on. Treachery that triggered those terrible memories. And as birds greeted the new day from the tops of the trees, she saw that Drakon's death was no accident. He'd been lured to that glade with cold-blooded purpose, his presence timed for the loosing of the volley.

Roxana's words floated back.

It grates, knowing the Hand of Athens moves among us, watching, listening, biding his time, while we dance to his tune like puppets.

She'd been referring, of course, to the various

merchants and emissaries who were gathered at the festival last night. But Roxana was wrong. Very wrong. The Hand of Athens did indeed move among them – but the hand moved from within.

It was surely no coincidence that both Drakon and the cavalry horses died under a rain of arrows, but why had no one drawn attention to this? In fact, Niobe was quick off the mark to dismiss it, perhaps a little too quick. Who knows, maybe it was simply a question of damage limitation, politics, politics, politics. But given that timing was the crux of Athens' campaign, who else knew enough about the Festival of the Fountains to suggest using it as a cover? Whether Niobe was in Athens' pocket or not, though, she could not possibly be working alone. As the reflections of the water rippled off the bronze doors of the shrine, Iliona considered her companions. Little plump Silas, who blinked and who bobbed. Phillip the thief, overshadowed in more ways than one by his big bear of a friend. Educated Talos, hot-headed Roxana, Jocasta, who hated them all. Any one of these could be a traitor. Every last one had the opportunity and the means.

But only one of the group had motive...

Lifting her eyes to the haze of green hills, Iliona watched wisps of white smoke from Mount Aetna coil up into a cloudless blue sky. With all her heart she wished she was wrong, that she could put the pieces together and reach a different conclusion. But it all boiled down to one question: who would benefit from a toppling of power? Not Silas. He'd still remain in bondage, simply serving a different master. Talos? Manetho? Phillip? Roxana? None would be remotely better off under Athens. If there had been any doubt in her mind, one only had to ask: Apart from Iliona, who else would Drakon have obeyed without question when it came to stationing himself in that glade?

The one member of the group who was noticeable by his absence this morning.

The Commander of the *Krypteia*.

She should have been shocked. She should have been outraged. But Iliona had been here before—

Like her father, Lysander would not consider his actions as betraying his country. He'd argue that sooner or later Athens would have her empire in place, he was merely making the inevitable work to Sparta's advantage. The hell he was. The cold-blooded bastard was using leadership, friendship, loyalty and trust to advance his personal ambition. And, as the candle of enlightenment continued to burn, Iliona realized that the real High Priestess of Alphaeus, the Lady Chloris, also had to be dead. Killed somewhere between leaving Arcadia and arriving in Sparta, because in the end, Lysander was working with Athens, not against them. He could not allow her to live.

So what was his plan?

Why this charade about sending a team to clear Sparta's name, only to pick them off one by one?

What on earth could that achieve? But before the question had even formed in her mind, she knew why Lysander had been watching the Temple of Eurotas for so long. Why he'd hung on before calling in his debt.

Just as she'd needed a scapegoat for the spring equinox, so Lysander needed one for his plan...

Already proven to be a traitor by helping deserters, Iliona was second cousin to the King, who had personally appointed her to the post. Obviously she wouldn't have the resources, the power, much less the inside knowledge to act alone in this treachery, and since no one would believe that an organization as feared and respected as the *Krypteia* would sell out their country, the blame must therefore lie with the King.

Drakon and the others were nothing more than sacrificial lambs, though Lysander would have different plans for Roxana. To give credence to his allegations, he'd need a truthful, dependable and objective witness to testify at Iliona's trial – and who better than the girl who'd dedicated her virginity to the State?

Apart from Iliona, who else would Drakon have obeyed without question when it came to stationing himself in that glade?

Dammit, he'd had her under surveillance for so long that he knew she'd baulk at being guarded and watched. He knew she'd try to fragment the group, and now Roxana would be able to testify, hand on her heart, how she'd also been ordered to leave her post. And since it could be

98

proved that Niobe had told Iliona about the volley fired into the dawn, a snippet she'd passed on to Talos, how could she deny asking Drakon to wait for her in the glade?

The wolf had set his trap in such a way that the finger of suspicion could only point in one direction. Once Iliona was found guilty, the King would fall, his Council with him – and while Sparta tore herself apart from the inside, the shadow of Athens would darken the landscape. A hero in the mould of Leonidas would be called for. Step forward the Head of the *Krypteia*...

From the spring of fresh water rimmed with papyrus, the tears of Arethusa bubbled gently to the surface.

Twelve

Hyblon the shepherd boy laid down his pan-pipes and stretched in the shade of an outcrop of rock. High in the distance, muffled by the thick forests of oak, beech and juniper, the rhythmic thwack-thwack-thwack of an axe floated down, as woodsmen felled timber which would be weathered then carried on chains behind bullocks down to the shipbuilding yards. But here, gazing across to the Great Burning Mountain rising up in the distance, the bleating of his contented flock combined with the scent of the thyme on the sun-sodden hills to make Hyblon's young eyelids heavy.

He let his mind drift. He was Heracles. Heracles, sent on his first Labour to kill the lion of Nemea, whose pelt was impervious to bronze, stone and steel. Hyblon had never been to Nemea, but he imagined the mountains would be similar to his own, and in his fantasies he followed the lion's giant tracks, scattered with the remains of the men it had slain, until he arrived at its lair.

Like Heracles before him, Hyblon the Hero loosed a flight of arrows, but they bounced off the beast's blood-spattered pelt like raindrops. He tried running it through with his trusty sword, but the sword bent, and his club of wild olive smashed into splinters against the lion's skull. Cornered in its cave, the lion turned. Snarled. Hyblon saw fangs as long as a dagger. Smelled its hot, foetid breath. As it sprang, Heracles launched himself at its neck and, with just the strength of his bare hands, choked the monster to death.

The little hero sighed happily, raised himself up on one sleepy elbow and checked that his flock had not wandered off, that none of his lambs were gambolling their way towards the ravines. Satisfied, he scanned the sky for circling eagles, but the only thing drifting against the backdrop of blue was the smoke from Aetna's great peak. Hyblon lay back again, folding his hands behind his head, listening to the droning of the bees among the wild herbs and the hymn of pipits on the wing.

Now he was Theseus, deep in the bowels of the labyrinth, bearding the Minotaur in its den. Half-man, half-bull, all cannibal, the Monster of Crete pawed the ground in impatience as Hyblon tracked his prey through the dank, dark, sub-terranean chambers—

The change was subtle. A flutter of wings. The bleat from a ewe. The cessation of birdsong close by. Individually, they were nothing, but to a shepherd boy raised in the hills, together these things signalled danger. Hyblon sprang to his feet, but before his hand had closed over his cornel wood staff to fend off whatever predator was stalking his flock, a giant shadow fell over the hillside.

The shadow started, as though surprised to see the lad pop up from behind the rock, but Hyblon didn't notice. Like a coney mesmerized by the glare of a cobra, he was transfixed by the eye. The eye in the middle of its forehead.

As the Cyclops turned towards him, Hyblon reached for his sling. Loading a pebble, he was ashamed to find his little hands shaking. Slithering backwards down the hillside, not daring to take his eyes off the Cyclops, he let go. But his shot went wide and the distance was closing. He loaded another bullet into his sling. This time, he thought. This time I—

A giant paw lashed out to grab him. Suddenly Hyblon was whirling through the air. He could see the glaring disc of the sun overhead. Heard the Cyclops's roar of triumph in his ears.

But before he could scream, he heard a mighty crack, and Hyblon's little world plunged into black.

'You shouldn't be wandering around without a bodyguard,' Phillip said, slotting into step alongside Iliona. 'Not that I'm suggesting the city's unsafe – anyway, who'd be stupid enough to attack the Arcadian priestess? But a woman on her own's always a target, and streets like these carry more risks than most.'

If the agora, with its law courts, temples and all those other fine structures that constituted civic order, was the commercial wheel upon which Syracuse turned, then the artisan quarter was its axle. Both had been oiled to operate smoothly, admittedly one with elbow grease, the other more with the greasing of palms, but while both contributed equally to the city's success, the industrial district was the heart from which the blood pumped. In the afternoon heat, the smell of leather fused with scents of sacking and willow. Scraps of hide miraculously turned into purses and sandals, multicoloured withies became baskets at the flick of a few nimble fingers, bone needles tacked up the seams of the salt sacks.

'Your protection is much appreciated,' Iliona lied smoothly.

'*My* protection?' Phillip's teeth shone white when he laughed. 'My lady, I'm even thinner than you and a whole hand span shorter. If it came to a fight, I reckon you'd end up defending me! No, no, it's his protection I'm talking about. That ugly lug trailing behind.'

Manetho nodded back as she thanked him, but for all that, the tracker's face could have been carved from an oak.

'Can't say I blame you, wanting to get away from all that dirging,' Phillip was saying. 'It's depressing stuff, death. Not that I don't feel sorry for Drakon,' he corrected quickly. 'I do. We all do. There for the grace of the gods go the rest of us and all that. But the point is, I wouldn't want people getting miserable over me when I'm dead.' His nose wrinkled. 'No good comes of hanging round mortuaries. Better to be out and in the thick of it.'

She wanted to warn him. Grab his arm, put her lips to his ear, tell him to trust no one, no one at all. But he'd laugh in her face, because youth is invincible, and would probably still be creased up when he repeated her ravings to Lysander.

'Quite right, Phillip. We should embrace life and respect death. Heaven knows, it comes soon enough.'

Too soon, if Lysander even remotely suspected that she was on to him. But as long as he believed he had the upper hand, Iliona was safe. Once more, it was a case of holding her nerve.

Watching the dexterity with which a carpenter turned wood with his double-edged saw, she reflected that change had come at breakneck speed. Within half a generation, temples had risen from the ashes of war. Peace had blossomed into an age of poetry and music, sculpture and

103

drama, of brand new technologies, even medicine. But its principal impact was the explosion of the democratic system. Gone were the dictators and tyrants that had held the scattered states in their grip and kept them poor and repressed. Suddenly citizens no longer accepted authority without question, but haste spawned problems of its own. Thirteen years of peace had most certainly changed the face of Greece and the way Greeks thought about themselves. But by the same token, it had brokered more greed and ambition than had ever been seen before. Lysander was merely one shining example.

And on the face of it, it seemed nothing could stop him.

Under the baking sun, Iliona's head throbbed. She was damned if she'd stand back and let history repeat itself, the way it had with her father. For one thing, Lysander wasn't a patriot. He was a self-seeking hypocrite who craved power at all costs, happy to sell his country out for his own ends. And for another thing, Iliona was no longer a child. But even assuming she had the means, the opportunity and, more important, the courage to kill him, he'd amassed so much evidence concerning her aid to deserters that the King and the government would still topple. All right, Lysander might not be around to watch Sparta fall apart. But his death wouldn't stop Athens from milking the crisis. The situation would be every bit as bad.

'Well, well, well!' Phillip chuckled. 'Would you look what that poor merchant dropped.'

'Give it back.'

'Seriously?'

'Seriously.'

His face rumpled as he grudgingly returned the drawstring purse, then brightened as the merchant rewarded his kindness with a bright, shiny drachma. 'Who says crime doesn't pay?'

Behind them, Manetho grunted.

'Ignore him, my lady,' Phillip hissed behind his hand. 'He's in a foul mood, and all because he'll be up there, scouring for traces of the Cretan archers, while we're attending Drakon's funeral down here.'

'It's bad luck, not sending the dead off properly,' the tracker growled.

'You and your bad luck. I've known virgins on their wedding night who aren't half as superstitious as you, mate.'

'You mock, little flea, but there's an entrance to Hades on this cursed island. Just make sure you don't take the wrong turn.'

'I've told him, my lady.' Phillip shot her a wink. 'On a still night in those hills he'll be able to hear the jangle of harness from the invisible chariot of Death, and jump at the crack of its whip.'

'One more word about blood-sucking fiends that haunt those bloody caves or witches that steal minds while men sleep, and it'll be you riding side-saddle to Hades, my young friend.'

'Even then you'll overtake me, thinking the thousand red hounds that tear wayfarers to pieces are chasing your big, ugly tail. Or will you be running from the ogre that blue-eyed Athene imprisoned under this island? They say that when the giant tries to shake off his chains, the whole of S-S-Sicily t-t-trembles like you.'

'Just because you haven't seen them yourself, don't mean those things don't exist,' Manetho protested.

Phillip skipped round a handcart loaded with thatching. 'Like the Cyclops, you mean?'

'Take no notice,' Iliona told Manetho. 'These are nothing but ancient fables and legends. Tales designed to frighten children at night.'

'With respect, ma'am.' The big man made the sign of the horns with his fingers. 'You want to talk to the farmers up in the hills before you dismiss them as myths. They've seen the Cyclops prodding their middens, snooping round homesteads after dark—'

'Yes, who knows how many folk have fallen foul of our nice friendly cannibal, ending up as supper instead of guest,' Phillip quipped. 'Mind, when he sees the size of you, me old mate, he'll think it's a banquet. All his birthdays rolled into one.'

'You think it's a joke?' There was a sober set to Manetho's jaw. 'How many other giants do you know of, with eyes in the middle of their foreheads?'

It was h-u-g-e. Alys's childish voice echoed. *I saw him once, he was ever so tall and I knew it was him because of the eye in his forehead.* Iliona remembered little hands spanning a circle the size of a melon. And when asked what colour

106

the eye was, *Blue, silly!*

'Let's change the subject,' Iliona said briskly. 'I'm already feeling my mind being sucked clean by your bickering.'

To her relief, they both laughed, the tracker braying louder than the ass that passed them on the inside, its panniers bursting with apples and figs. The deeper they encroached into the artisans' labyrinth, the more the soft smells of leather and willow gave way to the acid stench of molten metals, and Iliona was grateful for the wealth of hammers and hand-drills that put paid to any further conversation. Ostensibly admiring the embosswork on the tall silver candlesticks while cuirass-makers polished bronze to an eye-watering shine, she was painfully aware that the only solution was to expose Lysander's treachery herself. But how? Where could she even start? With no one to trust and no one to confide in, she had no idea where to begin.

Emerging into the agora, the change was dramatic. Suddenly the loudest sound was the grunting of men exercising in the gymnasia or the clickety-click of coins on the money-changers' tables, and in spite of herself, Iliona was impressed. With each city state minting its own design now, there must be a thousand different weights, shapes and sizes to calculate here. Copper *chalkoi*. Drachma, obols and staters of silver. Ephesus minted theirs in electrum, of course, Sicilians retained their fondness for bronze, and trust Athens to mint the biggest!

Buying three hot, honeyed pastries from a

street vendor, she was amazed at the speed with which the coins changed hands. How on earth did the money-changers keep track? Some were more easily recognizable than others, either displaying their patron deity – Arethusa for Syracuse, Athene for Athens – or else stamped with their patron deity's emblem. Pegasus on Corinthian coins, for example. But how many years did it take to distinguish the coinage of a thousand city states in differing metals, then change it all in the blink of an eye?

Biting into the crumbling pastry as deft hands flicked back and forth, Iliona wondered how the other states viewed Sparta's unique system of controlling its economy. On the principle that if money was hoarded, it undermined the whole financial system – better to keep it flowing and put it to work – the State compulsorily exchanged currency above a certain amount for its equivalent weight in bars of lead. Not the best country to settle in, if one's career choice was a miser, but at least it meant Sparta kept an accurate record of her assets—

Holy Zeus!

'Is something the matter, my lady?' Phillip had crumbs all round his mouth. 'You look like you've seen a ghost.'

'No, no, the pastry just went down the wrong way.' She tossed the rest to the pigeons. 'Will you excuse me?'

For heaven's sake, if the State could account for every last obol, then the coins could have been tracked to their source within hours...

meaning Sparta knew fine well her own treasury hadn't minted that silver. So why weren't they trying to find out who had?

Fashion me a bow, a fine silver bow,
And a quiverful of long silver arrows...

Drakon had been quoting from that part in the hymn where Artemis asks the Cyclops to lay down the task he is working on in his smithy.

How many other giants do you know of, with eyes in the middle of their foreheads?

It was h-u-g-e. I saw him once, he was ever so tall and I knew it was him because of the eye in his forehead.

The farmers have seen him, prodding their middens, snooping round their homesteads after dark.

There was no such creature as a Cyclops, but all myths started from a grain of truth. Now if Iliona was right (and it was still a big 'if'), there might yet be a way to bring down Lysander. And just across the way was the very place to find some answers! Without breaking her stride, she marched up the steps outside the Temple of Selene.

'Sorry, gentlemen.' A eunuch with a gleaming, shaven head barred her companions' progress with broad, outstretched arms. 'The moon goddess only admits female devotees.'

Manetho and Phillip shrugged as if to say, can't be helped, but Iliona had already forgotten about her male shadows.

109

Smoke and mirrors, it's why Lysander picked you.

Indeed it was – but not to carry out any smokescreen rites and rituals. He'd picked Iliona to be the centrepiece of his own personal illusion, but you can't fool a woman who sets riddles herself. Not for long. Illusion relies on the audience seeing what they've been primed beforehand to believe. The challenge facing Iliona was how best to debunk it.

Within the precinct of the temple, marble horses galloped and reared, the silver on their hooves glinting in the afternoon sun. Horses, of course, were sacred to the goddess. Their shoes represented the moon's crescent. So it came as no surprise to see thousands of silver-shod horseshoes set into the temple walls, gleaming, shining, glistening by the light of scores of oil lamps. And since the moon was also the source of all rain, water showered from a dozen silver cisterns into deep silver troughs, making music that jingled and chinked, while white doves cooed in their cage.

Silver, you notice. Silver, silver, everywhere. The metal of the moon—

Mingling among the novices and acolytes, the 'High Priestess of the river god Alphaeus' paid reverent devotions to Selene, inspecting entrails, dedicating a bracelet – and wasn't it only polite to converse with at least one of the nine priestesses who served the goddess?

'There must be lots of smiths on Sicily,' she observed airily, as the priestess ushered her inside the inner sanctuary.

It made no sense to mint the coins in faraway Athens. For one thing, the *lambda* would draw unwelcome attention. For another, unpredictable seas could easily sink the whole shipment. Far better to strike the coins here.

'You can say that again.' The priestess let out a suitably silvery laugh as she unlocked the door to show their honoured guest round a storehouse crammed with silver artefacts ranging from cats to griffons, cauldrons to urns, all set with blood-red carnelians from the deserts of Egypt or turquoises from Sinai, agates, amethysts and garnets. 'On the west coast alone there are over four hundred forges, working alongside the foundries.'

Too far away, and besides. The west was under the control of the Phrygians, and if the Phrygians sided with anyone, they sided with Persia. Athens' arch-enemy!

'Local silversmiths must be in abundance, too.' Iliona ran her hand over the gleaming flanks of a pony. Production on this scale must keep plenty of craftsmen in work.

'In truth, the more exquisite items tend to be imports.' The priestess covered her nose with her veil against the overwhelming smell of polish. 'Donations from Syracusian merchants that they picked up on their travels, though wealth does have this wonderful habit of rippling downwards. For most of the lower orders, monetary donations are all they can afford, and would you believe, they've increased almost fivefold in as

111

many years.' She rolled her eyes. 'You wouldn't *believe* the number of coinsmiths that have sprung up.'

Something bucked inside Iliona's chest. She recognized it as hope.

'We have to punch holes in the coins, to take them out of circulation, or else we'd be knee-deep in thieves—'

'I didn't notice a coinsmiths' quarter in town.'

That had been the point of this afternoon's walk. To locate the district where coins were struck.

'That's because there isn't one.' The priestess confirmed Iliona's findings, as she locked the depository door behind them. 'Why rent shop space when all one needs is a recessed anvil, a punch and hammer? The process is so simple, one could probably train dogs to strike the wretched dies.'

Cyclops. Silver. Smithies. The pieces finally slotted into place.

'Thank you,' Iliona said, kissing the woman's hands. 'Thank you, thank you so much.'

'Don't go yet,' the priestess called after her. 'I still have three further storehouses to show you.' But she was wasting her breath. Iliona was already well out of earshot.

You want unimpeachable witnesses, Lysander? Then unimpeachable witnesses are what you shall have.

I saw him once, he was ever so tall and I knew it was him because of the eye in his forehead.

Alys hadn't imagined the Cyclops, any more
112

than the farmers up in the hills had. But this was no creature of legend. It was flesh and blood they'd seen prowling around, and what's more flesh and blood of Thracian origin.

And the eye? Not a third organ of vision. What they'd seen was a tattoo of concentric blue circles – the ancient sign of the Thracian bronze-smith. The massive build of this race, coupled with the fact that they tended to work in isolation, gave rise to the myth of the Cyclops. Over time, these big, brawny mountain men extended their scope to meet the increasing demands of neighbouring Macedonia's silver and gold mines. It followed that sooner or later one would cross the ocean to Sicily, and for such a craftsman, minting coins could be done in his sleep.

As Iliona scurried back home along the waterfront, her veil pulled low over her face, she knew that if she could deliver the Thracian to Sparta, there would be no place for Lysander to hide.

The days of the *Krypteia*'s treachery were finally numbered.

Thirteen

With mud matted into his hair and his skin stained in streaks with soot, Lysander rattled his begging bowl with a convincingly palsied hand as merchants, poets, philosophers and bards swarmed through Syracuse's north gate.

'Alms! Alms for a poor wounded cripple!'

The cries of the beggar on Lysander's right would have carried more weight had he not stopped to shift his bandages to the other foot, since the one he was standing on was growing weary. Beside the fountain, the waif mewling pitifully took advantage of a lull in the traffic to lift the bloodied patch from her eyes to make a swift count of her takings.

'Won't you help a blind orphan girl?' Not enough, obviously. 'Won't you, sir? Please?'

They weren't all fakes. Too many lined, empty faces testified to too many sad, ruined lives. Lepers. Battle-scarred soldiers who'd drunk themselves into the gutter. Artisans whose injuries at the plane or the lathe had thrown them out of work with no prospects. It was no coincidence that they'd all clustered here. As the city's wealth and influence burgeoned, so did its prospects. Whether furriers from the mountains or

frauds with fake injuries, entrepreneurs flourish-
ed in this climate of riches.

'Can you spare a copper *chalkoi* for a poor
widow, mister?'

The old crone's voice was so thin, it didn't
carry over the clunk of wagon wheels and clatter
of oxen. When she turned her head, Lysander
tossed his own coins into her bowl. It wouldn't
be long before she'd need them for the Ferryman. The Fates who span, measured and cut the
thread of life were already sharpening their
scissors.

He stiffened as an armed guard approached,
breastplates gleaming, greaves jangling, the
plumes on their helmets bobbing with military
precision. But the guard marched past without a
glance at the scum under the arch, save one, who
spat into a cripple's bowl, sending the rest of the
unit into spasms of laughter. Lysander relaxed,
and the sun moved round in the sky as the smoke
from Mount Aetna made puffs of cloud in the
distance.

'Hey you!'

The crack of a bullwhip cleared a path through
the beggars.

'You with the red cloak. Don't I know you?'

'Who, me?' Lysander's voice became a whine.

'I *do* know you, dammit.' The rider dismount-
ed and no amount of expensive unguent could
disguise the stench of poverty and destitution
that he swaggered into. 'You used to be my
groom.'

'No, sir, not me.'

'Don't argue with me, man.' The stranger hauled Lysander to his feet by the scruff of his neck. 'I know my own slaves when I see 'em. Cost me half a talent of silver, you did.' He sneered at the empty bowl. 'Can't even claw an obol of it back. But you're coming with me anyway, you runaway bastard. The hard way or the easy way—' His hand covered his dagger. 'It's your choice.'

As he shoved Lysander through the gate towards the depths of the city, the *Krypteia*'s Commander hid his smile with his sleeve.

The Athenian had made contact at last.

In a cave in the hills, half-hidden by a scrambling fig tree, Theo curled his giant frame into a ball and howled.

Fourteen

'As ever, Niobe, you throw a truly magnificent banquet.' The City Elder, a broad-boned individual with a thick thatch of hair, bowed in homage to his hostess. 'The food melts in the mouth, the wine is *surely* Etruscan and I don't ever recall seeing such suppleness and poise from a dance troupe.'

'My three Graces?' Arethusa's priestess turned

her elaborate coiffure to the trio gyrating to a tune on the pan-pipes. 'Sublime, aren't they? I tell you, Periander, my temple cats could learn a thing or two from those girls.'

From the moment slaves swung open the oak doors embossed with bronze, Niobe's status shone through. Colourful tapestries hung on gaily painted walls, high-backed chairs with curving legs clustered round tables inlaid with ivory, and stars had been studded with prolific abandon between the fragrant cedarwood beams. Like a sunburst, rooms led off from the atrium in every direction, each boasting bold murals and cornices painted with garish geometric designs. Niobe did not favour subtle in, or outside, her palace.

'Acrobats, jugglers, astrologers, poets. Niobe, you have excelled yourself tonight. My only hope is that your rustic visitors appreciate the effort you've put in.'

'You flatter me, Periander, but then you are the City Council's chairman.'

Her companion laughed. 'What a wicked tongue you have on you. Why, were it not for your husband, I'd—'

'My husband's in Corinth, he's always in Corinth, and to listen to him you wonder how they manage without him. But before you make a complete ass of yourself, we both know I'm playing nymphs and satyrs with a boy half your age and that I have no desire to change that arrangement.'

'That empty-headed young stallion?' The

Chairman snorted. 'The lad has no brains, no conversation—'

'Exactly how it should be. Men are like cobblestones, Periander. Lay them right and you can walk all over them, and there's no danger of emotional involvement in such an arrangement ... Now do try a morsel of eel. My chief scribe owns the smoke house, so I can vouch for the flavour.'

'Mmm.' His eyes closed in pleasure. 'This is *delicious*. And those figs. Where the devil did you find them?'

'Wait till you try my sweet dessert wine. Quite honestly, if this isn't what the gods drink on Olympus, then the Immortals are being short-changed.' Arethusa's priestess linked her arm with her friend's. 'Now tell me something, Periander.'

'Anything you wish, dear lady, anything at all. After this feast of ambrosia, I would betray my own children. I can deny you nothing, Niobe.'

Laughing, she topped up his goblet. 'As much as it grieves me to waste such a wonderful opportunity, it's only your opinion of the Arcadian delegation I'm after.' She darted a glance to the far pillar of the room, where Iliona was holding court with two junior members of the city council. 'A moment ago, you referred to our spiritual cousins as rustic. Do you really find them bucolic?'

'Perhaps it's a sign of ageing, that my memory's not what it was, but now you come to mention it, no, this present contingent doesn't

118

seem as ... as ... *pastoral* as the last lot. Mind you,' the Chairman added with a chuckle, 'that was two years ago, and since I was heavily involved in plotting against tyrant rule at the time, my recollection might not be as clear as it could be.'

'Your recollection's just fine, Periander.' Niobe patted his arm. 'I simply wanted a second opinion. Now then,' she said briskly. 'What about this other business?'

'The Cyclops?' The Elder wrinkled his patrician nose. 'There's no doubting there's someone up in the hills, but what they're up to—'

'Some*one*, rather than some*thing*?'

'Let me put it this way.' Periander leaned towards her. 'I can't imagine a giant one-eyed cannibal disembarking in our harbour without at least one busybody drawing it to the Council's attention! But in answer to your question, quite frankly, Niobe, I don't know what to make of this business.'

'The homesteaders aren't imaginative by nature.'

'No, but they are superstitious.' Periander stroked his beard in thought. 'Which is why I was able to convince the farmers who came to petition me that we're only courting Artemis's wrath by picking a fight with a creature under her protection.'

'Explain to me, then, why there's a hunt being organized.'

'Ah, well, that's Athens's doing.' He popped another piece of smoked eel into his mouth. 'All

119

that class distinction plays havoc when it comes to finding ways of passing the time, and since their patricians have sod-all to do while they're here, being forbidden to engage in trade, they're bored out of their skulls. And who wouldn't be.'

'Come, come, Periander. We're talking about rich, powerful, but above all educated men who are more than capable of distinguishing between reality and myth. Why would they push to hunt down a Cyclops, knowing no such creature exists?'

The Chairman waved a dismissive hand. 'If they were back home, they'd be off in search of lion pelts to hang on their walls. Can't blame the poor buggers for having an itch.'

Niobe stared into her wine. 'You're going to let them scratch it?'

'Can't really stop them, my dear. And now I come to think of it, isn't your brother joining the hunt?'

'Any incentive to take his mind off his bladder stones.' Her smile was wan. 'I even bought him a new pack of hounds.'

'Then what's the problem? It'll be Athens, not Syracuse, who'll suffer, should Artemis vent her divine retribution.' He tapped the side of his nose knowingly. 'By letting them go off and do what they like, we keep our Attican friends happy, but more importantly, we keep them out of our hair.'

'I still don't understand this sudden rush of interest in a man who's no threat to anyone.'

'No threat? What about these young women

120

who have been disappearing at an alarming rate? Or that little shepherd boy who got himself killed yesterday? Hyblon, I think they called him. No, no, no. If the Athenians want to go out and bag themselves a "Cyclops", I don't intend to stand in their way.'

The shrewdness in Periander's eyes showed why he'd been elected Chairman.

'Whatever they end up killing, Niobe, one way or another, Syracuse will be rid of a monster.'

'What now, Bronze Man?' Jocasta continued to snip away at the stems of delphiniums, laying the heads lengthwise across her trug. 'A potion for your sprained conscience?'

'Conscience?' Talos scratched a puzzled head. 'Would that be found near those dangly bits at the back of the throat that you physicians refer to as scruples?'

'Those are tonsils. Scruples are the knives we use to put the terminally arrogant out of their misery.'

She swept past him to cut the white bells of rock lilies, carefully placing them between the delphiniums and a spray of yellow tulips. His shadow made her task difficult, even more so since light from the oil lamps tripled it in size. Behind them, music from the festivities was reduced to a muffle, the laughter no more than a murmur.

Everything King Midas touched had turned to gold, but Jocasta saw a broader approach to metal when it came to Niobe. Statues of bronze jostled alongside platters of embossed electrum which in turn rubbed shoulders with silver wine jars etched with green malachite. The effect ought to have been as hideous as it was overpowering, yet, like Niobe herself, it achieved the opposite effect, radiating exuberance wherever one looked. Exhibition for its own sake, and if there was a single item of furniture that wasn't either fashioned from rare wood and elaborately carved or else inlaid with jewels or ivory, Jocasta hadn't seen it. Every single lamp that hung from the candelabra was engraved with a different animal or bird. Beauty to be shared, not hidden away.

'I hear Niobe has asked you to have a look at her brother,' Talos said, leaning his shoulder against the pillar. 'I gather his bladder stones are no match for Syracusian doctors – or is it the other way round?' He rubbed his temples. 'My mind seems strangely fuddled tonight.'

'Unfortunately, it's nothing fatal. Merely the consequence of our hostess's light hand when watering her wine and a heavy hand when serving rich food.'

'Ah, but who can deny the logic of moderation in all things except what you enjoy? And anyway, I thought you herbalists were supposed to gather your herbally stuff in the mornings? Once the dew has evaporated, but before any essential oils leach out through the heat of the sun? And isn't it supposed to compromise their effectiveness, if you collect more than one species at a time?'

Jocasta moved on to the pink gladiolus. 'For a fuddled brain that claimed aboard ship not to be able to tell his decoction from his elbow, you suddenly know a lot about gathering herbs.'

'That's because I made it my business to find out.' He picked up a delphinium and peered into the violet-blue bells. 'Like, for instance, aren't these things poisonous?'

'Actually, I picked "these things" because I find them pretty. Or did you imagine I only went for thistles?'

Talos shot her a lopsided grin. 'You're not half as prickly as you make out.'

'Don't put money on it.'

One dark eye peered solemnly through his fringe. 'One thing I never do, Jocasta, is gamble.' Then the smile bounced back. 'So why aren't you having a wonderful, wonderful time like everybody else?'

'Who says I'm not?'

'Very well, then, I'll rephrase it.' He sniffed a tulip and seemed surprised that it was fragrant. 'Why aren't you inside, taking advantage of the lavish entertainment that's been laid on especially for our benefit?'

'The courtyard suits me nicely.'

He laid one hand over her scissors. 'Worried you'll get used to it?' he whispered in her ear. 'That too much high living might turn your pretty little revolutionary head?'

She snatched the scissors away. 'The only thing high living turns is my stomach.'

'Yes, of course. Who would want their feet

123

washed and oiled, when they could stay grimy and covered in mud and dust? And why would anyone want to inhale fragrant resins, when they could so easily breathe the stink of the city?'

'Live with me as a *helot*, then see how funny you find it.'

'Is that an invitation?'

Jocasta swatted a moth away from the flame of an oil lamp. 'Tell you what, Talos. Chew on these delphiniums for an hour or three, and then we'll discuss the matter further.'

His laughter echoed long after he'd left the courtyard. In the sky, the moon was just three days from being full.

The Serpent in Paradise coiled round the island and slowly started to squeeze.

Fifteen

Upstairs in her room, Iliona locked the door and then tested the catch. As usual, she was taking no chances. One person had already been murdered – two, if you counted Chloris – and while she had no doubt that Lysander intended to pin Sparta's betrayal on her, there was no guarantee that she'd make it home to stand trial, either. The slightest hint that she suspected he was anything other than he was pretending to be, and she'd be

124

passengering the same boat as Drakon to the Isles of the Blessed. The *Krypteia* would have no difficulty finding another scapegoat.

Dragging the clothes chest in front of the door, she unpinned her hair and loosened her girdle. Niobe had the same attitude to guests as Scythians had to their saddles. They simply cannot be stuffed too much. But though the gourmet delights should have tempted her taste buds, every mouthful tasted like sawdust. Wine, which ought to have slid down like nectar, could have been vinegar, for all that she knew.

Why couldn't the gods make things easy for once? Why was it always so bloody hard? Splashing her face from the bowl, she blotted it dry with a towel of clean linen and cleaned her teeth with a section of mastic. Iliona was under no illusions. Failure was far more likely an outcome than success, but with the testimony of the tattooed smith, Sparta might just have a chance to prove her innocence. Now even *that* was at risk, thanks to Athens' push to hunt him down! Absently, she rubbed a moisturizing balm of borage and marigold into her skin. What puzzled her was why, if the Thracian smith was such a thorn in their side, Athens had waited so long to eliminate the only witness to their political sabotage. Indeed, why had they even left him alive? Now it occurred to her that they'd been waiting for Lysander's arrival. More proof, if any was required, that the *Krypteia* was calling the shots.

She blew out the candle and lay back on the

pillows, moonlight streaming over the coverlet. Outside, the hoot of owls drifted on the night air, but sleep was a long way away.

There was no proof that the Thracian had murdered the shepherd boy, or even that Hyblon was actually dead. All they'd found at the scene was a large pool of blood, but the lad hadn't come home and in fairness the outlook wasn't at all promising. But whether the smith was responsible for the crime or not, how easy to exploit the fear of cannibalism among a superstitious hillside community and give impetus to the forthcoming hunt.

Listening to the repetitive hoo-hoo-hoo of owls in the pines and the gentle croaking of frogs, the Temple of Eurotas seemed a lifetime ago. Yet only a week had passed since Iliona was interpreting the chimes of the bronze discs in the plane grove, and consigning logs to the flame whose perpetuity protected her homeland.

I'll have you know, madam, this is not fat round my midriff. It's proof that gluttony lubricates vigilance.

Oh, Perses. From the day Iliona took office, he'd given loyalty without waver, support without question and opinions without reservation. What she wouldn't give, to have her old friend by her side now! But facts had to be faced. And while everyone knows that we enter this world alone and alone we depart it, they often forget that, for the large part in between, many of us also face adversity on our own.

Tossing and turning on imaginary lumps, she

126

thought surely there was someone? Surely she could find an ally here somewhere? She placed a handful of sleep stones close to her nose and inhaled their soothing, lavender fragrance. Jocasta would believe her. She'd even sympathize with her plight, but Iliona wasn't naïve. Generations of *helotry* had taken their toll, and if Jocasta thought there was the slightest chance of civil war on the horizon, it was all the incentive she needed. Sparta under Athens was one thing. A bloodbath across the Peloponnese quite another.

And Niobe? As the pale blue moonlight tramped round the room, Iliona reflected that the priestess's involvement, deep or otherwise, was irrelevant now. Syracuse was rapidly turning from a backward, rustic, dependent colony into an influential, international power. In this dog-eat-dog world of political change, it was every state for itself. Niobe would exploit every weakness that she could find.

In the dark, loneliness was colder than charity.

Gorged and replete on its feast of treachery and betrayal, the Serpent basked in the warmth of the sun. Too long it had been chained in the confines of Paradise, too long it had pulled at its chains.

But the first bite into the apple of freedom was sweet.

Now the Serpent wanted the orchard.

Iliona's thoughts were still on Niobe. For a long time, the priestess had been in conversation with the Chairman of the Council of Elders but, try

127

though she might, such was the lowered tone of their voices that Iliona had only managed to catch snippets. Did the Chairman suspect the delegation wasn't the real thing? Was that what Niobe was confiding? Twice she'd seen them glance in her direction. What were they talking about? She'd caught the odd word about Cyclops and Athens, but by the time she'd worked her way round the crowd, Arethusa's priestess had turned to toasting her honoured guests, her skin barely visible beneath the welter of cosmetics and gold jewellery that adorned it. Her exact words became muffled in recollection, but her laughter rang clear, as was the broad wink she shot at young Phillip. Then the Chairman strode up to the table, clutching a sackful of coins.

Mine, all mine, he roared, spilling them over the food, and as he did, everything on the table turned to silver.

Give that to me, shrieked the priestess of the moon. *That silver belongs to the temple*.

You must fashion me a bow, a fine silver bow, Drakon's tenor voice sang, *and stamp it with the sign of the* lambda.

That money's ours, cried the archers, notching arrows of gold. *We earned it killing horses, it made us rich men*.

As they lined up to fire off their first volley, a great bellow shook the banqueting hall.

My eye! Give me back my eye! roared the Cyclops, punching a hole in the door. *Those coins are my sight*, and as he strode into the room, a hundred feet tall, the building shook with his footsteps and plaster dust showered down from the ceiling. Yet even though he crammed Silas kicking and screaming into his mouth, all Iliona could see was the hole in his forehead, the hole where he'd been blinded...

She woke with a start. The nightmare had left her drenched in cold sweat, but to her surprise, moonlight had given way to golden sun and the sky was the colour of bluebells. Blame the late night, the stress and anxiety, but she'd slept longer than she'd intended. Swinging her legs off the couch, her foot groped for her sandals.

'The other's under the bed,' a gravel voice drawled. 'Allow me.'

Cold turned to ice. She counted to five, and when she finally spoke her voice was commendably level. 'How did you get in?'

'The problem is never getting into a lady's bedroom.' Lysander blew the dust off the shoe before handing it back. 'It's getting out without compromising her reputation.'

No wonder the mountain wolf smiled. Any man who looks that relaxed in a crisis has found someone to shoulder the blame. In this case, of course, they stared him straight in the face.

'How considerate,' she said.

How long had he been there? How long had he stood by the window, bronzed arms folded, watching her sleep...?

'Considerate was my parents' second choice of a name for me. Or didn't you imagine I'd know my father?'

He didn't wait for a reply. He probably knew the answer anyway.

'Syracuse isn't as bad as Athens, of course, who insist their women are locked away out of sight, the ultimate symbols of repression, possession and control.' He sat on the bed and made himself comfortable, banishing the lavender oil of the sleep stones with the scent of woodsmoke and leather. 'But considering their new-won democracy and the power this city's patron goddess is free to wield, I do find it surprising that Niobe hasn't followed Sparta's lead in giving women freedom and autonomy, don't you?'

'Enlightenment doesn't necessarily go hand in hand with power.'

In fact, there was nothing quite like equality to undermine one's own sense of superiority. Subjugation was irritatingly addictive.

'But you wouldn't have retained female discrimination, now would you?'

'Who can predict how one would react under hypothetical circumstances?' There was absolutely nothing in her manner to suggest that the High Priestess of Eurotas didn't regularly hold business meetings from her bed in a state of dishevelment. 'Speculation is pointless.'

'How true.' Measureless eyes fixed on the clothes chest that was still blocking her door. 'Are you frightened of me?' he asked quietly.

'Would you like me to be?'

'Hm.' He leaned back on the bed, folded his hands behind his head and stared up at the gilt-painted ceiling. 'It's come to my notice that you and the *helot* are taking a trip this bright, sunny morning.'

There was no point in asking how it had come to his notice. The household was large, the slave girls were pretty, easy prey for a man familiar with women in every sense of the word. Or did he think Iliona missed the way sharp eyes had assessed the hair that tumbled over her shoulders and the loose fall of an ungirdled gown over her breasts?

'The city is choking me, I'm used to the country, and since Jocasta needs to replenish her medicines, I've decided to accompany her.'

'You think that's wise?'

He closed his eyes.

She felt no less threatened.

'It would look odd if a priestess from land-locked Arcadia didn't show some curiosity in her exotic surroundings.' Amazing, really, how smoothly the lies flowed. 'After all, that's why you brought me along. To deflect attention with smoke and with mirrors.'

One lazy eye opened and swivelled towards her. 'Where did you get that idea from?'

'Phillip.'

'Then our young thief is mistaken.' A muscle twitched at the side of his mouth. 'I brought you along because you walk the winds and look down on the actions of mortals.'

'Meaning?'

'If you don't know already, I'm sure you'll work it out.' The eye closed again. 'You never

131

did explain why you brought the *helot* along on this trip. Did you fear I'd have my men storm the Temple in your absence, and deprive the poor and the needy of their only chance of passable health?'

Between his fingers he rolled a small scarlet seed, with a distinctive black spot like an eye.

'I don't suppose it occurred to you that I might want the company of another woman?'

'There's always my baby sister.'

Half-sister, she corrected mentally. There was a twenty-year age gap. 'Which only proves I don't walk the winds or look down on the actions of mortals, or I'd have known in advance she was coming.'

The muscle twitched again. 'You don't need to patronize me when it comes to Roxana. Kin or not, I'm well aware she's not the most feminine of creatures. Or the most endearing of female companions.'

'An agent in your own image, though. How proud you must be.'

He must have heard, surely he'd heard? But his breathing had deepened, his chest rose and fell, and the doves under the eaves cooed out their love song, and the sun drenched the air with its heat.

'It makes no difference,' he said at last. And no man who'd broached the inner sanctum at the shrine of Eurotas and the women's quarters of a foreign priestess was going to fall asleep on the job. 'Death, I mean.' He chewed his lower lip for a while. 'Whether it's carnage on the battlefield or the irony of watching a woman bleed to death as the price for giving birth, or even watching that same child slip into the void five years later as venom from a snakebite eroded his vitals, nothing changes.'

Was that his own story? Wife died in childbirth, son five years later? Hell, was it even true? His expression didn't change, his voice remained a monotone, and it wasn't beyond him to spin a tragic scenario to draw her deeper into his web. But at least his continuous goading proved he still believed he was pulling the strings.

'I'm sure those you assisted to the Isles of the Blessed were supremely grateful,' she said.

Something rumbled in the back of his throat. 'For the most part, I ensured their journey was quick.'

For the most part—

With a chill, she recognized the rumble as a warning.

'If you're talking about Drakon, he wouldn't have known what hit him,' she lied, eager to change the subject.

'Did that *helot* of yours spin you that fairytale?' He snorted. 'I've told you before, they're liars, those people. The angle of the arrows, the amount of blood spilled ... I assure you, my lady, Drakon died writhing in agony, and that's why I say it makes no bloody difference. Each time we confront death, no matter how often, a piece of ourselves dies as well.'

'Meaning?'

He shrugged. 'Nothing. I just thought it might

133

be of some comfort to you, since Drakon's voice seemed to reach into your soul.'

Iliona was not going to be drawn into sharing confidences, no matter how bleak or heart-rending, with a double-crossing, blackmailing hypocrite. Especially one who had gone to so much trouble to check up on his investment.

'I'm assuming you're not placing all your faith in a few puffs of my incense, Phillip's light fingers and whatever camp rubbish Manetho digs up,' she said crisply. 'That you have some other plan for clearing Sparta's name?'

'Iliona, Iliona.' He tutted and smiled. 'I *always* have a plan.'

With one bound he was off the couch and stretching the stiffness out of his arms. 'Enjoy your little expedition this morning. I hear there are herbs in those hills that don't grow in either Arcadia or Sparta. With luck, you might find a cure for broken hearts.'

'Yours?'

He laughed. 'I'm flattered you think I'd have one to break. But no, I was speaking generally. The condition seems to be so prevalent and so painful that its cure would heap riches on those who discovered it.' He paused. 'Then the King might take a more pliable stance towards the barley cakes and ribbons that are donated to Eurotas by the poor.'

Cunning. Maintain the pretence of normal life upon her return. Right down to the threat...

'In that case, I shall follow the trail of Eros's misspent arrows as tirelessly as you're following

134

that of the Cretan archers,' she said.

'Hm. Parallel investigations.' He stroked his jaw. 'Interesting notion, wouldn't you say?'

Something fluttered inside. He couldn't know. Unless she'd been talking aloud in her sleep, Lysander couldn't possibly know she'd worked out the Cyclops' secret.

'What's interesting,' she countered, 'is that you're not forbidding me to set off alone with a woman you openly distrust.'

'You make distrust sound like an unhealthy emotion, and anyway –' he clucked his tongue as he strolled across to the window '– accepting orders strikes me as contrary to your nature.'

'You're not even going to offer me a body-guard for protection?'

'Certainly not.' He seemed irritated by the question. 'With Drakon dead, my resources are stretched even thinner, and since there are no bandits on the eastern side of the island, you'll be perfectly safe.'

Iliona wasn't entirely sure this was true, but she understood his desire to get her out of the city, where she would not be in a position to stumble upon anything she wasn't supposed to.

'What about the one-eyed marauder?'

'Ah, but you're not frightened of myths, are you, my lady? Not the priestess who doesn't even believe in the demon over whom her own temple stands guard.'

Turning her gaze on the fishing boats spattered over the ocean like ink spots, hauling in baskets of octopus, sardines and crab, it crossed her

135

mind that Lysander might actually have added impetus to the hunt by killing Hyblon himself.

'I believe in the morality such tales engender,' she replied. 'As long as people fear the demon – or more importantly, its retribution – the world will not descend into lawlessness.' As though he cared. 'Which is why I think Athens should respect Artemis's creature,' she added stiffly.

'The Athenians have no respect for anything except power.' Lysander checked his dagger and adjusted his belt. 'But a word of warning, my lady. If anything comes to your ears, anything at all, or you have even the slightest suspicion, you tell me, do you hear? We're in this together, a team if you like, and teams never break rank. That is the code of the warrior.'

'I'm not a warrior.'

'Oh, but you are, Iliona. You are. Whether you like it or not.' He hooked one muscular leg over the sill and found a foothold in the scrambling rose. 'By the way.' He held the scarlet seed upright between his thumb and forefinger. 'Do you know what this is?'

'Should I?'

'Me neither, but here.' He tossed it across. 'You keep it. It's pretty.'

Then he was gone, and all that remained was an imprint on the damask and a faint whiff of woodsmoke and leather. Iliona would not need to lock her door in the future, or lug a clothes chest in front.

Lysander had made his point.

Sixteen

The bay of Syracuse twinkling gold in the sun didn't look much like a battleground, Iliona thought. But, like the Pass at Thermopylae, that's exactly what it was. And the soldiers there were betrayed by one of their own, too.

Plodding beside her and Jocasta, since the ground had become too rugged for riding, their horses paused from time to time to graze the meagre scrub, snickering softly as bees droned round the tall spikes of sea squill and crickets buzzed like wood saws. Long-horned, long-haired sheep chomped noisily around them, buzzards mewed as they spiralled upwards on the thermals and, far in the distance, the sound of pan-pipes floated on the breeze. Mystic, sweet and haunting.

'Tell me again why you've taken a sudden interest in gathering herbs?'

Watching Jocasta kilt her skirt above her knees to stop it snagging on the thorns, Iliona mourned the high, split seams that kept Spartan women cool on days like this, and allowed them complete freedom of movement at the same time. 'I told you. I'd had it to here with being shadowed day and night. A change of scenery seemed just the ticket.'

'And the real reason?'

'Sorry. I didn't realize fresh air had gone out of favour with you physicians.'

'Where does fresh air fit in with knocking on homesteaders' doors, while I'm busy stuffing my scrip?'

Wasn't it the Gauls who believed in reincarnation after death? In a previous life, Jocasta must have been some kind of terrier. 'It would be rude not to pay one's respects.'

Jocasta's lip curled. 'To think you had the nerve to lecture me about friendship, when the whole thing's based on honesty.'

'And trust,' Iliona reminded her.

Jocasta swung round, eyes flashing. 'Have I ever lied to you, even once? Have I ever made a secret of my feelings about *helotry*?'

True. At that very first interview, her attitude had been take me or leave me. 'Very well.' Iliona stepped over a butterfly sunning its wings. 'If you must know, I'm looking to pick up the trail of a one-eyed, man-eating colossus. Now does that make you feel better?'

To her surprise, Jocasta burst out laughing. 'The Cyclops? You?' She untied the ribbon binding her hair. Raven curls cascaded over her shoulders. 'That's one very powerful death wish you have.'

'I prefer to think of it as humanitarian aid.' Waves of fragrance were released by the buttercups, campion, columbines and mallow trampled underfoot. 'Athens have taken it upon them-

138

selves to kill the Cyclops, except you and I both know there's no such creature, and personally I don't find anything remotely amusing about hunting down a man with a tattoo in the middle of his forehead simply for sport.'

'I see. You're traipsing this wilderness of pot-holes and gorse to save the life of some freak whose favourite pastime is butchering women, not to mention small shepherd boys, who probably witnessed something nasty and needed to be silenced.'

'There's no proof of that,' Iliona shot back, but it sounded weak even to her own ears. Jocasta had touched on a nerve.

Part of her role as High Priestess was the need to be objective. Assuming she managed to track down the Thracian (and he didn't kill her in the process), it was her job to convince him that, if he returned to Sparta, no charges would be level-led against him on any issue. And, more impor-tantly, to honour that contract. The lives of thousands versus the lives of a few women. On paper, the balance was fair.

On paper...

Iliona pushed the hair out of her eyes. At some stage, she would have to face her own reflection, knowing she was sending god knows how many more girls to be ... what? Raped, tortured, brutal-ized beyond measure? Monsters like that never stop killing. If anything, the violence escalates in line with their victims' suffering. Their anguish is what drives them on. On the other hand, no Greek breaks an oath sworn on the altar. If Iliona gave him her word, which she would, she was effectively giving him free rein to continue his carnage. It might not be in Sparta, where he would be known, but there was nothing to stop him from moving on. Killing whenever and wherever he pleased.

She shook her head. First things first, one step at a time! The chances were that the hunters would get to him before she did, and who knows? They might be parading his massive corpse through the streets in triumph right now. Make no mistake, Lysander was good.

'What's happening about Niobe's brother?' she asked, as they approached the brow of the hill. 'Can you really cure his bladder stones, where so many others have failed?'

Jocasta shrugged. 'I've passed word via Niobe that I can, but apparently his physician holds a different opinion. It's just a question of waiting to see whether he'd rather continue writhing in agony, or swallow his pride and ask for my help. Personally, my money's on pain.'

'Don't be so cynical! Niobe told me he's been prescribed pastilles to expel them and all manner of vile potions to dissolve them, and none of the treatments had the slightest effect. She said her brother was so desperate that he got a surgeon to open him up last year, in an effort to crush the wretched things in situ.'

'Which would have worsened the pain, rather than eased it.'

'All the more reason for him to snap up your cure.'

Jocasta slanted her a sideways glance. 'That's a very nice pendant you're wearing. Gold or electrum?'

'Electrum.'

'Fancy staking it against a box of sharp scalpels?'

Scalpels? The most precious tools in a physician's surgery, both in financial and functional value. 'A bet is a bet,' Iliona warned. 'If you think I won't keep them—'

But Jocasta had already spat in her palm, sealing the wager. 'Well, now, if it isn't another homestead for you to go and disturb those poor sods from whatever it is they do to eke out a living.'

Iliona stared at the low, narrow hut in the valley below. In the winter, that humble abode would house not only the family, but the livestock as well. 'Do you want to come with me?'

'It's your death wish. You can follow it up on your own.' She patted her horse's flank. 'This great tub of glue and I are going to see whether there's anything other than thyme in this godforsaken wasteland.'

'Pastureland,' Iliona laughed. 'It's called pastureland, you horrible woman.'

'The hell it is.' With a toss of her raven-black hair, Jocasta turned her eyes on the shimmering heat haze. 'Pastureland is a pear-shaped valley cradled by hills, where orchards and wheat fields stretch to infinity, and where your parents carve their names in the bole of a chestnut. That's what pastureland is, Iliona, not this weather-beaten

141

lump of misery.' She pulled the horse round. 'See you back in the city.'

Watching *helot* and horse clamber away, Iliona mused that, in theory, both were enslaved to human masters, expected to jump at another man's bidding. In practice, of course, both were stubborn and spirited, and very much their own boss. In fact, the only difference between them that she could see was that Jocasta's wit was more highly developed. The ultimate irony, when you thought about it: that Jocasta possessed one of the finest examples of laconic humour that Laconia had never produced.

From the hills way over in the distance, smoke from the charcoal burners wreathed over the soft green canopy. Up here, though, the only trees that could gain a foothold on the soft, red pitted tufa were the occasional hawthorn gnarled by the wind or a twisted stump of juniper. Stiff-limbed and weary, Iliona made her way down to the cottage. Washing lay in neat heaps beside the scrubbing stones. A mattress stood propped against the outside wall to air.

'Anybody home?'

'Who's that?' A small squab of a woman came bustling round the corner, pulling up sharply when she saw her. 'Oh! Oh, milady!' The sun had shrivelled her skin to rawhide. Poverty had loosened her teeth to the point where she lisped. 'Well, fancy! What an honour.' She looked sixty, but was probably still a year or two short of her fortieth birthday. She introduced herself as Kyniska. 'Pray come inside and make yourself comfy.'

Daylight penetrated the single room at its peril, but by the glow of the fire Iliona noticed the ubiquitous cauldron suspended on chains, wafting out the smell from a stew that would bubble continuously for weeks on end, and which would only see meat two or three times a year. Beside the hearth, a stack of wooden plates were piled higgledy-piggledy. Kyniska straightened them with embarrassment.

'Can I offer you wine, marm?'

To accept would be to deplete precious reserves. To refuse would mortify the poor creature. 'A small glass would be lovely.'

Kyniska pulled up a stool with work-reddened hands, and while she went off to fetch water to add to the wine, Iliona's gaze ranged over the solid wooden tables, the neatly made pallet beds, the herbs that hung from the overhead beams. Thyme, rosemary and oregano, all doubling up as rinses for laundry, for disinfectants, for strewing, for medicine, for cooking, and which had clearly been added to tallow to make a sweet-scented polish. In fact, every home Iliona had called on today had differed only in the detail. Wooden chests spilling patched woollen blankets. Heaps of wool beside the family looms, waiting their turn to be weaved. More wool steeping in buckets of plant dye. Bright yellow juniper in this particular case, but in other cottages she'd seen dusky pink sorrel, rich creamy parsley, alkanet that turned everything red.

''Tis truly an honour, milady.'

Kyniska's face was flushed as she passed the goblet across, but now that Iliona's eyes had acclimatized to the gloom, she saw it was with unease rather than pleasure. Mindful that whatever story she spun had to stand scrutiny from all parties if she were taken to task, Iliona pitched into her now familiar routine. The Priestess of Arcadia, in Syracuse for the Festival of the Fountains, was exploring the countryside but had somehow got lost – could they give her directions? water her horse? et cetera, et cetera, et cetera. Oh, thank you, most kind, must admit she'd been worried, heard tales about giants, cannibals even, and she'd been nervous, up here all alone...

'With good reason.' Kyniska stared at her visitor with unnatural intensity. 'Especially now the Cyclops has took to eating shepherd boys in broad daylight.'

In a crib near the hearth, an infant stirred, blew a couple of bubbles, then gurgled itself back to sleep.

'Broad daylight?' That was a new slant.

'Aye.' Kyniska's head nodded firmly. 'You can see from here the place where the poor lad got torn limb from limb, if it weren't for that hill in the way.'

Under any other circumstances, Iliona would have laughed. 'You mean over there?' She gave a vague indication with a tilt of her head.

'Uh-uh. There.' Kyniska pointed a few degrees east of north. 'My man tells me there's a pool of blood the likes of which you've never seen. But it's the lad's mother you feel sorry for, don't you? I mean, we all have to go sometime, but ugh.' She shuddered. 'No one likes to think of their son's raw flesh being a feast for the Cyclops.'

She gave the cauldron a brisk stir with the paddle, checked the loaf in the oven and inspected the level of the water in the wooden butt.

'You're sure the boy's dead?' Iliona picked a straw doll from the floor and ran its hair through her fingers.

'No one lives after losing that much blood.' When Kyniska leaned close, Iliona inhaled the sweet scent of cloves from her tunic. 'Mark my words, milady, Hyblon's riding the Chariot of Death and the Cyclops is holding the reins.'

Outside, Iliona's horse whinnied softly, and frankly she didn't blame it. She stood up, shook her skirts and thanked Kyniska for her hospitality. 'How old's your baby?'

'Oh, he ain't mine.' Kyniska flashed a proud, gap-toothed smile. 'He's me daughter's bairn, and almost two moons, bless his little sweet heart.'

'Two moons? Well, there's a coincidence.' Iliona unpinned a gold-coloured brooch shaped like a peacock, the eyes of its tail feathers inset with metal painted over with blue. 'In Arcadia, we have a custom whereby baby's second moon is marked with a gift.'

Kyniska would have no idea where Arcadia was, much less any knowledge of its traditions and customs.

'Oh, milady.' Her eyes misted. 'Mi*lady*.' Squinting as they re-emerged into the sun, she untied the tethered mare and pointed in the opposite direction from which Iliona had come. 'You'll have no trouble finding your way back to Syracuse, now. Follow that track down to the cairn, then bear left, but mind you don't you hang about. The sun sinks fast this time of year, and there's no telling how much blood that ogre needs. You mount up as soon as the ground's fit for riding, then ride like the wind, d'you hear? Like the *wind*!'

Thanking her once again, Iliona set off down the path. Once out of sight of the cottage, it was her intention to double back and investigate the place where Hyblon had died, but with a shock she realized that time had run out. To cross this hill and then climb the next (shepherd boys don't pasture their flocks in the valleys) would take an hour, probably more. Then she'd have to search around until she found the spot ... by which time the sun would be setting.

'My lady?'

She turned to see a vision of loveliness running down the track towards her, clouds of red dust kicking up in her wake. Iliona smiled, remembering the days when her own hair was that fair, her own skin every bit as translucent. Thirty-four was by no means ancient. But it wasn't seventeen.

'I'm Helice, if you please, marm.' The girl bobbed a curtsy. 'You called on my mother and left this for my baby.'

Although not pretty in a classical sense, she radiated health through the clarity of her complexion, exuded vitality through the sheen on her hair. Right now, though, the brightness in her big blue eyes was clouded by anxiety as she pushed the brooch back into Iliona's hands.

'If you're worried the person you sell it to will think that it's stolen, you ought to know it's not gold.'

Helice looked shocked. 'Sell it?'

'Then I don't understand.' She'd only wanted to alleviate some of their poverty. Now it seemed they wouldn't dream of raising money from it. 'Surely this would help?'

'My lady, we're deeply honoured that you chose to visit our humble home.' Helice twisted her hands. 'But we don't want to offend you by taking your emblem, and we know that to accept would incite your displeasure.'

In the end, it was her very discomfort that gave her away. Flying in the face of relentless adversity, Kyniska's family remained uncomplaining and proud. Witness not only the gloss on the woodwork, but the bunches of horsetails piled on the table, ready to scour the trenchers once supper was over, the immaculately swept tamped earth floor. Yet these people – these practical, realistic, no-nonsense people who worked their fingers to the bone for a pittance – believed Iliona was the Queen of Heaven incarnate, disguising herself as a mortal. And all because Hera's emblem was the peacock!

The trick now was to disabuse Helice, without

undermining their ingrained superstitions.

'No, no, *this* is the totem of the river god Alphaeus.' She pulled off her ring. 'See?' In the bright sunshine, and at the speed which she flashed it, Helice couldn't tell it was shaped like a lion. 'And as for that brooch, to be honest with you, that was a gift from my ex-husband and you'd be doing me a favour by hanging on to the thing. It'll stop me being reminded of him.'

The girl blushed to her roots, a combination of relief, gratitude and probably shame. 'That's mighty kind of you.'

'Not at all, now you run along home. Your mother'll worry you've fallen foul of the Cyclops.'

'Tch, you don't want to listen to folk telling you Hyblon got eaten by cannibals! Stuff and nonsense, my lady.'

'Why do you say that?' Thirty seconds ago, she'd thought Iliona was Hera!

'Well, for one thing, it strikes me that an ogre would leave bones and brains splattered around, while there ain't nothing like that up there, only blood.'

Good point. All crimes leave some trace.

'And for another, the big fella lives in one of them tombs outside of the city. Leastways –' Helice shrugged '– that's where I saw him.'

Surprise knocked her sideways. *'You've seen him?'*

'Not close up, like you and me here. But I tell you, he could lift this horse of yours and sling it over his shoulder like it was a sack of turnips.'

148

A big man haunting the necropolis at night? Where pools of blood were found the next morning?

'What about the eye in his forehead?' Iliona asked quietly. It could still be coincidence.

'Well, that's why I haven't told no one 'cept you.' Helice's lip twisted. 'See, to me, it didn't really look like an eye. More a series of squiggles.'

Hope and terror brought Iliona's skin up in bumps. 'You're a very lucky girl.'

'How so?'

'Oh, come on. You must have heard about the women he's killed?'

'I've heard,' Helice said slowly. 'But me, I like to give folk the benefit of the doubt, and I've got to tell you, my lady, he didn't look like no butcher to me.'

'What did he look like?'

Helice thought about this a while. 'More lonely, I'd say.'

Iliona wanted to tell her the two went together. Instead she said, 'Can you tell me where exactly in the cemetery it was that you saw him?'

The sepulchres were spread over a vast area of hillside. It wasn't called the City of the Dead for nothing.

Helice turned to stroke the horse's mane. 'Why?'

'I – need to talk to him.'

'A minute ago he was a vicious killer. Now he's a lamb on a lead. Which is it, my lady? Because I might not have your education, but I'm

149

not bloody stupid.'

'I didn't mean to suggest you were. But regardless of his crimes, I need to get to him before the hunting party. This is very, very important.'

'That's why you came calling, wasn't it? To find clues as to his whereabouts.' The girl might lack education, but she wasn't short of insight. 'Which means you're either planning to kill him yourself, or sell the big fella out.'

'Hand on my heart, Helice, it's neither.'

Her eyes narrowed to hostile blue slits. 'You're still a High Priestess, though?'

'I am.'

'Then swear on the god that you serve that you won't sell him out.'

Iliona blocked out all the innocent young women that she'd be selling out instead. 'Very well. If that's what it takes to convince you that I mean him no harm, I swear on the river god—'

Say it. Say the word. Helice will never know any different.

'I swear on...'

It was no good. She'd made a contract to serve Sparta through the Shrine of Eurotas. To betray it was to betray the people who flocked to his temple and by all that was holy, she wouldn't swear a false oath.

'...on the river god Eurotas that I will let no harm come to this man.'

The colour drained from Helice's face. The hillsfolk might not know where Arcadia was, but everyone in the world knew Eurotas. 'You're *Spartan*?'

Iliona stared down her hostility. 'Helice, someone – no, not someone, dammit, Athens! – set us up by butchering your cavalry horses and planting coins on the archers to make it look like we were responsible. Now believe me, if there was another way to clear our name other than to enter Syracuse through the back door, we'd have done it.'

'Believe you? After you've deceived the priestess of Arethusa, the people of Syracuse and the whole bloody Council of Elders? Do I *look* green to you?'

'Helice, the reason your "big fella" has been forced into hiding is that he was set up by Athens as well, and you know bloody well there's a hunting party after his hide. I'm probably the only chance this man has.'

'Well, thanks a bunch for confiding in me. Because now, if Athens finds out I know your dirty little secret, they'll put me and my family to the sword as collaborators.'

Iliona pursed her lips. 'I'm sorry, Helice, but this is not about you, it's not about me—'

'No? Well, what about my baby? It's not about him, either, I suppose?'

'For gods' sake, do you think I enjoy putting you through this? Yes, I could have lied, kept up the pretence of being the Arcadian priestess. But don't you see? The lies have to stop somewhere. You, your family, you're good people, Helice. You deserve the truth, or I'm betraying you

151

every bit as much as Athens has betrayed you, throwing Syracuse to the wolves in the name of ambition.'

'Go to hell. I've got a bairn to think about.'

'Helice, please. The graveyard's a big place, I'm a stranger to this city, I wouldn't know where to start looking.'

'Tough.'

'So you're going to run away and let Greece go to the dogs?'

Helice took three more angry strides before she stopped. 'Let me get this right. Here's a man who goes round murdering women, yet Sparta's going to pardon him to save its reputation?'

'I didn't say it was perfect.'

For half a minute, Helice said nothing. But at least she hadn't stormed off. 'Here's the Avenue of Tombs as it faces the sea.' One sullen toe drew a map in the pebbles. 'The grotto's here. I came up this way. And I saw the big fella here.' She marked the spot by dropping a bright yellow buttercup on it. 'Now if you can't find your way round in the dark, then that's too bloody bad, because from here on in, lady, you're on your own.'

'Aren't I always?' Iliona replied, but Helice had gone. Only the wind heard her pain.

The Serpent uncoiled and licked its lips. Had it been a cat, it would have purred. Life was sweet.

Laconia was a great land, stretching from the peaks of Parnon in the east to Taygetus in the west to the surf-pounded cliffs of the cape. And did any mountain slopes teem with more game, any river yield more fish than the mighty Eurotas, or irrigate more fields for wheat, or feed lusher grazing for the best horseflesh in the world? Of course not. Nor could any forest provide better timber, bigger mushrooms or juicier berries, or offer a more plentiful supply of fuel for ovens and hearths. Sparta had everything any person, mortal or immortal, could desire, and it was beautiful.

Paradise.

A land where history and godhead ran through each Spartan's vein. A land given to them by Almighty Zeus, and it was the blood of his own son, Heracles, that was spilled each time they bled. Apollo protected them, Castor and Polydeuces were their heroes, it was from Sparta that Helen, wife of Menelaus, was abducted by Paris, sparking the Trojan War.

Ah, yes, war. War was the spine that kept Sparta straight, that kept her ever victorious. After Troy, she'd gone on to conquer neighbouring Messenia and put its people to *helotry*. The Peloponnese peninsula was hers now, her dominion extending even over the city of Argos, home of Jason of golden fleece fame. Under Sparta, old legends and heroes were crushed underfoot, as new legends and heroes were born.

And now it was time for another to rise from the dust...

Over the cauldron in which perfidy and cunning bubbled together, the Serpent sat watch and waited. Waited for the brew to distil into calculation, pure in its wickedness and guile.

For it is only the Serpent in Paradise who has the true power to wield. The others just bend with the wind...

Power was the energy that drove the Serpent on. The desire for absolute control. With the King and the Council out of the way, and Athens' hand on the tiller of Sparta, a new age would dawn. Chloris was part of that clearing of old wood. She was expendable and like the King, like Eurotas, like all the other leeches that sucked the State dry, her death was simply expedient. But with Drakon—

Oh, with Drakon, the Serpent discovered something new. Something it had never imagined.

The Serpent, of course, was no stranger to death. It had killed many times, but always – yes, always – in the course of its duty. Unemotional, necessary, it did not matter how. Manipulation for the greater good.

But with Drakon, that changed...

Power over a nation might be exciting. But control over a human being was nothing short of a thrill.

Writhing, twisting, the Serpent sloughed off its skin. The new body beneath glistened and gleamed, but the patterns that were revealed were subtly different.

To kill, or to spare?

To terminate life swiftly and cleanly, or inflict a lingering death?

To decide who, to decide when, to decide how,

to decide where! With the power at one's finger-tips to dominate the spirit as well as the flesh, it was no longer a question of wanting the orchard.

The Serpent was choosing the apples.

Seventeen

The sun's disc had almost slipped beyond the horizon when Jocasta slipped out of Niobe's palace. Alleyways that had earlier been lined with produce were deserted. Squares where the livestock had been sold now seemed double their size. But in place of the bustle of buying and selling, a new rhythm had taken over. Jocasta smelled baking. Heard babies bawling, dogs barking, plates scraping from behind the closed shutters. In short, the trappings of normal family life. How she envied them their simple plea-sures...

Picking her way through the maze of ware-houses, bath-houses, workshops and temples, she managed to cross the bridge to the mainland before the last vestige of light disappeared. From here on, it was easy. The white face of the quarry stared straight out to sea, it was simply a ques-tion of choosing whichever forks led that way. According to Silas, nothing stood between these cliffs and Egypt except for water. Jocasta sup-posed he would know about such things.

From time to time, she glanced over her shoulder. If Talos was behind her, she probably wouldn't know it, but it didn't hurt to keep checking. Below, the limestone frontages and blood-red roofs of the city had blended into the night. Now only a handful of lights twinkled out over the island, the rest shuttered away or blocked by oiled skins pulled over the windows. But the moon would rise soon, plump, bright and silver. The Festival of the Fountains was drawing closer.

Inhaling the scent from narcissus and hyacinth that proliferated the wayside, Jocasta took no pleasure in their perfume. Her mistake was believing Iliona, when she told her she'd been blackmailed into coming to Sicily. Right at the beginning, when Jocasta watched them take that slow stroll down towards the Pool of Reflection, she should have known they'd be plotting together. The priestess and the *Krypteia*. Had the affair started there and then, in Sparta? Or was it the exoticism of Syracuse that had added spice to their complicity? All Jocasta knew was that, when she saw a leg swing over Iliona's windowsill this morning, tanned and powerful in its masculinity, she'd been thrilled that Iliona had taken a lover. Good for her, Jocasta had thought, ducking into a doorway out of discretion. About bloody time she stopped mistrusting men. In fact, she was still smiling when Lysander dropped to the ground and blew a kiss to the open window on the tips of his fingers...

Jocasta remained in that doorway until long

after he'd gone. Yearning and bitterness twisted inside. Resolve hardened like stone. Until then, she'd thought of herself as a spider on the wind. Carried along, because to stay at Eurotas without its Priestess's protection would have meant being put to the sword. At least by coming to Syracuse, she had a fighting chance – but now that all had changed.

Passing through the quarries, Jocasta watched, sniffed and listened for any sign of the half-human fiend that haunted these hills at night. She was wary, who wouldn't be, but she wasn't afraid. All her life she'd faced death, it was failure that scared her. The knife in her hand would protect her.

Athens couldn't afford to take on Sparta outright, she thought, marching on with resolve. The world's mightiest land power versus the world's mightiest sea power? The result would be a war of attrition that would drag on for decades, and then probably still end up in stalemate. On the other hand, *helots* were growing impatient. The battle plans were in place, the motivation strong and they outnumbered citizens twenty to one. All they needed, and what they'd been waiting decades for, was a chink in their slavemasters' armour. War was no good. Productivity would then become crucial to Sparta's survival. With their men away fighting battles, the controlling of serfs would, by necessity, become harsher and even more cruel.

But with the Confederacy toppled, and Sparta's allies jumping to Athens like fleas, Sparta would be in no fit state to fight insurgency on top. So close, and yet so far away, she had thought. If only someone (she?) could nudge the balance in Athens' favour...

Then today, as she trudged the scrub with Iliona, pretending to believe her wicked lies, she had finally glimpsed that chink in the armour. A man with a tattoo on his forehead. Because if Jocasta could deliver the 'Cyclops' to Athens, events would spiral out of Sparta's control so fast that *helots* would have the upper hand before the summer was out!

Beyond the stone quarries, the path forked. To the right was the Avenue of Tombs leading up to the City of the Dead. To the left, a track led off through the meadows to a pine-ringed cupola in the hill. Confident that no one, not even Talos, was shadowing her, Jocasta branched purposefully left.

Lysander would never know that, with one tender kiss, he'd sealed his own death warrant, and Sparta's as well. Iliona wouldn't realize, until it was too late, that her own lies had brought her country down...

Due to its singular acoustic qualities, the City Elders were talking about turning this hollow in the Syracusian hillside into a public theatre, and it was these very acoustics that brought Jocasta up here tonight. Cloaked by the black wings of Night and cradled by the soft scent of pines, she closed her eyes and cleared all thoughts from her mind.

Born of Chaos, Night was the mother of Pain.

158

The mother of Strife and Deception. Under the protection of Night, dreams and death stalked the void. Adversity, Murder, Lawlessness and Ruin numbered among her grandchildren, yet for all that, Night also gave birth to the *Morai*. The Destinies, who obeyed the will of the gods.

Jocasta watched the moon rise as the stars tramped round the heavens. The Great Bear, the Little Bear, the Dragon. Personally, she was not convinced the *Morai* took their instructions from Olympus, any more than she believed that chanting spells over wounds and diseases would speed their recovery. But who could say what guided the future? So as the Pole Star glistened and the moon hid her face behind the trees, Jocasta gathered a bouquet of orchids, anemones, cyclamen and squills, and wove them into a circlet. Sprinkling the wreath with holy water from a phial that hung from her girdle, she gently laid it on a flat stone that would probably be a favourite for basking snakes in the daytime. Raising her arms in supplication, Jocasta began to chant the Hymn of Fate.

'O Daughters of the Night, accept this tribute,
Picked from virgin meadows,
Where no shepherd has ever pastured his flock,
No sword ever clashed, no harsh word ever
spoken.'

Thanks to the special auditory qualities of this bowl in the hill, her prayer would carry over the waters and up to the heavens. She waited for the answering nightingale call, that would tell her the *Morai* had heard her.

> '*Freedom is my destiny, and the destiny of my people,*
> *And the destiny of their sons after them.*
> *With all my heart, O Daughters of the Night,*
> *I beg you help me find a way to keep it.*'

Jocasta waited and strained for the song of the nightingale.

High in the hills, a wolf howled.

Iliona's back was starting to ache from crouching in the necropolis. The cylinder suggested the tomb's occupant had lived a happy, healthy and blameless life, but given that his occupation was also listed as that of attorney, she doubted it somehow. Night fell. Bats squeaked round the grotto. Mice rustled among the yellow marsh marigolds. But still no sign of the Thracian.

According to Helice, the big man had appeared lonely. Iliona wasn't surprised. A man on the run is always alone. But a murderer is surely the loneliest man on the planet.

Listening to a family of badgers gruntling through the undergrowth, she reflected that some killers grow more reckless with each victim they claim. In Iliona's view, such men secretly wanted to be caught. They hated themselves so much, were so ashamed of what they'd done and what they'd become, that they left trails of evidence in their wake that would eventually lead to their

160

capture. Others, however, took an obscene pride in their work, perfecting their skill with each murder. But these killers were arrogant, preening, self-obsessed hypocrites, so where did the Thracian fit? On the one hand, he was obviously adept at disposing of bodies and leaving no trace of his crime. On the other, he'd taken to stalking the necropolis in search of fresh victims, putting himself at risk every time. Why? Why the change? Presumably he'd been killing for years without anyone catching on, which suggested that it was only now, after he'd been routed and was effectively a victim himself, that he'd moved closer to town. And perhaps that was the key. The very familiarity of killing provided comfort in a world that had no place for him any more. Weighed against the need for emotional reassurance, risk came a very poor second.

But the City of the Dead was an odd choice, she thought. Thracians were famous for placing their dead on stiffened ox-hides, then strapping them to the tops of trees. Only when scavengers had picked the corpses clean did they purify their bones in fire, so what on earth possessed this big mountain man to stalk among tombs where the dead were contaminated by their own rotting flesh?

Iliona sighed. She supposed there were many questions to which she would never find answers. What was simply one more in the queue?

Close by, a frog plopped into the pool. Streaky clouds passed in front of the moon. Shadows fused into each other. She strained for the shuffle

161

of clogs on the path. Peered for signs of his approach. Surprise would be Iliona's weapon tonight. Surprise, and of course something else.

Shifting, she reflected on wild beasts brought down with arrows and slingshot, with daggers and spears, which is fine if you want to kill them. But to trap an animal and immobilize it requires a net. A net, but also a society which teaches its female citizens to fight like men, since its warriors aren't around to protect them. Iliona's hand tightened around her recent purchase from a local fisherman. The Thracian would not see it coming. Once he was caught in the webbing, she had ropes to bind his legs and arms, and then, when he was subdued, she would explain how she intended to smuggle him out of Syracuse—

'O Daughters of the Night.'

The voice made her jump.

'Accept this tribute, picked from virgin meadows...'

It came from everywhere and nowhere. Ethereal, haunting, unreal.

'...where no shepherd has ever pastured his flock,
Nor sword ever clashed, no harsh word ever spoken.'

Then Iliona remembered how the Elders were discussing turning the bowl in the hills into a public theatre that could seat thousands. Obviously a local Sicel girl, laying a wreath for her gods, with no idea her petition would be caught up in its unique acoustics.

The trouble was, if Iliona could hear her, so could the Thracian...

She crept out of her hiding place, leaving the net where it was. *Please don't let him take the life of another young girl.* Zeus was the only god with the power to overturn the Fates. *Not here*, she prayed. *Not tonight.*

It was too much to ask for not ever.

The further she tiptoed along the Avenue of the Tombs, the more the acoustics lost their exclusivity. The rest of the chant was lost to her ears. All the better to listen for other sounds—

From the corner of her eye, something moved. She spun round. Just a mourning ribbon draped over one of the statues. She held her breath. Waited.

High in the hills, a wolf howled.

How long she stood there, she couldn't say. Then finally, through the pines, she saw the silhouette of a girl hurrying back down the track. At that speed, Iliona had no doubts for her safety, and with a silent prayer of thanks to Zeus on Olympus, she made her way back to her vantage point, to settle down to her vigil. The moon, so nearly full, bathed the sepulchres in its silvery glow. The dead slumbered on. She dearly envied their peace.

'My lady?'

Iliona froze.

'Are you there?'

She forced herself to peer round the memorial. Maybe she was mistaken? Between the acoustics of the valley and her overworked imagination, why shouldn't she be wrong? But the blonde hair and shining complexion were unambiguous in the silvery light. Iliona's eyes stung. Poverty is a terrible master. Who could blame Helice for choosing a better one? By going straight to the Athenians, she'd be safeguarding the lives of herself and her family, and earning enough to set them all up for life.

'Hello?' she called again. 'Anyone...?'

The only response was the scuffle of a feral dog, searching about for its supper. Helice whistled it over, rubbed its ears and fed it a cake from the knotted cloth in her hand. The dog bolted it down, but cakes were not food. He trotted off in search of a rabbit. Iliona watched the girl make herself comfy on one of the stones, and strained for the sound of soldiers' boots. Should she make a run for it? *Could* she make a run for it? There were only three ways in and out. The path she came in on. The path Helice came in on. Or slithering downhill in the dark, knowing the slightest sound would be amplified.

Helice had turned to weaving strands of grass into the shape of a man. So it was she who'd made that doll in the cottage. Absently, Iliona wondered what had happened to the baby's father.

She could stay here, she supposed, but the Athenians wouldn't give up. Spartans masquerading as temple attendants? She prayed they hadn't stormed Niobe's palace already. Talos, Silas, Phillip, Jocasta, even Let's-Kill-Them-Right-Now Roxana. These people's lives depended on her. She owed it to them to get this right...

Finally, Iliona realized what she had to do. What had been staring her in the face these past twenty minutes —

'Oh, my lady! Oh, don't do that, you scared me to death!'

'Sorry.' She stepped out from behind the cylinder. 'I must have fallen asleep.'

There were no soldiers, of course. No swaggering Athenians or sacks of money. Just a courageous young mum with long hair like silk, and a heart of pure gold.

'Bun?' Helice held out one of the cakes she'd offered the dog, but Iliona's mouth was so dry, her stomach so tight, that she doubted she'd eat food again.

'Why did you come?'

'Well, for one thing, you don't know who you're looking for, and I do. But mostly, I suppose, it's because I wanted to make sure you kept your word.' Helice's chin jerked upwards. 'I'd rather see my boy orphaned but proud, knowing his family died for what they believed in, than have him rich and living in shame because his mother stood back and did nothing.'

'If Athens wins, he might still be orphaned and poor.'

Helice chuckled. 'You're only saying that to cheer me up.' She arranged the cakes in a neat pile on the rock. 'Here, are you crying?'

'No, I ... I stubbed my shin.'

'Aye, you want to be careful, some of these rocks can be spiteful. Now then.' She pursed her lips. 'Reckon this was just about the time when I saw the big fella. What say you and I make ourselves scarce?'

'You're very brave, you know that, Helice?'

She expected the girl to laugh again. Dismiss the compliment in a throwaway quip. Make light of it in some way. Instead, she stopped. Turned. Stared into Iliona's eyes for a count of three. 'I'm no coward, that's for sure,' she said evenly. 'But you...' Blue eyes narrowed. 'You're a fool, if you don't mind my saying so, marm. You don't see what's under your nose.'

In the moonlight, the High Priestess shivered.

Eighteen

When the disc of the sun peeped over the horizon, it was the cue for an eight-year-old novice at the Shrine of Arethusa to pick up his silver plate. Carefully he piled it with pomegranates and celery, then sprinkled it with a variety of seeds.

This was the first time Cimon had been tasked with the Feast for the Dead, and the responsibility had kept him awake all through the night. Suppose he scattered the seeds, those precious symbols of resurrection, before he split the pomegranates in half? Suppose something fell off the plate between here and the temple? Suppose the celery was pointing the wrong way? He knew it had to face west, towards the Isles of the Blessed, but his mind was so jumbled that he couldn't remember if it was the leafy end or the base. Would Drakon's soul go to Hell because Cimon got it wrong? Or would his shade just come back and haunt him?

In the cypress beside the gurgling spring, wrens chased each other in territorial combat. Cimon liked wrens, but daren't take his eye off the plate – which seemed to jump about in his hands – because she had a right old pinch when

167

it came to earlobes, did Niobe. He'd rather take his chance with Drakon's ghost.

As he approached the steps, the celery wobbled precariously, but to his relief it stayed put. He nudged the door open with his shoulder and heard the distinctive sound seeds make when they bounce. He must remember to gather them up before he went back. If Niobe found holy offerings littered over her precinct, he'd be in for a right old box round the ears.

'Hello,' he called. 'It's me, Cimon. I've brought the Feast.'

The Arcadians were supposed to take turns to keep vigil, it was their blooming dead, after all. Perhaps he'd gone for a pee? Or fallen asleep? According to his father, all Arcadians were slipshod and lazy, but then his father said that about anyone who wasn't from Syracuse. Cimon didn't know what to think. But when no one came forward or answered his call, he decided to carry on with the ceremony regardless. So he and his cargo quivered their way past terracotta plaques, bronze scrolls of poetry nailed on the walls, past figurines and flowers until they arrived at Drakon's bier. Right then. He rolled up his sleeves. Pomegranate – no, no, *seeds*. You scatter the *seeds*. Then he remembered that it *was* the pomegranates he had to cut first. Phew. Imagine getting that wrong! Licking the juice off his fingers, he wondered what was so blooming interesting that it kept the Arcadian away from his vigil, and decided his father was right after all. Lazy *and* slipshod. Still. While the cat was away...

Lamps flickered round the shrine, and though the thick fumes of incense were making him cough, Cimon saw no reason not to satisfy his curiosity about corpses. He'd not actually seen one before, so this'd be one in the eye for his brother! Pff. He squinted again. Was that it? Someone said the mortician had had to pick three thousand arrows out of the body. Well, that was a lie. You couldn't see more than a couple of scratches. Climbing back down, Cimon was so busy swallowing his disappointment that he almost missed the cellar door lying open.

Funny. It wasn't the flood season, when twice a year, the stuff stored down there had to be lugged up, and then returned.

'I don't see why the builders didn't cut steps in the rock,' Cimon moaned. It was a right pain, clambering up and down that ladder eight, nine times an hour.

'Because, young man, stone steps would become slimy and dangerous,' Niobe explained. 'Far better to use a simple rope ladder, that way you won't break your neck. Now you remember to pull it up, before you close the hatch.'

Peering into the void, Cimon wasn't surprised that, during the night, the Keeper of the Vigil got bored. That, for want of something to do, he'd decided to explore the cellar...

But he wasn't from Syracuse, was he? In Arcadia, they probably didn't have cellars that flooded. Theirs would have proper steps leading down, so when the Keeper of the Vigil stepped

169

forward, he wouldn't be expecting nothing but space.

No, Cimon wasn't surprised. Not at bit.

All the same, he screamed his head off.

Nineteen

'My Lord Myron has asked me to pass on his appreciation for your attending him, but wonders whether you could bear with him a few moments longer?'

Jocasta glanced at the sundial, which had already covered some distance. 'Perhaps you could remind My Lord Myron that I'm not charging him for this consultation.' Her smile was brittle. 'Unless, of course, he keeps me waiting much longer.'

The lackey's expression faltered, but was quickly mastered again. She did not believe humour was the cause of the lapse.

'I shall pass the message on.'

The flunkey retreated with a gesture that was neither unctuous nor subservient, but somewhere between the two. Jocasta's eyes continued their journey over gilded columns and richly painted walls, tapestries, fountains, embroidered drapes, marble shrines. With Niobe, wealth had been invested for display. Pleasure for all to enjoy. Her brother's was nothing more than a

170

flaunting of excess, and she thought of how the profits from Eurotas (as opposed to donations that went straight to the treasury) were ploughed back into the temple, that they might enrich lives at every level.

And the birds. Wild, magnificent cranes whose wings had been clipped for no other reason than to provide amusement to visitors – a practice, she noted, that was not merely confined to the cranes. Her eyes narrowed. The waste of money as aromatic resins burned in solid silver vases on top of bronze pedestals was one thing. But had Myron ever stopped to think how many families had been split up, just so he could have a different slave to attend his wardrobe, his massage, his bath? Spartans were mocked for what was austerity in comparison – but jewellery slaves? Sandal slaves? Slaves to wave fans? Slaves to call out the time? Watching them beetle about in identical livery, she searched for signs that the yoke choked their throats. But the funny thing was, it did not seem to bother them. Jocasta couldn't decide whether they'd been oppressed for so long that it no longer registered. Or whether combing another man's beard was preferable to fending for yourself, where you'd have to battle storms, disease, earthquakes and poverty to keep a roof over your head.

'Marm?'

With a gentle swish, the drapes to the *andron* parted and Jocasta was given her first glimpse of the room where the master of the house entertained his friends, his business associates, his concubines, his clients, but never – not ever – his wife. To aristocrats like him, women were simply more creatures to keep captive and caged. Her heart ached for the wives who rejoiced in repression as yet another symbol of status.

'Good of you to come, m'dear.' Myron beckoned her forward. 'Know you've got a lot on your plate, what with the Festival tomorrow and all that.'

Jocasta wasn't sure whether it was pain that clipped his voice or a career in the army. What delicious irony, if he'd been in the cavalry.

'Now then.' He indicated any number of stools and chairs that cluttered the room. 'Make yourself comfortable and— Hermes in Hades, what's that?'

'Sounds like a wagon overturning,' a voice oozed, at which point Jocasta realized there was a third person present. A sallow individual standing with his elbow on the bust of one of Myron's ancestors.

'M'personal physician,' Niobe's brother explained hurriedly, clapping his hands for a slave. 'Close the bloody window, chop, chop,' he ordered the boy. 'Can't hear m'self think for that row.'

The slave craned his neck through the gap. 'There's a child trapped beneath the wagon, my lord.'

'I don't care whether it's my own bloody wife underneath it. Close the fucking window, will you!'

'I think we should take a look,' Jocasta told the

physician, as the shutters closed on the child's cries.

'Bollocks.' Myron made a gesture for her to sit that brooked no disobedience. 'It'll live or die, makes no bloody difference, and you can tend to it afterwards, if you feel so inclined, but I'm a busy man, m'dear. Got a million things to fit in today. Now where were we?'

'You were about to tell me how you were feeling this morning.'

'Bloody awful,' he snapped, and it showed. If this man had good health to flaunt, then, like his wealth, he'd be trumpeting it from the rooftops. But his skin was tinged with a dull brownish grey and pain had etched irreversible lines in his features. 'So p'haps you'd be kind enough to explain to my physician here how you propose to ease this bloody agony.'

'The pain is merely a symptom,' she said. 'I intend to eliminate the stones, not mask the problem.'

'And exactly how do you propose to do that?' Her fellow medic's voice was soft, but the glint in his eye was harder than granite. When he leaned forward, she could see that his curls were thinning from the middle out, and that their colour had been enhanced by walnut juice.

'Last summer, when I was visiting the Oracle at Delphi, I encountered an eastern physician, who told me about a shrub that grows wild in Cilicia. Although its flowers are small and in-significant, the bush blazes with papery orange lanterns in autumn, and it's these lanterns which

173

contain the all-important fruits that will cure your patient's bladder stones.'

'You have proved their efficacy, of course?'

Jocasta was not entirely surprised to see him here. Had the roles been reversed, she'd have been keen to discover new cures, too. She smiled. 'Patients with persistent bladder stones aren't exactly thick on the ground where I come from.' It was only rich men with rich diets who let it get this far.

'I see.' The physician steepled his fingers over the marble bust. 'And you imagine chewing a few foreign berries will dissolve what I cannot expel and the surgeon was unable to remove?'

He addressed his remarks to his patron, not her, and, to her fury, it was to his physician that Myron replied. 'There are nights when I cannot sleep for the pain, and days when I can hardly move.'

'I am sure the Arcadian physic means well, my lord.' Dyed curls gave a patronizing tilt in Jocasta's direction. 'Nevertheless, my experience suggests this is nothing but mumbo-jumbo, that will more likely poison than cure.'

She refused to descend into a slanging match with this supercilious medic. She'd made her case clear, it was now up to Myron. And how strange, given their inbred capacity for oppression, that her silence did not make either man happy. Indeed, the physician's contempt for this foreigner, a woman at that, pulsated across the room in such waves that she could practically reach up and squeeze the juice out of it. But her task was to cure, not mollycoddle. Niobe's brother was perfectly capable of making his own decisions.

Time passed. She counted the cherubs painted between the beams on the ceiling. Traced the geometric maze on the cornice. Followed the bloody exploits at Troy as swords slashed and axes hacked and was not at all surprised to find that Ajax bore a striking facial resemblance to her host. Outside, the muffled cries finally stopped.

'You, uh...' Myron cleared his throat. 'You say these berries were sold to you by a Cilician physician?'

'On the contrary, he sold me the shrub.' She'd planted it outside her chamber, where it had produced a stunning display through last autumn.

Myron raised a quizzical eyebrow in his physician's direction. 'I presume you've heard of this bush with the papery lanterns?'

'I have heard of many shrubs, my lord.' He shot Jocasta a reptilian smile. 'These eastern charlatans can be very persuasive.'

Myron sighed. 'I fear you are right.' He leaned across and gave her arm a conciliatory pat. 'I'm sure you are perfectly sincere in your belief that these fruits can cure my problem, m'dear. But since we have no proof of their efficacy, I think we'd best leave it to proven science, don't you?'

Jocasta shrugged. What did she care? She'd got an electrum pendant out of the deal.

Iliona did not go straight back to the palace after
175

her fruitless vigil. Instead, she paid a call to the fisherman who'd sold her the net and who'd carried it up to the necropolis (these things were surprisingly heavy). Being a man who reputedly would do anything for money, he'd agreed, in return for a gold choker, two rings and, after much haggling, a brooch inset with beryl, to convey the netted Thracian down to the harbour and smuggle him aboard a ship bound for the Peloponnese. Iliona needed to tell him that his services wouldn't be required just yet. He upped his price to include both her earrings.

By the time she returned to Niobe's house, applewood logs were being stuffed inside greedy ovens, and the smell of freshly baked bread wafted tantalizing aromas over the courtyard. To ensure the floral displays remained at their magnificent best, slaves upended jugs of waste water over the tubs. Laundry maids sang as they folded the washing, and the guard dog gnawed on a bone large enough to have been an unfortunate burglar.

Of Niobe herself, though, or any of the others, there was no sign. Iliona was extremely relieved.

Up in her room, every soft silky cushion seemed to beckon her over. The scented damask all but drew itself back. She yawned, slipped off her dusty robe – and knew that as long as the Thracian remained on the loose, sleep was out of the question. It had been optimistic to hope he'd turn up on the first night, but time was fast running out. Tomorrow was the Festival of the Fountains. All she had was the next twenty-four hours, and unless she reached the Cyclops before the Athenians, her next sleep might well be for ever. Plunging her face into a bowl of icy cold water, she—

'You *promised*!'

Even without the sooty streaks round its eyes and messy red blobs on its cheeks, the scowl round the door unmistakably belonged to a pixie.

'Zygia says she hates you, she hates you, and she'll *never* believe anything you tell her again!'

Oh, no! She'd promised to show Alys her ceremonial robes! 'Darling, I am so sorry.' Contrition revived her faster than any amount of iced water.

'We waited, but you never came, and you did, you swore on your oath.'

'I know, darling, but ... there were reasons.'

'Grown-ups always say that.' A tiny lower lip started to tremble, but the blaze in her eyes didn't falter.

Iliona kneeled down. 'You're cross with me, and do you know what, Alys? You're fully entitled to be. What I did was unforgivable and no amount of apology makes it right, does it, Zygs?'

The flame of anger was replaced by astonishment. This was the first time anyone had actually talked to her imaginary friend, and it took only the briefest hesitation before the child was conferring in Zygia's ear between her chubby cupped hands.

'Zygia says, no it doesn't, but she says to tell

177

you she likes you, so she's forgiven you.'

'Thank you, Zygia,' Iliona said solemnly. 'But what about you, Alys? Have you forgiven me?'

Tiny shoulders shrugged. 'Suppose so.'

'Would you like me to show you the robes now? They're very pretty. Purple and gold, shot through with silver, with lots of gorgeous embroidery.'

'Psst, psst, psst,' went Alys to the door jamb, then: 'Zygia says that's very kind, but there's no time.' She tilted her froth of curls on one side and listened. 'Any minute now you'll hear the bell calling me down to the loom, where I have to learn *spinning* for two hours, *weaving* for two hours, then,' big eyes rolled, 'it's how to run a *house*, how to beat *slaves* – oh-oh, there it goes.' Shooing the imaginary Zygia along the gallery like a goose-girl, Alys turned abruptly at the top of the stairs. 'Zygs wants to know if you have any bedtime tales you could tell us?'

'Hundreds, darling. I have hundreds.'

'Oh, we don't need *that* many to send us to sleep,' she said, as she clumped down the stairs. 'Zygia thinks three's enough.'

The first thing Jocasta noticed when she returned from Myron's was not so much something that was there, as something that was noticeable by its absence.

She'd been so used to seeing him behind her, beside her, leaning casually against a pillar – half shifty, half wholesome but always inscrutable – that she actually stopped to look round.

178

Mistaking her interest, the guard dog abandoned his bone and came loping over for a pat. Once he realized it wasn't forthcoming, he returned to his crunching with no hard feelings. Jocasta shrugged. Maybe there was no point in following her any more? Maybe Talos was sufficiently familiar with her habits to know exactly where and when to slide the knife between her ribs? Maybe he was waiting inside for her this very minute? It didn't matter. Jocasta was ready for his strike, when it came. And she had no plans to row the Styx alone.

All the same, it was odd not having that triangular grin follow her round the courtyard, or hear his cultured voice teasing in her ear. At least he'd make a good companion on that ferry ride, she decided. They might even enjoy themselves, down there in Hades.

'I'm just back from seeing Niobe's brother,' she said, knocking on Iliona's door. 'You owe me that pendant, remember?'

There was no answer, so she put her ear to the door, listening for the sound of a mattress bouncing on the other side or sweet whisperings of love. But nothing. Only silence. She tried the catch. The door wasn't locked. Jocasta slipped inside.

The room was large and luxurious, and smelled of lavender and roses, in fact it was everything Jocasta's own room was not. Such things didn't trouble her. Without wasting time, she drew a knife from the folds of her gown and made a series of gouges in the windowsill. The next time the *Krypteia* swung his leg over, at least he'd pick up a few splinters. She then set about sifting through Iliona's belongings. It took just seconds to find the seed.

Small, scarlet, and with a black spot like an eye. Deadly when filed to a point.

So then. She sat on the same bedspread upon which Lysander would have sprawled naked so many times with his lover, and wondered what whispered secrets these pillows held. Whose idea was it that Iliona should steal the seed? What did they plan to do with it? Who were they plotting to kill?

Not her. Iliona might be many things, but she wasn't a cold-blooded murderess. All the same, it was a puzzle. Still in two minds whether to steal it back or leave it, Jocasta became aware that she was sitting on an immaculately made bed, but that a dusty robe was pooled upon the floor and a bowl of dirty water sat on the table. Now Iliona wasn't slovenly. And a palace of this magnitude doesn't tolerate sloppy housekeeping...

Jocasta examined the milky water, then turned her attention to the dust on the discarded gown. It was not the one Iliona had worn yesterday, and in any case the dust in the hills was red. She drummed her fingers on the maplewood table. If the bed hadn't been slept in, where had Iliona spent the night? There was only one place in Syracuse that kicked up white dust. The same dust that had marked Jocasta's own hems. But why would Iliona spend the night up by the quarry? Jocasta was certain she hadn't been followed. Coincidence? As a physician, she rarely believed in coincidence, but whether Iliona had overheard her or not, Jocasta was on the road to fulfilling her destiny. Nothing and no one was going to stand in her way.

Freedom is my destiny, and the destiny of my people,
And the destiny of their sons after them.
With all my heart, O Daughters of the Night,
I beg you help me find a way to keep it.

No nightingale had answered her prayer in the grassy cupola last night, but the Destinies were pleased with her chaplet of flowers. She knew this, because on her way home last night, she'd been passing a tavern when a drunken wag placed an empty wine cup to his forehead, pretending to be the Cyclops.

'What goes best with young shepherd boys?' he'd roared. 'Mustard? Or a chutney made from wild mint?'

'With that level of blood loss,' his fellow drinker quipped back, 'he'll be so chewy that you'll need to tenderize him over the fire.'

'Gives a new dimension to getting stewed in the taverns.'

'Or getting a good roasting from rolling home drunk!'

Jocasta had been horrified by their insensitivity – but before her head had hit her pillow, she realized it was the *Morai*'s way of answering

181

her prayer. Find that pool of blood, they said, it might lead you to the Thracian. It occurred to her, as she replaced the seed and slipped out of Iliona's room, that one motive for Hyblon's murder was that he'd stumbled upon the fugitive's hiding place. And if so...

She skipped down the stairs and out to the stable yard.

If so, Jocasta had brought a full range of potions with her on this trip, and it didn't matter how big the Thracian was. She had the means at her disposal to render him as helpless as a kitten. After that, it would be easy.

'A donkey?' The groom craned his head so he could not be mistaken in his hearing. 'You did say donkey, miss?'

'Yes, you know. Big grey things with sad eyes and twitchy ears.'

'Aye, but...' He frowned in disapproval. 'They ain't what you'd call *elegant*.'

'I'd rather have sure-footed than elegant over rough terrain.'

'Sure-footed, but not what you'd call *stately*.' He scratched his head as he studied this stylish young woman with raven-black hair and a gown of soft apricot linen. 'I dunno what the Mistress would say, I really don't. Her honoured guest going off on an *ass*?'

Jocasta slid a coin into his hand. 'My guess is that the Mistress never gets to hear about it.'

The groom perked up as the coin disappeared into the depths of his tunic. 'No, miss, now you mention it, I don't reckon she will.'

When he smiled, she saw both his teeth.

The Serpent rejoiced. As news of the body in the cellar went round, it could feel its heart swelling with ecstasy. With every howl from the wailing women, satisfaction pulsated against the wall of its chest and the Serpent hugged its delight to its breast.

They had no idea. These people driving out evil spirits with their flutes, splashing holy water, they had no idea how exhilarating control over an individual could be. More thrilling than the power to change the future of nations. More satisfying than anything they could ever imagine.

The second apple had been selected, toyed with, and finally dropped – and this was only the start. Wait till it worked its way round the orchard!

Twenty

The uplands might be wild and windswept, but the air was warm and it carried with it the sweet scents of broom and narcissus. Bees droned in and out of the bindweed that coiled round whatever it could find to cling to in this hostile scrub, crickets rasped in prickly junipers, lambs bleated in defiance of the vultures that cruised the skies above. From time to time, Iliona stopped to let her horse chew on a rare clump of juicy grass or quench its thirst from a narrow beck, but in truth, this was as much to catch her own breath as for her stallion's benefit. Swallowtail and Apollo butterflies flittered over the scrub. At the sight of her shadow, lizards scuttled under their stones.

The sight of another human being surprised her. It was a woman further on up the hill. She was riding a donkey, and although it was too far away to be certain, it looked for all the world like someone she knew.

Iliona would never know what stopped her from calling out. At the time, she would have said she was afraid she'd alert the Thracian smith to their presence. Later on, she wasn't so sure. But she kicked her heels in the horse's flank and closed the distance in silence.

'Jocasta! What on earth are you doing up here?'

'Me?' It wasn't often the *helot* could be caught by surprise, but she covered it well. And quickly. 'Looking for you, of course. What else?'

She was lying.

'Why?'

'I had no one to talk to, for one thing. Some kerfuffle or other over at the temple. But don't ask me what.'

'It must have been important to fetch everyone over.'

Jocasta shrugged. 'You know how much I care about their affairs.'

Her voice was light, but there was something not quite right about the physician's smile. In fact, forced was the word that sprang to mind. 'What was the other reason for looking for me?'

'Many hands make light work, as they say.' Her grimace wasn't forced. 'I want this business over and done with as quickly as you.'

Across the scrub, a rock partridge called. A thin *wit-wit-wit* as it bobbed.

'How did you know where to find me?'

'I took a chance that this'd be the start point for your search.' Jocasta ruffled the donkey's long bristly ear. 'Me and Hector just hit lucky, I guess.' She smiled again, and if anything Iliona's unease increased. 'After all, that's what friends are for, isn't it?'

'Friendship costs nothing, that's for sure. But it's funny how many people can't seem to afford it.' Betrayal was everywhere, she could trust no one – but Jocasta? Jocasta hated the *Krypteia* with every fibre of her body. She'd die cursing the Secret Police with her final breath. 'Though you might regret your offer to help me search,' she added lightly. 'These hills unfold for ever.'

'Ah, but you count the grains of the sand on the seashore. For someone who sees through the eyes of the blind, a needle in a haystack can't be too hard.'

'The trouble is, I'm usually too busy measuring the seas in the oceans,' she quipped back, but the hairs at the nape of her neck had started to prickle. Lysander had turned manipulation into an art form, and as they plodded on over the brow of the hill, a scenario formed in her mind.

Do you remember Pausanias, Jocasta?

Iliona could almost hear his gravel voice echoing round the physician's chamber, and that one name would have been enough to capture her attention. Pausanias was Jocasta's hero.

He was a Spartan. A brilliant young general whose tactics at Plataea had annihilated the Persian army and ended their domination once and for all. But Pausanias had needed *helots* to fight at Plataea. In return, he'd promised them their freedom...

Remember, too, what happened to him?

Iliona pictured Lysander leaning against Jocasta's consulting couch, reminding her of the State's fury at this outrageous promise.

Victory notwithstanding, Jocasta, the Council accused him of treason. To avoid arrest and to

186

allow himself time to draw up his defence, Pausanias sought sanctuary in the Temple of Athene.

Jocasta would have shuddered at what followed. How the Council bricked her hero – Sparta's liberator – inside the temple, and how it was only when Pausanias was too starved to move that he was taken outside and left to die, rather than defile sacred ground.

High above them, buzzards mewed. Iliona wondered, what else would Lysander have needed to bring her to his side? That there was no place for *helotry* in the new Sparta? That under his leadership the country wanted slaves like the rest of Greece? And that, although she may not approve, it was individual ownership he was pushing for, not increased burdens on the State?

Take it or leave it, Jocasta. Slavery isn't going away in your lifetime or mine, so you can either swallow your morality and give your own people freedom. Or watch while they're sold off as slaves.

Would Jocasta have been tricked by his version of history? That we all see what we're conditioned to see?

Pausanias wasn't a hero. Yes, his tactics defeated the Persians, and yes, he did take Byzantium afterwards. But only to serve his own ends. Like Lysander, Pausanias craved only power and in the end was corrupted by it. For years, Spartans were loath to believe the accusations of treason that time and time again were levelled against him. Preposterous! The general who'd liberated Greece from the Persians now seduced

187

by the enemy himself? He adopted Persian dress and copied oriental ways for his own comfort and convenience, nothing more. And even when he lost Byzantium (to Athens, as well!) the people stayed loyal. But, in the end, his own letters condemned him. They proved he'd sold Sparta out.

Not that Lysander would let truth stand in the way of ambition. As Head of the *Krypteia*, he would 'prove' to Jocasta that the letters were forgeries and the evidence falsified, another reason why it was important to overturn the old order and institute one of his own. Of course, that was pure speculation. Just one scenario that ran through her mind. All the same, she wondered how desperate Jocasta was, when it came to leading her people to freedom. As they picked their way over the rugged terrain, their mounts plodding alongside them since it was too rough to ride, Iliona saw determination shining in Jocasta's eyes. And she asked herself, was determination the same thing as desperation?

Jocasta stopped to rub the small of her back. 'Why didn't you ask Manetho to track down the Thracian?'

'The Festival of the Fountains is tomorrow,' Iliona reminded her. 'I'd have to ride out to the caves behind where the horses were killed, waste several hours trying to find him, then ride all the way back again.' As if he'd believe her anyway! 'And listen. Either the Thousand Red Hounds of Hell have found another wayfarer to tear apart, or that's the baying of the Athenians' dogs

188

coming closer. Time is not on my side.'

Neither was luck. Their only reward for trudging the hill was sheep droppings on their sandals, grasshoppers up their skirts and an angry wasp that got a kick from Jocasta's ass. But, as Lysander said, persistence pays off.

'Kyniska was right.' Iliona bunched her sleeve across her face to block out the stench. 'This *is* a pool. I've never seen anything like it.'

Jocasta didn't seem to notice the smell. Kneeling beside the congealed obscenity, carelessly swatting away blowflies with the back of her hand, she examined the area. 'See the jagged point on this rock?'

Iliona forced herself to look. 'Yes.'

'Now see that arc of blood? It indicates the direction of spurt.' She stood up and walked around to the other side. 'In my view, this spray is consistent with a head wound. Foreheads gush like fountains and if he tripped – ooh, I don't know, in the dark...?' She paced the scene, peering at the ground with sharp, assessing eyes. 'I don't understand why there's so much blood pooled here, but no trail leading away.'

Iliona took the opportunity to remove herself upwind and explained that the hill farmers had already asked themselves this particular question. It was why one missing shepherd boy plus one tattooed giant equalled one cannibalistic feast.

'Let me tell you what I think happened.' Jocasta measured the air with her hands the approximate height of a boy on the brink of puberty. 'I think Hyblon tripped here.' She indicated a fissure an equal distance from the blood pool. 'He was coming downhill, you can tell that from the arc, and he must have been running to have hit his head that hard.' She pointed to the offending jagged rock. 'Like I said, head wounds gush.'

No one had ever denied she was a damn good physician.

'And you're suggesting the boy might be alive?'

'Last night I heard a man suggest that shepherd boys were chewy and tough. Maybe the Cyclops feels the same way?' Jocasta tossed her hair over her shoulders. 'All right, so it's not funny, but honestly. If the child was dead, why move the body? It's only decent to leave it, so his parents can bury him, and given that neither of us believes in man-eating monsters, there's no other explanation.'

'You're saying he took him away to tend his wounds?' In spite of herself, Iliona was impressed.

'Having wrapped the boy in – oh, I don't know, his shirt or something, which would explain why there's no trail of blood.'

'So far, so good,' Iliona said, looking around, 'but the hillspeople have searched this area thoroughly. Where on earth did he take him?'

There were as many caves in these hills as grains of sand on the seashore. As many caverns as drops of water to measure the oceans. Iliona would need a damn sight more than to hear the voice of the voiceless or see through the eyes of the blind if she was to find the big Thracian. At least, find him in time.

The traitor laughed. No one could stop the avalanche that was rolling. Lie back. Relax. Enjoy the sun, the sea and the wine...

Peering into another dark, dank cavern, knife clenched in her hand, Jocasta reminded herself that what she was doing was for the good of the cause. That it was Iliona who'd betrayed *her*, not the other way round.

Freedom is my destiny, and the destiny of my people,
And the destiny of their sons after them.
With all my heart, O Daughters of the Night,
I beg you help me find a way to keep it.

Just keep remembering that. Just keep remembering the Morai have shown you the path to freedom. They never said the road would be easy.

She breathed a sigh that was both relief and frustration that the cave contained nothing but spiders. The Thracian was ugly, lonely, a killer, a monster, but he was also a nurse and a victim. When democrats vote, they cast black pebbles for no, white for yes, but nothing else in life is clear-cut. It's the shades of grey that cause all the problems.

Outside, she paused in the shade of a bent-over

191

arbute, running her hand down its brown bark and fingering its laurel-like leaves. The wood from the arbute produced the best flutes in the world, but, of course, the music is only as good as the flautist.

It went against Jocasta's calling to put a man to death, but now she had Iliona along, what choice did she have? Dead or alive, Athens wouldn't care, and in truth his days were already numbered. At least she was in a position to ease his journey to the Isles of the Blessed by making it painless.

Freedom is my destiny, and the destiny of my people,
And the destiny of their sons after them.

Yes, you keep remembering that, young lady. What was one life against the lives of hundreds of thousands?

Prodding the overgrowth round yet another cave in the tufa that had been eroded by weather and ancient man, she saw the road to sedition opening up. It might not be this year, but next year, next year for sure, she would visit her homeland for the very first time and trace her parents' names on the bark of that old chestnut tree with the tips of her finger. She saw herself kissing the pasture that was her birthright. She saw herself marrying, bearing sons, starting a new life in Messenia.

But as a free woman.

Not a slave.

* * *

The sun was high and the shadows short when Iliona first heard the moan. Soft and low, she wasn't quite sure. But the second groan left no doubt. She waved her arm to beckon Jocasta. Together they tiptoed on up the hill. So many caverns, which was the source of the sound?

'Hyblon?' she called. 'Hyblon, is that you?'

The moaning stopped. Abruptly. As though a hand had clamped over a small mouth to gag it.

'Over there,' Jocasta mouthed. 'Behind that scrambling fig.'

But as they crept up the hillside, Iliona realized that, if they barged straight in, the Thracian would be on the defensive. Already in fear for his life, he was more likely to harm the boy as he lashed out. Taking a deep breath, she signalled for Jocasta to step to the side. Then she squared her shoulders and lifted her chin.

'Hear me, for I am the High Priestess of the river god Eurotas,' she said authoritatively. 'I count the grains of sand on the shore and measure the seas in the ocean.'

Nothing.

'You don't believe that I walk the winds and look down on the actions of mortals? Then hear this. I know you are no Cyclops but a smith from over the waters in Thrace. I know it is no third eye in your forehead, but a tattoo of concentric circles in blue. And I know you struck coins for masters who betrayed you, just as they betrayed the archers they affected to befriend.'

Silence. And this time her hands were sweating.

'Thracian, I can hear the voice of the voiceless and see through the eyes of the blind. Through these eyes, I see that you did not harm the shepherd boy, but brought him up here for tending. Through these eyes, I see that he is badly wounded, and it was because of my visions that I have brought my temple physician along, that she might heal the boy's head.'

This time the pause was hers.

'Now do you believe I see what you cannot?'

Slowly the scrambling fig was pulled aside and the gap filled by a giant of a man dressed not in a light linen tunic, but in brown leather pantaloons tied round his ankles. In place of the usual shaven skin, a rug of black hair covered his forearms and chest. His muscles bulged out like melons. But for all that, it was the tattoo that mesmerized Iliona.

Well, you've got him, Jocasta thought, ducking past him into the cave. You've got your damned Cyclops, even if he does look like the wolf man.

But now you've got him, what are you going to do with him, eh?

She looked at the boy. What indeed.

Twenty-One

On the dockside at Syracuse, two merchants each shook the other's wrist and lapsed into the dullest of small talk. Around them, sacks of beans were unloaded and melons discharged in exchange for Sicilian timber. The merchants nodded, smiled, wagged fingers and heads, and after a while the subtext of their talk was lost in the haggle of goods and the squawking of geese in their crates. If anyone had been listening, which was always a risk, all they'd have caught was the odd snippet.

'...everything is going according to schedule...'

'...the package will be delivered into your hands tomorrow...'

'...confidentiality guaranteed...'

After they'd concluded their business, the two merchants clasped wrists in farewell. Only the sharpest eye would have noticed that the long-hair merchant had grey eyes and battle-scarred limbs, while the other wore a cloak-pin fashioned in the shape of an owl that was also the emblem of Athens.

No coins exchanged hands, not even discreetly, but then this wasn't about a few paltry gold pieces. This was about power, corruption, ambition and greed.

Lysander's smile was pure wolf as the Athenian left.

Pushing the scrambling fig aside with hands as large as a cheese paddle, Theo stepped into the light. Blinking at the sudden rush of sun, he opened his mouth to tell the High Priestess that he couldn't help it. That terrible things had happened, he was sorry, so sorry, but she must understand, none of this was his fault, he couldn't help it. But before he could speak, a dark force rushed past, like he didn't exist. The dark force started to shout.

'LIGHT! I NEED LIGHT!'

Baffled, he turned to the Spartan priestess, who walked the winds of knowledge. By Bendis, she was lovely. Hair like honey, eyes like—

'Stop gawping,' the dark-haired creature hissed, 'and lift this boy close to the cave mouth. I need to see before I can work.'

In his arms, the shepherd boy seemed shamefully light.

'Water.' The fierceness of her expression lent speed to his response. 'Not enough,' she snapped. 'I need more.'

'There's a small stream over the way—'

'Then stop wasting time telling me and go fetch it!'

He blinked. He'd never met a physician before, but he hadn't imagined them to be human wasps. 'Yes, ma'am.'

'And for the gods' sakes, get a move on!'

'Yes, *ma'am*.'

Snatching up two goatskins, he hadn't expected the Spartan priestess to accompany him. 'Don't worry, I won't run away.'

Her gown was like gossamer. Her eyes bluer than the ocean on a clear day.

'I'm sure you won't,' she said, and her voice was like the honey of her hair. 'But Jocasta's always more comfortable working alone.'

Theo ran a paw over his mouth. 'Are all physicians like her?'

She smelled of rosewater and lemon balm, and her skin was softer than vellum.

'Unfortunately not.'

When she laughed, the sound seemed to him like silver and gold rushing together. He longed for it to never end.

'But once you get past her temper, you'll find that woman's the best healer you'll ever meet. If anyone can put Hyblon back on his feet, she can.'

'Hyblon.' Theo rolled the sound round on his tongue. 'So that's his name, is it? Hyblon.'

And all the time, he couldn't help thinking, was there ever a greater contrast between two women? Darkness and light. Tetchiness and serenity. One healing bodies as the other heals souls – though his own was beyond salvation. Together they filled the goatskins with water. The ache in his heart was like fire.

'What are his prospects?' In the strong light of day, the boy's colour didn't look too good. More like no colour at all.

'I don't know where the hell you found these—' The medic waved the bloodied poultice that he'd laid over Hyblon's head wound.

'It's only yarrow and oregano,' he said quickly.

'I know what they bloody well are,' she snapped back. 'What's your name?'

'Theophanes.' He gulped. 'Theo.'

'Well, Theo, since you asked, I will tell you.' Unsmiling eyes bored into him, colder than ice. 'These herbs saved his life.' She beckoned him forward and probed the wound with a damp cloth. 'As you can see, it's deep. Right down to the bone. But your compress staunched the bleeding and prevented the wound from becoming infected. Because once poison slips into the blood, it kills slowly through fever, but it kills all the same.'

Theo wondered how she'd have looked at him, had he *not* saved the boy's life.

'The crisis is far from over, though.' She drew a range of potions and herbs from her scrip. 'So if you two would get the hell out of my light, I might actually be able to see what I'm doing.'

Theo decided he'd rather be flayed alive than spend time with this woman. He edged back from the cave and wasn't surprised when the priestess joined him.

'I've ... done bad things.'

She looked at him for a long, long, very long time. 'I know, Theo.' Her sigh was like the wind in the reeds, and carried the weight of the world. 'I know you have.'

She would, of course, he reminded himself, as

198

a kestrel hovered over the scrub. She knew everything, this blonde, beautiful, fragile creature, whose collarbone cast shadows that dappled her skin.

'Do you ... want to talk about it?' she asked.

The kestrel dropped, slewed, then flew off to tear its prey apart in a juniper tree. He watched until the bird finished eating. A vole, he thought. Or maybe a mouse. Then shook his head. Why would he? Why would anyone want to open a wound and spill out the poison? Air things that were better kept in the dark? Face monsters that were best run away from? But oh, her skin smelled of lemon balm, and wasn't her hair the colour of honey?

Theo ran his hands over his face. 'Why not?' he said.

His soul was damned anyway.

Lysander stared up at the sky – blue, boundless, eternal – and stretched his arms sideways. Oh dear. Another poor acolyte meets with an accident, but then what do you expect, with the cellar door wide open? They don't know their way round the city or our customs, these foreigners, and besides. Everyone knows Arcadians are stupid.

As the sun warmed his skin, the *Krypteia*'s thoughts turned to the speeches, poetry and parades tomorrow. To the music, singing and dancing that would deflect their attention. To the marriage of Arethusa and Alphaeus that would be re-enacted by torchlight, to the sacrifices and prayers, the feasting right through to dawn, to the wine that would flow through the streets. What was one dead stranger among that? On a scale of one to ten, it wouldn't even rate a mention.

He cracked his knuckles and decided that if there was a better climate in which treachery could operate unhindered, he was damned if he could think of one. Truly, yes truly, it was perfect.

But there was no time to waste applauding the advantages of flawless timing or the joys of masterly planning. Complacency is a breeding ground for sloppiness and error. He needed to concentrate on the impact of this latest death on his fellow Spartans.

So far, neither Iliona nor Jocasta was aware of the tragedy. That was something he'd need to work on. But, as this mission's leader, Lysander was more than capable of influencing the minds of his team. He really did not foresee a problem. At least not in the immediate future. Which is why he'd ridden into the hills behind the plain where the cavalry horses were slaughtered—

'Manetho?' He cupped his hands so his voice would carry further. 'Manetho, it's Lysander, can you hear me?'

Twenty-Two

Jocasta blotted her patient's forehead and thought, already there's an improvement. His body was still limp and his skin remained cold to the touch, but no signs of a fever had manifested themselves. His was simply the inevitable chill that follows blood loss, and disorientation from cracking his skull. But then Hyblon, of course, was a child of these hills. Tough by nature, tougher by outlook. He'd pull through, would this shepherd boy.

But what of the man who had saved him?

She leaned back on her knees. A mountain man who knew how to heal, how to hide, and how to kill. Someone who lived outside society and had compassion for the boy. But none whatsoever for his victims...

She sniffed the poultice for signs of infection. It was clear. Hyblon's breathing was already more regular from the potion she had slipped him. It had also dulled much of the pain.

She'd applied for the job at Eurotas in order to treat those who needed physicking the most. In other words, the *perioikoi* and her fellow *helots*. But by the same token, working at the temple allowed the same State that had enslaved her to fund her medical research, and the irony was sweet. Thanks to Sparta, the more Jocasta experimented with new techniques and untried medicines, the better qualified she would be when her people finally broke free. Not only better placed to tend their injuries, but also, once some kind of normality was established, to offer a whole range of cures to counteract sickness and disease.

And that was the problem, wasn't it?

Jocasta was a healer. Her vocation was to make sick people well, to improve their quality of life, and sometimes, yes of course she had, she'd helped them on their journey. But only those who'd suffered unimaginable pain and for whom there was no cure. She had never looked a strong, healthy person in the eye and decided she must kill them.

Particularly one who'd save the life of a child who would otherwise have bled to death.

'Drink some more of this,' she said, tipping the boy's head back.

It was blood she'd drained from a vein in Iliona's horse. That, and the water, were doing Hyblon the power of good. Finishing what the yarrow poultice had started—

Enough! What was more important?

With the mountain man dead, Athens would be free to mix its mischief and give Messenia a very real chance to regain its independence. Jocasta could make that journey to the pear-shaped valley in her homeland. Search out that ancient chestnut where her parents carved their names. Gouge her own name in its bark.

Repeat. Theo might have had compassion for the boy, but he had none whatsoever for his victims.

Her resolve hardened. Now all she needed was the right moment to strike.

It would come.

With the smell of thyme and oregano drifting on the breeze and the sea as blue as cobalt in the distance, it was impossible to imagine horror stalking these hills. But it did. And it stalked them in many different guises.

Iliona heard the baying of the Athenians' hounds on the breeze. Pictured the pack, as high as her waist, their senses honed by starvation and cruelty. She shuddered.

'Is something the matter, your Highness?'

For a moment, she'd almost forgotten about Theo. Almost being the operative word.

'No, no, I'm fine.'

Highness? The word jarred. Too reverent, too respectful, too damned overdramatic. How reverent was he with those girls in the cemetery? How respectful when he sliced them to ribbons...?

'There is, there's something wrong. That's twice that you've shivered.'

He'd been counting. Watching her from the corner of his eye. And counting, and watching, and counting—

I've done bad things, he'd said, and foolishly she'd asked if he'd care to get it off his chest. *Why not*, he'd said, so out it came...

Once upon a time, Syracuse was just another small community that made its living out of fish. Then someone noticed three things. First, it was just one day's sail to Carthage. Second, it was right next door to Sardinia, Gaul and the Italian peninsula. And third, its double harbour offered perfect anchorage for merchantmen and warships.

Under Gelon the Tyrant, trade became the linchpin of the city's success. Treaties were negotiated as to who was allowed through the Straits at what price, and such was its prosperity that the local Sicels were either forced into serfdom to work their own land or sold elsewhere as slaves. And since no city state could achieve worldwide influence, Gelon the Tyrant set out to rectify matters.

Unfortunately, there was a problem. During the Persian Wars, he'd refused to send aid to Greece unless he was given command of either the naval forces or the army. Now, whether he genuinely believed his support was so critical to victory that Athens would instantly surrender her immense naval power, or that Sparta would have no qualms about serving Syracusian masters with no infantry experience, no one will ever know. But when Greece managed to defeat Persia that very same summer without Gelon's help, it was a gamble the tyrant lived to regret. Trade remained in everyone's interest, but when it came to helping Syracuse increase its political influence, Gelon found a thousand scattered city states with a single common grudge. They banned their coinsmiths from collaborating.

To his credit, he didn't give up. Short on allies but still long on ambition, he extended his recruitment drive to the furthest reaches of the Hellenic world, where, to a Thracian smith with a wife and young son, Syracuse was the land of opportunity. A boat sped them round the Cyclades, through the Sea of Crete and then across the wide Ionian, and even though they'd never seen an ocean and were sick from start to finish, it was worth it. Well used to biting winds and snow-capped peaks (Thrace was home to the North Wind, after all) they settled easily into the rough hill country, where their forge churned out drachma after drachma, stamped with Gelon's mark.

For the son, every day was an adventure. With forests to roam and caves to explore, Theo was never lonely, and on his tenth birthday, when he was inaugurated into the apprenticeship of a craft that would take twelve years to master, the moment was marked in the usual way. By his father branding his forehead with the Magic Circle. And because Theo was an apprentice now, he didn't stop to question why his mother no longer took him with her when she went into Syracuse. He assumed it was because the boy had turned into a man.

Time passed, and so did the Thracian smith, though death did not come riding swiftly. For the mountain man who'd sailed from the far side of the world, the journey was as agonizing as it was lingering. A torment for those who loved him, as much as for the sufferer. Eventually, though, his naked corpse was stretched out on an untreated hide for the vultures to pick his bones clean. And, thanking Bendis that the apprentice had managed to qualify before the master died, Theo continued with the official commissions.

More time passed, but this time the chariot came without warning. Breaking for dinner one day, Theo found his mother dead on the floor, her hand still clutching the heart that had failed her. The smith was alone. But now he was busier than ever, doing the job of two men as well as keeping house. Loneliness was not a concept Theo understood.

Until the soldiers came marching in.

Seizing the stamped coins and the unworked metals, they ransacked his forge, ravaged his cabin and explained that Gelon was dead, his successor expelled, and that a quarter century of tyranny was now at an end. And since all this information was relayed at the point of a sword, Theo also understood that private contractors such as coinsmiths were considered supporters, rather than workers. At the time, he felt lucky to have escaped with his life.

But with no money to fall back on, his savings having been confiscated as well, Theo needed to find work. A strong ox like him? And nothing he wouldn't turn his hand to? As he set off down to Syracuse for the first time in eighteen years, he was confident of finding a job in the docks or the artisan quarter. Accustomed to the cool scent of the hills, the soft tread of the forest floor, he'd forgotten what it was like to walk on paved streets. To see towers of stone. To smell the smokeries, the incense, the arsenals. In fact, so preoccupied was he by the vast changes that had taken place since he was a boy that, when people shied away or made the sign of the horns, he paid no attention. Thracians dressed differently, he knew that. Instead of tunics, they tucked shirts into pantaloons, and nothing, but nothing, would make them shave off their body hair. They were mountain men, not bloody eunuchs!

Then someone screamed. What, he wondered? Had he forgotten to remove the black leather patch that shielded one eye from the sparks of the forge? A necessary device, since no smith could afford to be blinded in both eyes. But no, he'd left his eye patch at home. So what then? And what was all that claptrap about Cyclops? Then he caught his reflection in one of the fountains. Saw the tattoo that proclaimed his craft—

Until that morning, Theo had worn his branding with pride.

Ever since, he'd worn it with loathing.

'I see.'

When Theo agreed to tell Iliona his story, she'd braced herself for what was about to spill out. A cathartic confession. An admission of guilt. Remorse for what he had done. She was as prepared as she'd ever be for its horrific revelations, the knowledge that she'd be reliving his victims' terror, humiliation and suffering without being able to show any emotion, for it was only his belief in her supernatural powers that made Theo trust her.

What she wasn't prepared for was what he'd leave out...

There was no mention in his tale of women. No blood. No creeping round tombstones after dark. But killers were cunning. And even though furtive glances confirmed he was holding something back, Theo played on Iliona's sympathy. And to be fair, he'd done a bloody good job.

'I thought, if I could find a way to pay my fare to Thrace,' he said, tucking into the goat's cheese that she'd unwrapped from her satchel, 'I could work in the mines in the hinterland.'

You had to admire Lysander's cunning, too. Shunned and feared, desperate for money and craving any form of human companionship, however distant or brief, Theo must have snapped his hand off when he made his approach. But then Lysander was an expert at choosing soft targets—

'You must have been suspicious of an Athenian wanting coins stamped with the symbol of Sparta?'

In the distance she could hear the howl of the tracker dogs, surely closer than she'd heard them before? At the cave mouth, Jocasta was bandaging Hyblon's head with a remarkably grim set to her jaw.

'Aye.' Theo combed his thick tangle of hair back from his face. 'Like I said, I've done bad things. But business is business at the end of the day, and he even promised to book my passage home, to spare me the embarrassment of going into town.' His smile was without cheer. 'The funny thing was, I actually thought what a nice chap he was.'

'If it's any consolation, a lot of Spartans feel the same.'

'I had no idea it would be that bad, though. Not until I noticed an unusual burst of activity among the hill farmers, as they dashed from one cott to the next. That night, I crept up to their doors and listened.'

'Which is how you heard about the cavalry horses on the Kedos Plain? How it was Sparta's doing, because the archers carried silver coins stamped with the *lambda*?'

'My coins. Aye.' Theo swallowed the last of the cheese and wiped his mouth with the back of his hand. 'And not only did the bugger not pay up, I happened to be coming home over the hill when I noticed men armed with spears and daggers behind my cabin.'

The scent of juniper carried on the air, and from somewhere close at hand a whinchat scolded.

'You're not the only one who's ever been duped.'

Forget the girls. Your job is to save your country, Iliona told herself. Not bloody moralize.

'Probably not, but with all due respect, your Highness, until you find yourself alone, with no one to turn to and no one to talk things through with, you can't understand.'

'You'd be surprised.'

His expression suggested that indeed he would.

'At first I thought, so what?' Calloused hands wrung back and forth. 'I'd been paid, hadn't I? But then I got to thinking, what use was money, when I had nowhere to go? I reckoned that if those archers had been betrayed, then the minute I tried to board a ship, I'd stand no chance either. They'd label me a Cyclops and – well. That's exactly what they've done.'

Me, me, me, she thought. Only ever thinking of himself. And when he stood up, Iliona was cast into shadow.

'You say you're from Sparta,' he said, 'but aren't Spartans unwelcome in Syracuse?'

'Very much so, but since we obviously *didn't* bribe those archers and have no desire to see the Confederacy smashed—'

'What Confederacy?'

'You don't know?'

To her, it was inconceivable that anyone could have lived so utterly sheltered from reality, but of course, he was an outcast as much as a recluse, and he'd probably used more words today than he'd spoken in five years. She checked the position of the sun. The politics was complicated, but unless Theo knew exactly how deeply he was involved in this mess, he wouldn't know what was at stake in getting out.

And she saw it in his eyes. He hadn't ruled out that this might still be a trap...

'Athens wants the whole of Greece under its

control,' she explained crisply. 'Their first step towards creating an Empire was to form the Delian League, but they pushed too far, too fast. Sparta equalized the scales by forming a Confederacy of her own.'

'And it's this coalition that Athens undermined, when it wiped out Syracuse's cavalry capability?'

'Exactly.'

'Meaning Athens doesn't just weaken the Confederacy, it gets to settle its score with Syracuse in the process.' Theo scratched his chin. 'I was four years into my apprenticeship when the Persians stood at Athens' gates. Athens asked Gelon to send warships in support, and he agreed, but only on condition he commanded the whole navy.'

'To which Athens replied, if I remember correctly, that they'd rather be overrun by barbarians than give in to some snide little opportunist bastard,' Iliona said, which was precisely what had happened. The Persians sacked their city and burned it to the ground.

'Twelve years isn't that long when you're harbouring grudges,' Theo said. 'I've heard Athens is good at serving revenge icy cold.'

Not as good as the Spartans, she thought.

'Anything else I ought to know about?' he asked.

Good question, because how much should she disclose? The more she confided, the weaker Iliona's position. Then again, the greater the lack of information, the greater the lack of trust.

211

'Sparta is officially Syracuse's enemy, so I'm here under false pretences, but I have to be honest, Theo. You're the only person who can clear my country's name.'

'*Me?*'

Trust. The only element binding them together, and she dare not let her mask slip. Not for a minute. Not a second.

'Your testimony is central to proving our innocence.' Half hidden by the scrambling fig, Jocasta was putting the finishing touches to her patient's bandages. Iliona fixed her eyes on them. 'I need you to return to Sparta with me.'

Theo frowned. 'Sparta?'

'You have my oath that you'll be free from prosecution.' She paused. 'On all issues.'

'Will there be work for me there?'

Me, me, always bloody me. 'I think it would probably be better all round if we repatriated you to Thrace.' Anything to get this monster out of her homeland, where he couldn't contaminate the air with his wickedness.

'And you want me to go now?'

'No.'

Too late to smuggle him off the island today, the sun was sinking rapidly now. And tomorrow, of course, was the Festival of the Fountains, and Iliona daren't alert Lysander by her absence. It only needed a message on a different ship that took a different route and benefited from better winds for his version of betrayal to arrive ahead of her.

But obviously Theo couldn't accompany her to

Syracuse, either.

She looked round. 'How sure are you that this cave is safe?'

Giant hands made a sweep of the landscape. 'I know these hills upside down, inside out and backwards. It's safe.'

Oh, dear god. He'd carried his victims up here. Toyed with them, tortured them, buried their bodies under the shale...

'Then stay here until I come for you, but only me, do you understand?'

Theo nodded. 'You, nobody else.'

Iliona managed to stagger out of his sight before she was sick into the gorse. 'Just the heat,' she told Jocasta, waving the physician away. 'I'm fine now.'

But she wasn't, of course, and never would be. In giving life to Sparta, she'd be condemning more women to a horrible death and the fact that they'd be Thracian girls did not make it better. Out of sight was not out of mind.

Alone in his cave, Theo should have been pleased to be leaving this island. Returning to Thrace, to live among people who wore the same clothes, worshipped the same gods, followed the same customs and drank beer, rather than wine. In Thrace, his size would be normal. In Thrace, his mutilation would be a symbol of pride. In Thrace he would not be a freak.

And he thought of the priestess, the beautiful priestess, whose skin was softer than vellum and whose eyes were bluer than the ocean that

213

circled the world. Aye, she was lovely. Perfect in every way. And she counted the grains of sand on the shore and saw through the eyes of the blind.

But there was another girl, a younger girl, who could supplant her beauty, and when he closed his eyes he was back among the marble figures that guarded the tombs. In the moonlight, he saw hair that hung down her back, the colour of corn silk. He could hear her step, bouncy and light on the path, and the song she'd sung to herself.

'From the Great Burning Mountain
To the pastures and streams
Where the oxen of the sun god would graze.'

And aye, her skin had been perfumed with the oil of sweet lilies...

'Oh, isle of the gods,
Sweet isle of the Sicels,
Let it be here where I end my days.'

Alone in his cave, Theo howled.

On the far side of the hill, treachery watched the blood-red sun sink below the horizon. It was there, in the Gardens of the Hesperides, walled by Atlas and washed by the rivers of purity, that the Evening Star made his home and the Nymphs of the West lulled mortals to sleep with their soft, soothing lullabies. It was also where Hera herself had planted a tree of golden apples, and set Ladon, the many-headed serpent, to guard it.

Gifted with the power of human speech, Ladon was a child born of Night, and though some claimed he had a thousand heads, others just a hundred, there was no dispute over who had sired him. Ladon's father was the fabled Old Man of the Sea, a prophet who could change shape at will. Homer had written about him. Drakon had sung about him:

At high noon the Old Man of the Sea
Emerges from the salt and makes for shelter on
the strand.
Then his briney sons, the flippered seals,
Heave themselves from the surf to sleep beside
him on the sand.

Seals might sleep, but serpents don't. At least, not those who guard the apples in the orchard. The name Ladon means Embracer and, slithering among the stones, the Serpent of Treachery embraced the new order it was unleashing. Coiling up on the Stone of Conviction, it basked in the heat of destruction.

Twenty-Three

'My baby, my baby!'

Jocasta pulled Hyblon's mother away before she finished off what a jagged lump of rock could not.

'Praise be to Zeus, to Hera, Apollo, Demeter!' Tears of joy streamed down her face. 'We thought the Cyclops had ate him. We thought–'

'He tripped, that was all, and now he needs rest. Rest and quiet,' Jocasta added firmly.

'But how did you find him?' the woman asked, crushing her son to her breast. 'We searched everywhere—'

'Head wounds are notoriously disorientating.' Partly true. 'He ended up some considerable distance from the site of the injury.'

'And he crawled all that way by himself?' Hyblon's mother switched from hugging him to death to smothering her boy with kisses. 'I can't imagine how there weren't no trail to follow, marm, I really can't.'

'It would appear your son had the presence of mind to wrap his tunic round his head to staunch the bleeding.'

'Really? What a brave little boy!' She blew her nose on her sleeve. 'You'll never know how grateful I am for bringing him home. It's a

216

miracle, marm, truly it is.'

Miracle be damned. It was hard bloody work on that donkey.

'I should warn you, though. This type of head injury can cause delusions.'

'What sort of – oh, look, he's stirring. I'm here, ma wee lamb. Mammy's here.'

'Hey.' He'd lost a lot of blood, so his voice was faint. 'Hey, Mam, guess what? I saw the Cyclops. He had an eye in his forehead that was bigger than a shield.'

'Ah.' Hyblon's mother laughed as she ruffled her son's hair. 'That sort of delusion.'

Night might have fallen by the time Iliona's horse trotted into Syracuse, but you'd be hard pushed to tell. From the harbour to the agora, cressets flickered on every corner, lighting the way for the thousands of pilgrims that were flooding into the city to celebrate the Festival of the Fountains. Cymbals and castanets clattered in welcome. The market place had become a theatre of jugglers, dancers and balladeers performing by the light of flaming rag torches. Stalls of olives, bread and cheeses had been laid out to tempt the hungry hordes, and in a bid to catch the visitors' purses as much as their eye, hill farmers fluffed their thickest fleeces and sandal makers dangled their leatherware from long poles.

'Pretty bracelets, milady?'

'Perfumed unguents?'

'A diadem for your hair?'

Steering her horse through the seething mass, Iliona wondered what the real Priestess of Alphaeus would have made of all this. Was Chloris the type of woman who relished the hustle and bustle of city life, or was rural Arcadia more to her taste? What of the banquet held in her honour the other night? Would she have enjoyed, or endured, the Chairman of the Council's gushing speeches, rubbing shoulders with the cream of Sicilian society?

Iliona sighed. It wouldn't just have been Chloris who'd been killed, either. Her guard would have been eliminated at the same time, only for gods' sake, how many were doomed to enter that dark, lonely world – a world where the clinking of goblets never penetrated and the gaiety of harps never reached – before Lysander's lust for power could be stopped? Chloris. Drakon. Seventeen Cretan archers. Where was it going to end? Swerving round a troupe of tumblers, she tried to tell herself that Theo's testimony would be reducing the growing list of orphans and widows – but what of the women who would never marry, because of her? What of the children that would never be born, because the High Priestess of Eurotas had let their mother's killer walk free?

'You can't deny the ingenuity of these charlatans, can you, my lady?'

Turning, she found herself face to face, or rather shoulder to face, with a froth of curls encircling a shiny bald head, and Silas's unmistakable avuncular smile.

'See that stall by the gymnasium?' She'd forgotten how much the little man bobbed. 'The fellow's dispensing rat's tongues to reverse baldness, and weasel fat to cure warts.'

'Are you supposed to swallow the stuff or rub it in?'

'I doubt it matters, because on the adjacent stall you can shortcut the prognosis by having your horoscope drawn up by a gentleman who claims to have been the astrologer to Assyrian suzerains, Parthian priests, even the King of Tartessa, wherever that is.'

'Oh, I'm sure you know where it is.'

'Actually, I do, yes.' Rosebud lips pinched in embarrassment. 'Tartessa is situated on the southernmost coast of the Iberian peninsula, on the far side of the Pillars of Heracles. Beyond it lie rich silver mines, with copper mines found even deeper in the interior, and our knowledge of this kingdom only came about because Colaeus of Samos was blown there in a storm—' He broke off abruptly, staring at a point over her shoulder. 'I talk too much, don't I?'

'Far better too much than too little.'

'I can't help it. Once I start, facts tumble out, even though I know that level of detail bores people rigid. Mind you.' He smiled sheepishly. 'Colaeus eventually got as far as Libya, you know.'

'Good for him,' Iliona laughed, noting that the queue for the astrologer was three times longer than any other. 'But a word of advice, Silas. Never apologize for your training.'

'You think not?' Small eyes blinked furiously. 'The trouble is, when one is trained to repeat facts like a parrot bird, one forgets how to think for oneself.' His face turned scarlet. 'I am very lucky to have found a wife who understands. Oh, and Lysander, of course.'

'Of course.'

And dammit, if the *Krypteia* thought he could send this man to Hades, the *Krypteia* had another think coming. But it was a sobering thought that the lives of Silas, Phillip, Manetho, Talos, not forgetting Jocasta and Roxana, depended on her. Her and the Thracian smith...

'Moreover, this other business has really unsettled me, which makes the problem ten times worse,' he confessed.

'What other business is that?' she asked absently, because you'd think people might at least stop to question why, if the astrologer's predictions were so amazingly accurate, the suzerains let such a treasure go.

'You know. The unfortunate accident that occurred during his vigil in the temple last night.'

Around her, the lights of Syracuse suddenly dimmed. 'What unfortunate accident?'

'You mean you haven't heard?' Piggy eyes goggled. 'How, when it was his turn to stand watch over Drakon's body, he mistook the void for a flight of steps in the dark and fell headlong into the vault? His neck was broken, as you would expect. Fourth and fifth vertebrae, the mortician—'

'Who, Silas?'

Who had sustained another 'tragic accident'?

'Oh, Lady Iliona.' The little man wrung his hands in apology. 'I thought you knew. I – dear me, dear me, I thought *everyone* knew. It's Phillip.' His face twisted miserably. 'Our little thief fell into the cellar.'

Returning to the city, Lysander pulled on his fake bandages and became a cripple, whining his way through the crowd. There was blood on his clothes, but so what. You can't slice a knife through a windpipe without spurting blood, and since he was a vagrant, a drifter, a beggar, an outcast, what else would you expect but dirty clothes?

This was a dream. Any minute she'd wake up and doves would be cooing softly in the grove of sacred plane trees, the sunlight would reflect off the slow-flowing Eurotas, and through the open window she'd catch the scent of water mint, myrtle and hyssop. Frogs would be croaking, the wind would rustle through the reeds, and she'd rise from her bed, ready to exchange the usual banter with the Guardian of the Flame about his children, his wife, his flatulent dogs, consign another ritual log to the tripod and all would be well with the world.

Except this wasn't a dream. There were no doves. No frogs, no mint, no whispering reed beds. And the sky overhead was pitch black. As black as the fear in her heart—

Lysander had managed to eliminate a second member of his team and pass it off as an accident. Phillip, Silas, Talos, what did it matter which one? Whoever had drawn that particular vigil would have paid the price for his ambition.

And Iliona had not seen it coming.

Worse, she'd been congratulating herself that the smith's testimony would prevent others from crossing the Styx. Without realizing the Ferry had already sailed...

Isn't it wonderful? To be a thief and a spy and be paid for it, too!

And now the same fingers that had plucked the choker from her neck and Manetho's buckle from his belt were stealing the coins from the Ferryman's pocket.

'Are you all right, my dear?'

'What? Oh. Oh, yes.'

She had no idea how she got to the shrine, much less what she'd done with her horse or why Niobe should be shouting with hands cupped against her ear. All she could see was an angel-faced youth hurtling headlong into the void.

'It's just the smoke from the tar on the torches,' she said. 'Always makes my eyes water.'

'Not as much as this racket, I'll bet.'

A gold-bangled wrist indicated the fountain house that adjoined the shrine and supplied households on the island with fresh water. And suddenly Iliona realized that Niobe hadn't been raising her voice to drown the keening of the wailing women that had set every guard dog in the vicinity howling. It was to carry over the crowd of pitcher girls that had gathered round the spring and were banging vigorously on the side of their empty pots.

'One can understand their frustration. They can see the water glistening in the cisterns, so near and yet so far and all that. But what these lazy creatures can't get through their skulls is that the spring has been defiled by death every bit as much as the temple. I'm sorry, but that fountain house remains out of bounds until the purification rites are finished. Honestly!' Niobe rolled her heavily kohled eyes. 'As if I'm going to let their having to lug water from the mainland take priority over the damage this double catastrophe has done to our city!'

Through doors flung wide to admit the purifying dirges, the bronze spouts shaped like boar's heads sparkled in the torchlight. Like the marble statue of Arethusa herself, they were wreathed in yew. The death tree.

'I ask you, my dear, who's going to want a Lucky Arethusa now?' A beringed hand wafted in the direction of a stall set up near the portico, where a battalion of wood nymphs stood forlornly in a whole variety of colours, heights and poses. 'We spent the entire winter carving these for tomorrow's festival, and then what happens?' Niobe raised her voice another notch. 'Word goes out that Arethusa has stopped protecting Syracuse.'

Twelve years isn't that long when you're harbouring grudges. Athens is good at serving revenge icy cold.

Oh, the wolf was clever. He'd killed Drakon and Phillip in quick succession, so when their bodies lay together in the city's leading shrine, Athens could fire off their second shot in the propaganda war. Iliona stared down the marble portico towards the other spring that welled up in the sea and thought, sorry, Lysander. You may think you've loosed your poisoned arrow in the wind, but I walk the winds, remember?

'You need to make an announcement,' she told Niobe. 'Tell them Arethusa hasn't abandoned her people, rather that Alphaeus has displeased her, hence the retribution on his priests.'

'Don't you think it sounds a tad thin?'

'It's fiesta time, Niobe. People are prepared to believe anything.'

Providing action was taken early enough, Lysander's nasty little plan would fall flat on its belly, and time was not on his side to come up with decent alternatives.

'Oh, and one other thing.' Iliona felt a thousand years old. 'Assure them, won't you, that Alphaeus will put things right. Tomorrow, here, at the Festival of the Fountains.'

It had to end. The carnage had to stop, and it had to stop now. Any hopes of sailing home to Sparta had been dashed with Phillip's 'tragic accident', so where better to expose the *Krypteia*'s treachery than before the entire population of this budding city state? Tomorrow night Iliona would summon the Thracian smith to bear testimony, and somehow she must also make sure that Lysander was present at the smith's disclosure.

It was too late to save Phillip. But so help her, no one else was going to be sacrificed on the altar of this bastard's personal glory.

As he slithered and snaked through the crowds round the shrine, he saw his sister, hair shining copper in the light of so many torches. Ah, Roxana. His beautiful, strong, virginal sister. Lysander stopped, drinking in the toss of her head, the proud, athletic stance. Product of his father's own loins, Roxana was the epitome of Spartan womanhood and youth. A warrior in his own image.

He watched her for several long minutes, oblivious to the pitcher girls clanging on the side of their pots and the acolytes who purified the air with fragrant incense.

After a while, she turned. Caught his eye. Nodded.

He nodded back, and thought, oh, Roxana, Roxana. What a perfect, unimpeachable witness you'd be...

Standing before the shrine while solemn hymns were chanted, Roxana felt the hackles rise on the back of her neck. It was part of her training, an integral part, to know when she was being watched. She turned, scanning the crowd with expert eyes. There was nothing on any of the faces that warranted further attention, but she remained stiff and on the alert.

Then she noticed the beggar. Dirty, dishevelled, but unmistakably familiar. Green eyes met with grey. A message passed between them. She nodded. He nodded. It was agreed.

She blinked. When her eyelids fluttered open again, he was gone.

Squashed between the garland stall and that of the sausage seller was an untidy tent made from a patchwork of brown and orange linen that was fraying badly round the edges. It didn't help that next door were displaying ribbons to eye-catching perfection, hoping to tempt pilgrims to add brightly coloured streamers to their floral crowns, or that the sausages on the other side were hot and sticky with dark, honeyed spices. But mainly the lack of interest was because no one had faith in the stallholder's relics. If that was a genuine oar from the Argonauts' voyage, or a real lock of Aphrodite's hair, why were his tent poles riddled with woodworm, and why couldn't he afford the price of a bath?

'You, sir. How about a splinter from Heracles' club to bring you good health?'

The charlatan couldn't have chosen a worse target. The gentleman in question was a banker, who employed two men full time just to mark the corner stones of properties he mortgaged, and he wasn't going to be fobbed off with a chunk of pine, when Heracles wielded olivewood.

'Madam?' The stallholder hoped to have better luck with a flax merchant's wife. 'A tail feather from one of Hera's own peacocks? Only two obols, you know.'

'Two obols, you say?' The merchant's wife fished deep into her purse and shot him a radiant smile. 'Well, here's what you can do with your two obols, you fraud.'

She tossed them into Lysander's begging bowl and stomped off. The stallholder grunted without malice or surprise, and turned to pushing his stock of authentic dragons' teeth.

Lysander tapped his forefinger against his lip. So close. So very, very close now, but the paradox was still there. What had to be done, had to be done. It was a question of expediency. A means to an end. Stay detached.

Except ... He ran his hand over his jaw. It was no longer that easy, was it...?

'Lucky griffon scales, my lord? Snake from Medusa's own head?'

'I'll take the snake,' Lysander said.

'You will?' The stallholder quickly recovered. 'It'll cost you two obols. Mind, for that I can jab it with a stick and make it writhe.'

'What say you take the lot,' he said, emptying out the bowl. 'And forget the party tricks.'

The man leaned over his trestle. 'Won't really turn you to stone, mate.'

'There are many who believe it already has,' Lysander said, but the stallholder was too busy biting on the coins to pay attention. By the time he looked up again, the beggar had vanished.

* * *

227

Beyond the gymnasium, he set it free.

And the Serpent wriggled in pleasure at the anticipation of its new life.

Twenty-Four

'Come, come, ladies, you know the rules.' Niobe clapped authoritative hands. 'Arethusa's purity has been compromised by the grim hand of fate and you all know that, until these two young men leave this temple for their final journey to the Islands of the Blessed, the fountain house remains cordoned off.'

Her explanation only served to infuriate the pitcher girls, who couldn't grasp how water from the spring, whose conduits completely bypassed the shrine, could possibly become contaminated by two foreign corpses lying inside.

'Here!' One of the older women stepped forward. 'We didn't mind trudging the whole length of the island and over the bridge to the next fountain house for a day or two, love, but this ain't on.'

In no uncertain terms, she told the High Priestess where she could stick her precious cordon.

'And to think Niobe called them ladies.'

Roxana sidled up to Iliona, as the banging increased to fever pitch. Her hair hung loose in mourning, just as it had done for Drakon two days earlier, but for all the femininity of curls tumbling round her shoulders, it was her muscular grace that stood out. That, and the passion in her eyes.

'My brother would never allow civil disobedience to get out of hand.'

'I'm sure he wouldn't.'

'Discipline. Those women need discipline,' Roxana spat. 'Lack of it is a direct consequence of consumerist policies. They wouldn't get away with this in Sparta.'

'Only because we don't have pitcher girls.'

'Precisely. We have *helots*, and *helots* know their bloody place.'

'Which I think you'll find is a country called Messenia.'

There really is no place like home.

Green eyes flashed. '*Helots* know the punishment for mutiny.'

'The fact that they fear the *Krypteia* doesn't stop them plotting rebellion, Roxana. It simply makes them more cautious.'

'Our intelligence is sharp, my lady, and our knives are even sharper. Insurrection doesn't bother me.'

'Your brother has trained you well.'

'Thank you.' Roxana's smile was pure pride. 'If I'd been born a man, I'd have aspired to be exactly like Lysander. As a mere woman, I have to content myself with modelling my principles on his.'

'*Mere* woman? In Sparta, men and women are equals.'

'Not physically, they're not, so in dedicating my virginity to the State, I hope to set an example.'

Iliona felt so very, very weary. 'But what about children? Don't you want babies, Roxana?'

Emotion flickered on the girl's face and then was gone. But not before Iliona recognized it as longing. 'Look.' Roxana was grateful for the distraction. 'Niobe's finally called out the guard, and not a moment too soon, in my opinion. That's a nasty riot swelling out there, so if you'll excuse me, I'll go and keep vigil over the biers in case they storm the shrine.'

Iliona frowned. Roxana abandoning her duty as bodyguard? If she wasn't so tired, she might have smelled a rat. Instead, she was simply relieved to know that Roxana would be inside the temple, where, praise be to Hera, lightning wouldn't strike twice. Not that Lysander was likely to kill his little sister. Or, at least, Iliona didn't imagine he would. But when it comes to power and control, the rules of engagement are few. Corruption makes its own laws.

All the same, it was Roxana's emotional health she feared for more than her safety. What would happen once the poor girl discovered her idol was a traitor, and not the hero she worshipped and believed in? Closing her eyes as harpists eased Phillip's cold, lonely journey and flautists banished any malevolent spirits that might threaten his shade, her thoughts drifted back to the Festival of the Stags.

Think of it not so much as stealing, Lysander

had said about Phillip's light fingers. *More finding things before people lose them.*

He'd been sipping from her goblet at the time. Rolling the thick, dark Etruscan wine on his tongue and no doubt savouring its richness and vintage in the same way he savoured his treachery. What goes through such a mind? she asked herself. What manner of monster cracks jokes about someone, knowing he intends to kill them the very next day?

One could argue that Phillip had also practised deception, but his was a different kind. There was nothing underhand about his code of ethics. He wore his skills as a thief with pride, and it kept him relentlessly cheerful and happy.

You won't need to tell Manetho twice. She could almost hear his distinctive laugh above the pitchers and the chants. *His favourite food is seconds, and even the nags in the stables fear for their nosebags, when this man's in town.*

This from the thief who'd steal the belch from a drunk.

Ah, but I'd sell it on for a profit, mate, that's the difference.

Manetho had loved him. *If you ate more, little flea, you wouldn't rattle so loudly. Let's see if we can't muffle some of that clattering.* And the sad thing was, Manetho didn't know his friend was dead.

Iliona made her way along the marble portico, a curious oasis of peace and serenity. Would she have acted differently, had she known this morning that this vibrant youth was dead? Would she still have gone into the hills, instead of blessing his remains and staying with him through the rites that purified his sticky-fingered soul? Of course not, so perhaps ignorance was a blessing. At least this way she'd found the coinsmith before the Athenians and—

'Those pitcher girls have really pissed off the stallholders and street artists.' With her black hair and black robes, Jocasta was one with the column's shadow. 'I mean, who wants acrobats and trinkets when there's the potential for a riot?'

When she stepped forward into the light, Iliona saw that her skin was drawn from too little sleep and too much strain, and for the first time she understood, really understood, what it was like to live in constant fear for your life.

'They still rank higher than waves slapping against the rocks or freshwater springs rising up in the ocean,' Iliona said. 'Tranquillity is dull.'

'Tranquillity is never dull,' Jocasta retorted. 'But what's new to us is ordinary to these people. Stand them on the banks of the River Eurotas, and it would take their breath away.'

'What about pear-shaped valleys cradled by hills, where orchards and wheat fields stretch to infinity?'

Jocasta's lips pursed but no word passed through them. Outside the fountain house, the captain of the guard tried to reason with the women, the horsehair on his helmet ruffling in the evening breeze.

'Did he tell you about the girls?' she asked

eventually. 'What he'd done with their bodies?'

'No.'

'Did you ask?'

'No.' Iliona bit on her lip. 'But I apologize for lying to you about why I went looking for him.'

Hardly her intention to blurt out in public that he was the smith who'd minted the coins that were then planted on the Cretan archers, but standing there, hearing Hyblon's pathetic whimpers and knowing how close they were, she didn't feel she had a choice. But it did explain Jocasta's granite expression as she tended the boy.

'I suppose you knew all along?'

'I knew he wasn't a Cyclops.' Iliona leaned on the parapet and watched the ships out in the bay. 'After that, it was more a series of leaps in the dark.'

'He's a conundrum, isn't he?' Jocasta leaned the small of her back to the wall and stared down the flickering portico. 'A monster, who shows no compassion for his victims, yet saves the life of a child.'

'A male child.' Iliona wasn't sure he'd have been so accommodating had Hyblon been a girl, and in a twisted way she was almost disappointed. How much easier to deal with a man who'd ruthlessly silenced the only witness to his butchery. 'We must take care not to be drawn into the compassion net ourselves.'

'Yes.' Jocasta's eyes bored into hers. 'Yes, Iliona, we must.'

Beside the fountain house, frustration bubbled

233

over, optimism proving stronger than reality. The guard found no trouble pushing back the surge, and the wider its circle, the thinner it became. Defeated, the women began to disperse.

'Oh, good. My eardrums have rediscovered the joys of nuances,' Jocasta said.

Iliona smiled, praying Niobe would have the same luck calming Syracusians embittered by Lysander's vicious slander. But if anybody could convince them this was no more than a lover's tiff (and the Immortals were famous for their capricious sulks and tantrums), Niobe was the one. And Pericles wouldn't want the double tragedy laid at his door, either. Implausible or not, the City Council would back her claim.

Who knows how many folk have fallen foul of our nice friendly cannibal, ending up as supper instead of guest? Phillip's teasing whispered to her on the wind. *Mind, when he sees the size of you, me old mate, he'll think it's a banquet. All his birthdays rolled into one.*

Iliona sighed. In battle, casualties are inevitable, but the war still wasn't won. Lysander might have ostensibly despatched Manetho to scout the caves behind the plain, but if the Athenians had no luck finding Theo, the *Krypteia* would have no qualms about setting his own superstitious team member on the 'Cyclops's' trail. And in obeying, Manetho would have no idea he was signing his own death warrant...

She stared at the moon, so nearly full, and prayed to Zeus to keep Manetho safe.

'Just another day,' she whispered, 'just one

more day and then it will be over.'

It's bad luck, not sending the dead off. If Manetho felt resentment at missing Drakon's funeral, it would be nothing compared to his anger at missing the little flea's burial. And, dear god, once he found he'd placed his trust in a man who was bent on bringing Sparta down—

Sweet Selene! If Lysander could talk Drakon into standing in that glade to catch a volley full of arrows and then dupe Phillip into standing over an open hatch, how easy to persuade the tracker to reveal himself to his Commander among the caves above the plain.

Lysander hadn't sent Manetho on a wild goose chase at all, she realized. It was simply an excuse to isolate him from the others.

Manetho was the next man on his list.

What exquisite pleasure, choosing the apples! Rolling them round in your hand, weighing them, rubbing them, smoothing them, shining them.

Plucking them from the bough whenever it pleased you...

Twenty-Five

Far above the city, above even the white cliffs hewn by thousands of chisels over the years, Helice approached the Avenue of Tombs with neither fear nor trepidation. In her hand was a posy of flowers for her brother. Arabis, campion and lilies of the field. When a storm capsized his fishing boat last spring, there'd been no grave to mark him, so she'd taken it upon herself to find a stone up here, in the City of the Dead, which she could dedicate to Esmon's memory. The one she'd eventually decided on was near the grotto, a wide, flat stone large enough to sit on, where she could bring flowers, cakes and pome-granates, listen to the fountain and talk to him.

There was lots to say tonight. For a start, Jason was smiling all the time, and although he'd been a bit colicky last week, he was better now – Esmon would have loved to see the little mite blowing bubbles in his sleep, or laughing at the way his face twisted just before he burped. Then there was the Spartan priestess to tell him about, and the laugh they'd had when Iliona said she wasn't exactly flattered at being mistaken for a goddess who condones the seducing of virgins and the raping of nymphs, no matter how elevated her husband's position, thank you very much. Helice sighed. Esmon would've liked Iliona, probably had a crush on her as well, but most of all, Esmon would have known what to do about the big fella. He'd have set her right.

Taking a shortcut through the tombs, lit almost as bright as day under the moon, Helice thought, how strange that it was only last night when she and Iliona had sat here, among the dead, waiting for the big fella to show. So much had happened since, of course, starting this morning when she'd tried to convince her mother that Iliona wasn't Hera come to earth disguised as a mortal.

'Why the devil would she trek all this way from Mount Olympus,' she'd asked Kyniska, 'just to check up on you?'

For that, she'd received a backhander from her father. 'Don't you mock the gods, my girl. Not in my bloody house.'

The slap woke Jason up, but when Kyniska rushed across to soothe his crying, her father grabbed her by the shoulder and threw her to the floor.

'I've told you before, you don't touch that little bastard when I'm around, y'hear?' To make his point he'd bunched his fist. 'It's bad enough knowing I've raised a daughter as a whore, and if it wasn't for providence, and the fact it's a boy, it wouldn't be here in the bloody first place.'

'He's Jason, not "it",' Helice shot back. 'I don't know how you can live with yourself, your own grandson—'

This time the blow sent her reeling. 'That little

237

bastard ain't no kin of mine.' Her father shook his wrist from where the swipe had jarred it. 'I told you to get rid of it, I even gave you the money to go to that woman in the hills, but your body was too strong for her potions. It didn't reject the brat like it should've, and that's fair enough. We're sound stock, us. But I told you straight, if it was a girl I'd expose the bitch on the hillside. If it's a boy, then it's free labour for me, and you count yourself lucky I didn't throw you out. To work the docks, with the other whores.'

Helice stumbled, and realized that the reason she'd nearly bumped into one of the tomb markers was the tears that blurred her vision. Hurriedly, she gulped them back, ashamed of letting them get the better of her.

'Oh, Esmon,' she sighed. 'This never happened when you was here.'

Esmon had always stood up to the old man, and the old man respected him for it, too. But when Esmon died, he went mad with grief and took out his rage on Kyniska and Helice.

'Like we weren't grieving ourselves!'

That was the reason she went with that charcoal burner from over the way. He was gentle and sweet, funny and handsome, and his love-making let Helice forget, yes it did, but most of all it made her feel cherished. In the dark days after Esmon died, she'd lived for those secret trysts in that old abandoned shepherd's hut, and when she found out she was carrying, she was over the moon. She never once doubted he'd do the right thing. It came as quite a surprise to discover he had a wife already.

When she could no longer hide the bump, her father hit the roof, but if he thought Helice was going to swallow some potion that would flush the baby from her body, he had no idea. And god help her, she'd have killed him before she'd let him tear her daughter from her breast for the wolves to rip her to pieces.

At Esmon's stone, she arranged her posy so that the white flowers sat on a bed of blue and red, and anchored the stems with some pebbles. For a second, she thought she heard the snap of a twig, but she waited, and listened, and when nothing moved, she shrugged and settled cross-legged on the rock, bathed in the white light of the moon.

'You'd have loved playing with Jason,' she told Esmon, smoothing the loose strands of her hair with her hands.

She could see him now. Tucking his little shawl round his neck, running his finger down his wee rosy cheek! But Esmon's bones were being washed by the sea, weren't they? And now her big, handsome brother would never know babies, never know love, never experience happiness ever again.

To keep the sobs at bay, Helice began to sing.

'Sleep, my baby, close your eyes,
Sleep soundly till the sunrise.'

Jason loved that little song. He'd gurgle and—

This time, there was no mistaking the sound. Helice turned.

Just as a giant figure blocked out the moon.

Twenty-Six

Sleep. More than anything, Iliona needed sleep. Drakon's murder had tormented her first night with horrors, and last night she'd had no sleep at all. True, she snatched catnaps whenever she could, but these were nowhere near enough to restore the emotional and physical energy that was being expended. Mind and body screamed for reprieve – but was a small child locked in her loneliness any less important?

Rubbing wine lees into her cheeks and eliminating the purple hollows under her eyes with chalk, she knew she would die before breaking her oath a second time. She'd promised Alys a bedtime story and by heaven—

'Not Arethusa, *ple-e-a-s-e*.'

Whoever thought an ivory comb would tame those pixie tresses was a romantic in the extreme. It had turned tight curls into a bright golden froth with a mind of its own, that spread over the covers like a sunburst, and had more spring than Alys's bolster.

'Zygia's *so* fed up with happy endings!' Alys pushed her tongue between the gap where her two front teeth should have been. 'She wants to hear about monsters and fiends.'

Why was Iliona not surprised?

'Very well.'

She settled herself on the edge of the couch and her heart ached. In a palace this size, where servants bustled like ants and silver was as common as clay, Alys lacked for nothing. Rich murals covered her walls, there were furs to keep her warm in the winter, fans of peacock feathers to keep her cool in the summer. She was draped in linens so fine they could only have come from Egypt, and scented with lavender that did not grow wild in these hills. The girdle that belted her little robes was gold. The amulet that hung round her neck was set with amber.

But where was the love? Where were her toys? Where, for gods' sake, was the child's mother? Everything had been so carefully tidied away that, had it not been for the tiny bed, this could have been a guest room when it should be a playpen.

Where, in everything that was holy, was the laughter and warmth in her life?

'A long, long time ago in Eastern Thrace there lived a king called Phineas,' she began. 'Now Phineas was a very good king, but he was also a seer who predicted the future so accurately that it made the gods angry.'

'Because then people would know what the gods were up to before they'd even done it?'

'Exactly. And the gods don't want mortals to know what they have in store for them, so they

241

blinded poor Phineas.' Encouraged by a ghoulish lick of the lips, she continued. 'But that wasn't the end of Phineas's problems.'

'No?'

'No. He was plagued by harpies. Do you know what they are?'

'Oh, yes. They're horrid winged women with breath so vile that it rots everything they come into contact with.' Alys's eyes were like saucers. 'Like King Midas, only the other way round.'

'That's right. So at mealtimes, down they'd swoop, these horrible harpies, and snatch up as much as they could in their claws, but because the rest was rotten and putrefied, poor old Phineas was starving to death.'

'Was he saved?'

'By the sons of the North Wind, the only men who could fight the harpies in the air, and they chased them right back to their native lands.'

'Gosh.' The pixie's eyes widened. 'That's *really* exciting. Do you know any more wicked women stories?'

Iliona resisted the urge to say the girl's mother, for abandoning her daughter to over-zealous carers, and Niobe for not seeing what was under her own bloody nose.

'Far away,' she said, 'on the coldest slope of Mount Atlas, there lived a woman by the name of Medusa. Instead of pretty hair like yours,' Iliona gave the wild tangle a playful tug, 'Medusa had live snakes growing out of her head, and she was so hideous that one look was all it took to turn any living creature to stone.'

'Even men?'

'Especially men.'

'Monsters are always so *gross*.'

'Not in real life, Alys. In real life they look just like you and me.'

'But you're *beautiful*.'

Iliona laughed. 'Thank you, young lady, but so were the sirens, and you know what their favourite pastime was?'

'Tell, tell!'

'Luring ships on to the rocks with their singing, just so they could watch the sailors drown.'

The smile became a frown. 'Why?'

'Sadly, Alys, there are people in this world who kill purely for the pleasure of it.'

'That's horrible.'

'Yes it is.' She leaned down, kissed her forehead and went to blow out the candle. 'Luckily for us, those people are few and far between. Now you go to sleep—'

'Not yet,' the pixie pleaded. 'One more, oh, please. I *like* your stories!'

'Gruesome child,' she chuckled. 'But it's well past your bedtime and since I don't know any more stories—'

'I know one,' a gravel voice rumbled, and instantly the smell of freshly scrubbed childish skin was banished by woodsmoke and leather.

'Men aren't allowed in the women's quarters.' Alys giggled and goggled in equal proportions as she pushed past Iliona to sit up again. 'How *did* you get past the guards?'

'It's not the getting in,' Iliona murmured, 'it's

243

the getting out again. Isn't that right?'

'Hm.' Lysander scratched the side of his cheek.

'What's your story?' Alys asked, bouncing up and down on the bed. 'What's it about?'

'It's about a bat,' he said, 'and a weasel.'

Chubby hands clapped in delight. 'Goody.'

'Bats are quick little creatures,' he said, leaning his shoulder against the door jamb, 'but weasels are cunning, and one day the weasel catches the bat.'

Grey eyes held the child captive, but Iliona had no doubts who this tale was intended for.

'Now, the bat knows there's no point in begging for mercy, because she can see the meanness in the weasel's face, so she tells him *I'm not a bat, I'm a mouse*. And since the weasel likes mice, he lets her go.'

'I like that story.'

'Ah, but it's not over, because the very next day—' he snapped his fingers – 'the bat is caught by a different weasel. One who doesn't like mice.'

Tiny hands clamped over a rosebud mouth in horror. 'And he *ate* her?'

'No, he didn't. You see, the bat is learning from the weasels. She tells the second one *I'm not a mouse, I'm a bat*. And so she fools him and flies free.'

'That's a clever story,' Alys said. 'Did you make it up?'

'A chap called Aesop did, a long, long time ago.'

The pixie hugged her knees. 'Will you come back and tell me some more of Master Aesop's tales tomorrow?'

'Tomorrow's the Festival of the Fountains,' he said.

'So it is!' Her eyes lit up. 'And it's Drakon's funeral in the morning and that should be fun, because I overheard Nurse telling her sister that Drakon had more arrows sticking out of him than a porcupine had quills and I've never seen a porcupine, have you?'

'You'd be surprised what I've seen on my travels,' he drawled.

Alys wasn't interested. 'Just think! Two celebrations in one day, and maybe I'll even get to see some poor people, too! Have you ever seen a poor person? Nurse says they have scabs and lice and that's why I must keep away from them, but I have a scab, look!' She stuck a leg out from under the covers to reveal a minuscule graze on her knee. 'Nothing scary about that, is there?'

Lysander heaved himself away from the door jamb and peered closely. 'No, there's nothing scary about that.'

With a flick of his wrist, a ball of wood with a groove in the centre materialized in his hand. A piece of string had been wound tight into the groove, and when he let go, the ball bounced down on the length of its string, and with another flick of his wrist ran back up its own plumb line.

'*Gosh!*'

'Gosh, indeed.' He tossed the toy so it landed on her pillow. 'Now go to sleep, or you'll be too

245

tired to play with it in the morning.'

He blew out the candle and Iliona thought, yes, in real life monsters do look just like the rest of us.

The only difference was, when Lysander looked at himself in the mirror he would not see a villain.

He'd see a hero looking back.

'Do you always keep a yo-yo in your tunic for emergencies?'

Unsurprisingly, he'd followed Iliona to her room. Teasing, toying, enjoying himself.

'That was Alys's own toy,' he said. 'I noticed it poking out the side of a chest. But as you know so well, my lady...' he shot her a tight smile, 'quickness of the hand deceives the eye.'

Strolling across to the window, still unshuttered against the night, he tested the scrambling rose with his hand. 'Are you still cross because Jocasta saw me leaving yesterday?'

What?

'The instant she spotted me, of course, the situation was compromised. I decided to make the best of a bad job.'

Oh, you bastard. Not enough that he'd blackmailed her into coming to Syracuse. Not enough that he intended to brand her as the instrument of Sparta's downfall. He wanted to humiliate her in the process. First, by exploiting the vulnerability of a woman asleep in her own bedroom (and he wasn't to know she had not undressed). Now the same man who could turn himself into smoke and vanish in the breeze made sure Jocasta saw him skulking out through Iliona's window.

Her smile gave nothing away. 'Yes, I'd forgotten you were incapable of making yourself invisible.'

A muscle pulled at the side of his cheek. 'You mean you *don't* like the idea of a dashing lover peppered with rose thorns just to get to your bedroom?'

'You really like yourself, don't you?'

'Someone has to.' He rested his hip against the table and tapped a finger against his lower lip. 'That was an interesting choice of story you told Alys back there.'

Iliona tensed inside. 'Medusa always goes down well—'

'No, the one about the harpies.' He rubbed his jaw with a slow, sinuous movement. 'Phineas was a king in *Thrace*, you say?'

Iliona closed the window, since the night air suddenly seemed chill. 'Eastern Thrace,' she said. 'By the shores of the Black Sea, I believe.'

'Hm.' He nodded. 'Though that's not where the harpies were chased back to by the sons of the North Wind. That's *Crete*, I think you'll find.'

According to certain philosophers, the subconscious overrides the conscious in times of acute stress. And sometimes the subconscious makes a person reveal their innermost fears through thoughts and actions without being aware of what they're doing. Iliona believed she'd picked that story out of the air, yet it would seem that

247

Phineas's brush with the harpies was nothing more than a manifestation of her inner turmoil. Her mind had quite literally chosen the story for her.

'Crete?' she echoed innocently. 'I thought that was the Minotaur's home?'

She'd need to tread even more carefully from now on. She could not afford to give anything else away through sloppy words or actions. Lives depended on it. Including, of course, hers.

'Him, too,' Lysander said, prising his hip away from the table and taking his muscular thighs over to Iliona's bed. A slave had already turned down the coverlet, and when he ran the back of his hand over her pillow, she shivered.

'The *Krypteia* will be poorer without Phillip,' Lysander said quietly, and in the lamplight, his oiled skin glistened. 'That boy could steal a shadow.'

Expressionless eyes focused on the delicate embroidery his finger was tracing, but she wasn't fooled. He'd brought up the subject of the smith, then added in the archers, and now he'd turned the conversation round to murder. But—

The bat is learning from the weasels.

Iliona strode across to face him and hoped never to smell leather or woodsmoke again.

'This mission is cursed,' the High Priestess of Eurotas intoned solemnly. 'First, the arrows of Artemis rained death upon Drakon as a sign of her displeasure. When the warning was ignored, the floors of Arethusa opened up in anger, for I'm sure you need no reminding that Alphaeus tried to seduce Artemis before pursuing Arethusa. Or that it was Artemis who, at the wood nymph's request, changed Arethusa into the fountain that she is today.'

'Are you telling me these deaths are divine retribution because a handful of Spartans had the temerity to impersonate some obscure Arcadian river god in their desperate search for justice?'

Iliona wished he'd stop caressing her pillow. 'What is important to one person is not necessarily a priority for another.'

'I can't argue with that.'

'You can't argue with the gods, either,' and it was a credit to her upbringing as well as her vocation that her voice remained commendably neutral. 'The message from the gods is clear.'

His tongue flickered round his upper lip. 'I do hope you're not about to suggest I abandon this mission.'

'If you don't, more of our people will die and the gods will hold you responsible for their deaths.'

In calling his bluff, she had braced herself for any response. Any response that is, except the Commander of the *Krypteia* leaning so close that his nose almost touched hers.

'You,' he whispered, and she could feel the brush of his breath in her hair. 'You have no idea.'

On silent feet he padded to the door. He turned, and though his face was cast into shadow, she knew that he was smiling.

249

'Tell me, Iliona. Are you frightened of me now?'

The Serpent was a child of the Night, and its brothers were Pain, Deception, Panic and Discord, Hardship, Lawlessness and Ruin.

Every last one of them enjoyed a good fight, especially when the opponent was worthy.

And the best way to ensure that was to bait it.

Twenty-Seven

Sitting with his back against the warm wall of the grotto, moonlight pooling silver on the stone, Theo listened to the scuttle of the rats.

In his hand, the arabis, campion and lilies of the field were dwarfed.

A fox barked in the distance. An owl hooted to its mate. Listening to the water trickling and splashing in the basin behind him, he wondered how little Hyblon was coming on. She had all the charm of a wounded bear, that medic, but Theo believed the High Priestess when she said Jocasta was good at her job.

'I've had a lot of practice lately with boys who've lost copious amounts of blood,' she'd snapped, when he asked if Hyblon'd be all right just draped across her donkey. And although he assumed these other boys had also lived to tell the tale, Jocasta didn't seem any the happier for all that.

But the fact that Hyblon wasn't dead changed nothing, did it? He'd seen Theo's size, and it had scared him. He'd seen the tattoo and mistaken it for an eye, and since all Cyclops made their homes in caves, he'd taken off like a bullet.

It was because of Theo that the lad tripped and fell.

He stared at his hands in the moonlight. Bigger than cheese paddles, them, and his body covered with hair that the Greeks liked to shave off because they claimed it was primitive as well as unhygienic. Even so, he thought. If he trimmed off every whisker and took to wearing tunics instead of pantaloons and sandals instead of clogs, it still wouldn't make him one of them.

He was a freak.

He would always be a freak.

Running his finger round and round the circle in his forehead, he cursed that something so ugly could be so revered back home in Thrace. It traced back to the days when bronzesmiths were considered sorcerers, conjuring bowls, helmets, ritual masks or whatever from a simple disc of metal. Magicians? That was a laugh, Theo thought. All they did was describe a series of concentric circles on the flat metal with a compass. The guide from which they then hammered outwards from the centre. Hardly sorcery, but the circle, the original magic circle, had become the symbol of the smith. Just as metallurgy was still accompanied today by incantations counted out on the fingers of the smith's right hand.

But what use was such a skill to him?

Suppose he gave evidence for Sparta? What then? He was seven when he left Thrace and couldn't remember one damn thing about it, except that his mother had cried. Somewhere, he supposed, he had relatives. Uncles, cousins, nephews, aunts. But Thrace was a vast country, where the mountain peoples lived in isolation. How would he find his kin? In any case, their lives were established. Who was going to make room for a stranger?

Across his knees, a stream of golden hair glistened in the moonlight. He longed to stroke it. Feel its silkiness running through his hands softer than spider silk. Smell its perfume. Bury his head in its loveliness. He remembered the way her voice, so light and sweet, brought life to this grim, dark city of the dead.

Sleep, my baby, close your eyes,
Sleep soundly till the sunrise.

A lullaby. A lullaby that she'd sung how many times for her child? A hundred? A thousand? He pictured her husband, sitting by the fire. Babies tugging at her skirts. Dogs nuzzling her hand.

There would be no peace for Theo. Not in this life. For this was no life at all.

He placed the point of his dagger to the artery in his neck.

And the stars tramped oh so slowly round the heavens.

Twenty-Eight

In contrast to her treatment room, where box-wood containers with papyrus labels stood in neat array beside hinged bronze boxes and ceramic pots, and where phials of pewter rubbed shoulders with minute copper flasks, the palace kitchens seemed cluttered. Jocasta didn't care. Providing she had the pans and skillets to herself, there was a certain familiarity in the rows of gleaming scoops and spatulae on the walls. And in spite of ladles and strainers dangling in place of catheters and clamps, bowls and mixing jugs were universal, plus a pestle was a pestle was a pestle.

'Tell me,' a cultured voice murmured. 'Are you cooking a late supper or an early breakfast?'

'Taste it and decide for yourself,' she invited Talos. 'All three broths are poisonous.'

He watched as she gave the henbane a professional stir then checked the pot of mandrake simmering beside it on the gridiron. 'Has anyone ever told you that having a conversation with you is on a par with rolling naked in a bed of stinging nettles?'

He hoisted himself on to the adjacent work bench. His thighs were muscular, his skin midway between deep olive and burnished copper.

Not an unattractive combination, all in all.

'Then don't do it,' she said.

'Were it not for the passionate encouragement you give me, I wouldn't.' His nose wrinkled as she transferred the hellebore with a set of wooden tongs to prevent its juices from blistering her skin. 'Though I'll bet you didn't intend your face to show pleasure when it saw me outside the shrine tonight.'

'Don't flatter yourself, Bronze Man.' She gave the mandrake a sharp stab with the skewer. 'What you saw on my face was surprise, not delight. I thought it was Silas's shift to watch over the dead.'

Liar. When she'd returned to the city after handing Hyblon over to his mother and heard that another member of the delegation had died ... And with Talos not hanging around in the courtyard this morning...

'Being short-handed of late, our turns seem to come round a lot faster. Though keeping vigil seems to be a dangerous business.' One eye glittered through the fringe. 'Which reminds me. Where were you last night?'

'More to the point, I'd have thought, is where were you?'

As the physician drained the hellebore, something in the *helot* started to niggle. No stranger to warning signals, Jocasta tried to pinpoint the source of her unease. It wouldn't come. She blamed the need to concentrate on her medicines.

'If I asked what you plan to do with those evil-

254

smelling poisons, would you tell me the truth?'

'It's no great secret.' She shrugged. 'Niobe's brother can't sleep for his painful bladder stones. This concoction will put that right.'

'I trust you'll carve the recipe on his tombstone, so others might share his relief.'

A soft snort of laughter escaped against her will. 'I'm preparing an anodyne, not a murder weapon.'

'What a wonderful occupation, being a physician,' he said, sighing. 'If things go wrong, you simply bury your mistake.'

'It saves dealing with the customer's complaints.'

This time it was Talos's turn to laugh out loud, and as Jocasta's steady hand measured out two *cythera* of mandrake broth and stirred in the henbane a dribble at a time, she thought that, tempting as it was to toss a coin between force-feeding Myron those wretched oriental berries to prove that arrogant physician of his wrong and simply leaving him to wallow in his self-inflicted agonies, in the end it was just as easy to cure him.

Promising Niobe that she'd prepare a night-time sedative that would at least allow her brother the sleep he so desperately craved, she didn't add that it would rid him of his painful bladder stones at the same time. But if that little creep of a personal physician got the credit, then Justice was as blind as Messenian sages said.

'That's a very pretty pendant,' Talos said. 'Is it gold or electrum?'

'Mind your own business,' she said, swatting his hand away. But in its wake his skin left a faint aroma of pine cones, and the pendant was warm from his touch when it fell back against her throat.

'Tell me something else.' He lifted the lid of the terracotta breadbin, pulled off two chunks of a fig loaf and passed a piece across. 'As a physician you spend all your time fighting death, and as a woman you spend all your time fighting life.'

Jocasta placed the fig bread on the table. 'Is that supposed to be a question?'

'The question,' he said munching, 'is why.'

Carefully she extracted the berries from the papery orange lanterns, then crushed them in the mortar.

'You haven't answered,' he said after a while.

'Who said I intended to?'

Talos pulled two more chunks off the loaf and found a log of goat's cheese and some dried apricots in the cellar. She placed these offerings alongside the first piece of fig bread.

'Let me tell you my theory.' He poured water and wine into a bowl then swilled them round. 'My theory is that most people, if you asked them, would imagine that, for someone who's lived with the threat of death hanging over her for her entire life, death would hold no terrors. I believe those people are wrong – Oops.' He bent down to pick up the pestle that had unaccountably slipped through her fingers.

Jocasta snatched it from his hand. 'Why don't

you go and find a scab to pick?'

'Seems I already have,' he said, tipping the wine into a pair of goblets. 'And apparently it's weeping. At least on the inside, which explains why the exterior is so crusty. It's the accumulation of salt.'

'A pinch of which needs to be taken with everything that comes out of your mouth.'

'Yes, talking of mouths,' Talos spiked his dark fringe with his fingers. In the courtyard, the moon turned the artemisias to silver and made the wings of the moths round the night stocks quite translucent. 'Aren't you even the teeniest bit hungry?'

'I work in a temple, remember.' Jocasta pulverized a handful of the corn cockle seeds that would relieve the inflammation in Myron's urinary passage. 'So whenever I see a lamb being petted and fed the way you're treating me, I know that lamb's on its way to the slaughter.'

'Funny, spirited, very much her own woman.' He addressed the ceiling beams as he leaned his elbows on the work bench and cupped his chin in his hands. 'By thunder, this girl possesses all the qualities one needs to cook up a ... what's the word?'

'Banquet fit for a king?'

'Rebellion,' he said, switching on his most wholesome smile. 'That's the word I was looking for. Rebellion.'

Like she said. Slaughter.

'Of course, I'm only repeating idle gossip, but from what I picked up from chatting to various shepherds and huntsmen, it seems insurrection is a popular topic of conversation among the *helots* lately.'

'Sparta's a long, long way away, Talos.'

And if he needed confirmation of just how far it was, the proof was right here, in her hands...

'The *Krypteia* is relentless in its quest to root out insurgency,' he said levelly. 'Though you'd think the *helots* would see that a full-scale revolt would not be to their advantage. I mean, sure they outnumber citizens and *perioikoi* by twenty to one, but pitted against Sparta's military might?' He snapped his fingers. 'The revolution would be doomed from the outset.'

Not if it had a nudge in the right direction, she decided, transferring the viscous liquid into phials. A nice spot of political turmoil was just the thing to spread the troops out thinly, because drilled and deadly as they are, even Sparta's famous hoplites can't be in five places at once.

'So if you're not anxious about the outcome, why bother talking to me?'

'Well, for one thing, rolling in nettles can be deeply addictive. And for another...' He clucked his tongue. 'I come from a long line of wealthy landowners, and if there's one thing the aristocracy understands, it's obligation. To its country, its traditions.' He paused. 'To its slaves.'

'And naturally no landowner would want to see his workforce depleted. Imagine the impact it would have on the harvest.'

'Sarcasm is only as effective as the vessel it's poured into, Jocasta. The impact would be dire

258

without men to bring it in.'

'Sparta would starve, but at least it would starve equally.'

'You think so? Citizens would at least have the wherewithal to buy supplies from abroad, but where will *helots* find food, once the grain has rotted in the fields? Where will they find shelter in the winter from the snows?' He rubbed his hands briskly together. 'But what do a few herdsmen know, eh? And as you so rightly say, why lumber you with my troubles? You're a physician, you're above that kind of stuff, and it's not like some paltry uprising in oh-so-far-away Sparta is going to change the course of world history. Not the way Athens dominating the whole of Greece would, for example.'

'The issue is still slavery,' she said, capping the phials.

'A point Athens has taken great pains to drum into Syracuse by leading them to believe that the members of the Confederacy are not, as we Spartans like to claim, allies, but in fact subjects under our control.'

'Wiping out their cavalry capability was a masterstroke,' she admitted.

'Up to a point, and it's all very well them laughing off this nonsense of rich Athenian boys having nothing better to fill their idle hours than chasing mythical monsters across the country-side, but...'

'But what?'

She upended the dregs of her pans into the waste bin, ready for the midden boys to empty.

'Right now, Periander's happy to let his Attican associates do whatever they want. It keeps them out of his hair. But suppose it came to his attention that there was *another* reason to hunt down this mythical Cyclops?'

'There is another reason.' She rinsed her fingers in a bowl of fresh water and dried them on a towel of clean, white linen. 'This mythical Cyclops has a penchant for butchering women, remember?'

'And Periander isn't stupid. If he can have someone else clear up that mess, he's laughing.'

And how, because it wouldn't be Syracuse courting Artemis's wrath by picking a fight with a creature that was under her protection. It would be Athens. Just as it would be Athens who'd suffer, should Artemis vent divine retribution.

'But what I'm driving at is this. Imagine Periander's reaction, should he discover that Athens has drawn up some delightfully detailed plans for the shattered Confederacy. Plans in which he no longer figures as Chairman of the City Council. Or indeed has any role to play.'

'So you're planning to blow our cover and come clean with him in the morning?'

Talos found a jar of pickled walnuts on the shelf, plucked one out and bit into it. 'That would be political suicide,' he said, munching. 'No city state would ever trust us again on the grounds that we must have had something to hide, or we'd have gone straight to the Council in the first place.'

'So who's going to tell the Chairman about

260

Athens' plans—? Oh, no! Don't you look at me like that.'

'I'm not looking at you like anything, Jocasta. In fact, if I'm looking at you at all, it's because I very much like what I see. But there's no need to break out in a sweat. I'm not suggesting you throw yourself on the mercy of the City Council, either.' The shifty expression took over beneath the fringe. 'I was rather hoping the Cyclops could do that.'

A trap. It was a trap. He couldn't possibly know that she'd located the smith, but he was up to something, the slimy bastard. With concentrated care, she copied out the dosage for Myron's prescription, then picked up the two goblets, standing so close to him that her shoulder almost touched his.

'You're brighter than you look, Bronze Man.'

As she handed him the wine, her breast somehow brushed his arm, and she knew from the way his pupils darkened that he could smell the rinse in her hair, as well as the borage that softened and scented her skin.

'In fact, if it wasn't for the Cyclops being a creature of myth, I'd say you were a genius.'

'Myth?' His voice was hoarse as he ran his thumb slowly down her cheek before drawing it across her lower lip. 'The Secret Police don't chase shadows, Jocasta.'

And as his mouth covered hers, she thought, Talos wasn't the only one who knew how to set a trap.

Or how to bloody spring them.

In the wee small hours, when exhaustion forced the acrobats and fire eaters into winding up their acts, when taverns had finally managed to squeeze in the last of the pilgrims like pieces of some crazy jigsaw, and when slumber stones in bedrooms right across the city soothed sleepers with their permeated oils, Iliona dreamed.

She dreamed of thwarting Athens. Of retaining civil order in her country. Of bringing down the Head of the *Krypteia*. No doubt whoever took his place would be ruthless to his marrow and every bit as cold, but at least his successor would not be a traitor.

So in her dreams she was back setting riddles, making inventories, dictating letters to her scribes. She was listening to the cuckoo in the oak. Blessing babies. Cursing the hot winds that blew in from the south and parched the earth.

And in her sleep, just as in her waking, Iliona was filled with confidence.

She'd devised a foolproof way of smuggling Theo into Syracuse because, like Phillip said, the quickness of the hand deceives the eye. Black his skin with charcoal to cover the tattoo. Amid so many entertainers, what was one more crank? And with so much bustle in the palace, who was going to notice a servant who came in but didn't leave?

The safest place for Theo was in Iliona's room.

All she had to do was go and fetch him.

On the other side of the women's quarters,

Jocasta dreamed alone. Talos had finally slipped away after they'd satisfied each other for the third, and nearly a fourth, time. The whole point of setting honey traps is that they're sweet.

In the morning she would take a horse and head into the hills.

Killing Theo would not be a problem after all.

In its bed of contentment, the Serpent also slept.

And dreamed of procreation in its own image.

Twenty-Nine

Poor Aurora might have the lowest shrine count in the whole of Greece, but the lack of altar fires didn't make her any less revered. Aurora was the goddess who ushered in the day, forcing Night and all its demon spawn back into the shadowlands where they belonged. With a shake of her rosy cloak, she released Hope and Peace from their chains, that they might reverse the wickedness that Pain and Anguish, Strife and Deception, Murder, Destitution and Panic had wreaked. What Aurora could not reverse was Death.

And thus it was an hour before the first soft glow of dawn that Drakon set off on his voyage to the Underworld, torches guiding his funeral chariot while flutes of alder bark piped a mournful dirge.

'As I see it,' Silas said to Iliona, as the procession wound its way along the narrow alleyways, 'Death is merely a chrysalis. Parallel to the way that the corpse of our young balladeer is sheathed in a mantle that tucks around his feet and binds his limbs tightly to his body, so a butterfly in the pupating stage of its life cycle forms a cocoon in which it lies dormant until the perfect insect inside is developed.'

It was a comforting idea, she supposed, that Hades was populated with swallowtails and fritillaries flitting joyfully from blossom to blossom. In reality, she thought, the butterfly's world was dominated by predators who saw it as food. In Drakon's case, the predator had found his meal particularly satisfying.

'And you think today is the day that perfection has been reached?'

Silas's cheeks bunched into a sad smile. 'It's as good a day as any, Lady Iliona. As good a day as any.'

As the convoy approached the bridge, the undertakers stretched out their right hands and turned them palm-up to the gods. Bearers sprinkled drops from Arethusa's spring before the hearse.

'That was the last straw, as far as the pitcher women are concerned.' Roxana stepped up to fill the gap that Silas left. 'They're madder than a nest of hornets, having to traipse right over to the mainland for their water, while the temple

264

attendants are allowed to fill as much as they like for some foreigner's funeral procession. I tell you, my lady, they're not happy.'

Iliona suppressed a smile. 'Actually, Roxana, I think you'll find that that's exactly what they are.' The guard had managed to disperse them easily last night ... but that was last night. Today Syracuse was celebrating one of the biggest festivals in its calendar, and how often were women that far down the social scale given a chance to be the centre of attention? 'Mark my words, those girls are playing for the crowd.'

'Well, I don't like it.' Feline eyes flashed. 'They're drawing far too much attention to this delegation, and I'm pretty sure Niobe suspects something, you know.' She leaned close as the hired mourners threw their hands in the air and the choir broke into ritual laments. 'She keeps asking me about Arcadia. What's it like in the winter? What manner of herbs grow? How deeply entrenched is the worship of Pan? And I've no idea how to reply. I've never been to Arcadia in my life.'

'Neither has she.'

'Really?' The freckles on Roxana's nose wrinkled. 'What about when the Festival was held there last year?'

'Niobe is a product of Syracuse's new-found democracy,' Iliona pointed out. 'Her appointment was purely political, and last year was her first year as High Priestess.'

'Oh, well! If she was just asking out of curiosity, I can improvise as easily as the next

265

person,' Roxana breezed. 'By the time she visits next spring, she'll be so grateful Syracuse isn't shackled to Athens that she'll probably wrap those enormous flabby legs of hers in goatskins and play the pan-pipes herself.'

Somehow Iliona hadn't imagined Roxana cracking jokes. 'Considering it's a funeral, you seem extraordinarily cheerful.'

'Why not? Don't get me wrong, I enjoy my work, you know I do, but Sparta's my home and Sparta's where my heart lies. Who wouldn't rejoice at the prospect of going home tomorrow?'

Iliona pulled up short. 'Tomorrow? What happened to the mission? What happened to clearing Sparta's name?'

The procession halted at the edge of the Burning Field. Across the clearing, a Corinthian merchant with measureless grey eyes and his long hair tied in a leather thong at the nape was chatting to the Chairman of the City Council. Periander appeared to be smiling.

'Don't tell the others,' Roxana begged. 'It's just our secret,' she whispered, but...' Her face beamed with pride as she watched her brother the shapeshifter play his latest role to the full. 'But Lysander told me everything's going to be settled tonight.'

Indeed it would, Iliona reflected. Just not in the way that he thought.

'Don't you find that rather extraordinary?'

'My brother has always been out of the ordinary.' Roxana clipped off a lock of hair as a mourning token for her dead comrade. 'Just as he's always been right.' There was not even a trace of doubt in her smile. 'Oh, don't look so worried. You're in safe hands with Lysander, my lady.' She patted Iliona's arm in reassurance. 'We all are,' she added confidently.

As she strode off, all grace and agility, youthfulness and hope, Iliona finally understood how far the *Krypteia* was prepared to go in his quest for power. Until now, she'd had no reason to fear for Roxana's life, for who could believe a man would sacrifice his own sister to achieve his goal? Now she saw that Roxana's love was the weapon with which Lysander intended to kill her.

Iliona prayed for the strength to disarm him.

As Lucifer the morning star announced the arrival of the dawn, the undertakers transferred Drakon's body from the hearse to the pyre and wreathed the bier with juniper and yew. It was said that the soul departed through the mouth with the very last living breath. An invisible wisp called the psyche, that could not return and had no desire to do so. It was also said that, by releasing the psyche, a new life was born that would live for ever in the apple orchards of the Far West.

And you see? With every step that it took, the Serpent was learning.

At first, this was purely a matter of power. Of having control over a nation, its people, its wealth and its destiny. Now it had become so

267

much more.

And so personal...

While the wailing women raised their hands in lament as Night slowly turned the Burning Field into day, the Serpent basked in the heat of the flames.

Eliminating Chloris had been an act of expediency, and it hadn't mattered one iota that it was carried out by others or conducted at distance.

But with the discovery that toying with a human life brought pleasure, the mood shifted. Drakon's murder showed that in choosing not only the apple, but the time and the place it should fall, the Serpent had become a god. No wonder the Olympians dangled mortals like puppets.

Someone, somewhere was delivering an elegy. Someone else was pronouncing that the organs of the sacrificial beast augured well for the soul of the departed. Who cared?

To kill or to spare.

To terminate swiftly or inflict a lingering death.

To decide who, when and where...

Having a human being at one's mercy was the greatest power of all, dangling the thread of life and dominating the spirit as well as the flesh was the supreme climax. Or so the Serpent believed...

Phillip had always been part of the plan.

He was a thief and a liar with nothing to say, and who had nothing to contribute to society in return. To eliminate Phillip would be like squashing a bug. His death would be doing the world a favour.

Choosing him over the others, though, that had been a genuine source of pleasure. Eeny, meeny, miny, mo, you're mine. And once the victim was selected, there followed the build-up. The foreplay, if you like. That delicious anticipation in which the thread of life was dangled back and forth over the dagger of death.

Now? Or in a minute?

Now? Or in an hour...?

Using trust, using guile, using loyalty, using comradeship, the apple was slowly rolled to the edge of the branch. Then the mood shifted again.

Forget psyche! Forget that invisible last breath escaping through the mouth! It was the *eyes*. That indescribable moment when the victim realizes that they've not only been betrayed, but that betrayal has brought their killer boundless pleasure. It was the horror in their eyes that was so unutterably exciting. Their terror. Their powerlessness.

Oh, how the Serpent enjoyed learning new things.

The protraction of death was a lesson that needed more practice!

'I realize this is an inopportune moment to intrude on your grief.' Niobe separated herself from the Syracusian contingent to station herself beside Iliona as the torch was set to Drakon's pyre. 'But I'm afraid the situation at the shrine has turned rather ugly.'

'So I'd heard.'

'The suggestion that retribution is confined purely to your delegation is cutting no ice with the pitcher women, who are positively revelling in their talent for causing a riot.'

Across the clearing, Periander's merchant companion had melted away. Iliona wasn't surprised.

Niobe sighed. 'According to the captain of the guard, half the city and nine-tenths of the pilgrims are behind the wretched girls' petition. He warns of a city-wide riot.'

'I'm sure if you—'

'There is no "me" about this, dear. It's "us".' A gold-weighted hand clamped on Iliona's shoulder to reinforce her solidarity. 'Nor can we afford to wait till sundown, when the Festival begins. I apologize for dragging you away, but we need you to help defuse the situation, although heaven only knows how.' She rolled her thickly kohled eyes. 'Appealing to their better side is a joke, and I'm reluctant to resort to violence, one simply doesn't know where it will end.'

'Indeed, Niobe, one does not.'

'I *wish* I knew the answer.'

'Funnily enough, I think it's standing over there.' Iliona pointed towards a little man, bobbing absently from sandalled foot to sandalled foot as he absorbed every word of the ovations. 'Silas trained as a recital slave. If you forget about trying to calm things down but let people be drawn themselves to his recitations, you'll have them eating out of your hand in no time.'

And who wouldn't be mesmerized by tales of two beautiful women turned into sea monsters, one dashing ships against the rocks, the other pulling them down to a watery grave, she added.

'Certainly not!' Niobe's eyes bulged in horror. 'That riot is being incited outside the shrine of which I am High Priestess and which plays host to a fellow High Priestess. I will not have my authority suddenly undermined by a man, especially not one of lower status!'

'Surely the whole point is that he lures them away without them realizing what's happened?'

'You have no idea how hard I've worked to reach this position,' Niobe hissed. 'Surely you, of all people, don't need reminding of how challenging it is to be successful in a man's world! I am not prepared to have the whole city watch a male slave achieve what I cannot. I insist you come at once.'

'I can't.'

'Oh, good heavens, you Arcadians don't honestly wait for the fire to die down, do you? That takes *hours*, and besides. If you feel that little fellow's capable of representing you in a riot, he's more than fit to stand in now.'

'Take Roxana instead. Then if logic fails, she can beat the crowd into submission.'

Her humour fell flat. 'Are you refusing to help?'

'Deferring assistance,' she corrected. 'Unfortunately, I have an even more pressing engagement.' Manetho must be moved out of those

271

hills. The Thracian must be moved down to safety. 'But I repeat, I will set the record straight tonight.'

Niobe snorted. 'By tonight those women will have stormed the fountain house, contaminating the purity of Arethusa's spring even further, and giving conviction to the lie that our patron has abandoned us.'

'I'm sorry, but this is important.'

'You desert your dead comrade, you desert your god, you even desert your religious obligations to go swanning off in the middle of a funeral while rebellion is cooking – and then have the audacity to tell me something is more important?'

'You have to trust me.'

'I would rather put my trust in a nest of vipers,' Niobe spat. 'This is the most unconscionable dereliction of duty I have ever come across in my life, and I am ashamed to be associated with you.'

She stormed off. Meanwhile the choir calmed the River Styx and steadied the Ferryman's oars, and dancers swirled in scarlet robes around an altar strewn with cherries, pomegranates and poppies. All red, of course, the symbol of resurrection. And there was a parallel, she thought. Not with Niobe's anger, not with blood, but in that something new was rising from the flames. A world of harmony and balance. Of peace restored. Of calm.

All that new world needed was the affidavit of a butcher.

As pine spat out its resins from the pyre, Iliona slipped away.

Kyniska was exhausted. All night she'd called and searched for Helice, but Helice hadn't come. Her man said, what do you expect of an alleycat like that? But her man was wrong. Helice was a good girl. Respectable. And if her father wasn't too bound up in grief to see what was right beneath his nose, he'd know it—
She stopped to blow her nose. Something must've happened to the lass, she'd said. An accident, like Hyblon had, you wait. You wait till you find her lying bleeding some place out there, her leg broke or her ankle trapped in some fissure in the rock. You'll be sorry then, she told her man, as they'd stood underneath the moon, calling her name. Helice'd never leave her bairn all night without telling.
All the same, a grain of hesitation wriggled in her mind. Helice was upset because they'd rowed. Because her father hit her, which he shouldn't, and which, although he never said so in as many words, he was sorry for, and if the Cyclops got to her, he'd never forgive himself, not ever. But the point was, Helice was upset. And the last time she was upset, she'd taken up with that dirty, scheming adulterer across the way. Not that Kyniska would ever let her man in on the name of Jason's father. That was her secret, hers and Helice's, and she'd take it to the grave. Just as she knew her daughter hadn't taken that wicked potion to abort the bairn, or

where the lovers used to tryst.

But no, oh, surely not. Helice weren't daft enough to fall for his sweet talk a second time. Were she—?

'I'll check she's not with me sister,' Kyniska said, but in any case, her man had set off to search the dried-up river beds before the moon had set. She didn't need no telling that he'd also check in the ravines.

And as the pale light of dawn brought colour to the landscape, Kyniska was reminded how the dew was formed. That it was Aurora's tears falling on the grass as she wept for her beloved son, killed at Troy at the end of Achilles' spear. Kyniska prayed her own tears wouldn't wash these hills. The tide would flood the city, that's for sure.

'Helice? Helice, are you there, love?'

Her heart was heavy as she approached the shepherd's hut, long since abandoned once the roof blew off. Now mildew painted frescoes on the stone, moss had begun its silent, soft invasion. She took a deep breath, then another. You never know, she thought. Passion makes fools of everyone. And with hope still flickering inside, she pressed on up the weed-infested path. The door had fallen off its hinge, there was a strong smell of sheep-dip in the air, which was odd, considering there weren't no sheep up here any more. And yet—

Like the desperate animal that she was, Kyniska refused to give up.

'Heli—'

As she opened her mouth, a hand closed over it. 'Not a word,' a voice whispered. It was low and full of warning. 'Not a word, if you'd be so kind.'

Kyniska looked up and saw the single, blue eye staring at her without emotion. She prayed to Hera that her man would take pity on his grandson, claim him, feed him, cherish him. Tell him how his grandma loved him so very, very much. Slowly, Kyniska nodded.

'Good.' Theo nodded, but made no move to release his grip. 'Now then.' He clucked his tongue. 'What do you think we should do next?'

The Serpent was also in a quandary.

Now? Or in a minute?

Now? Or in an hour...?

In Phillip's broken spirit, it found pleasure beyond measure in watching terror dance in someone's eyes. In making them understand that their death, and the manner of it, was in someone else's hand. That they were utterly, helplessly, ridiculously powerless.

So as the sun rose over the island of Sicily, casting its light on the slopes of Mount Aetna and bringing softness to the orchards and olive groves, the Serpent basked in happy indecision. *Now, or in a minute? Now, or in an hour?* For the longer the cusp between life and death stretched, the more precious it became.

For both parties.

Thirty

Iliona had rehearsed her speech so many times that she was in danger of doing Silas out of a job. But it was vital she convinced Theo that he would be safe from Athens' reprisals, just as he would be free from prosecution and (this was the hard bit) from any other crimes. He'd made no mention of his victims and given no hint of contrition. That's what made him evil. And even though he believed she walked the winds of knowledge and knew every damn thing he'd ever done, he hadn't so much as skated round the killings. Too ashamed? Possibly. Too scared to admit it, even to himself? Almost certainly, so 'immunity from any other crimes' left it vague and open. All the same, she approached his cave with trepidation.

'Theo, it is I.' Her hands shook as they pulled away the scrambling fig. 'The High Priestess who counts the grains of—'

'Save your breath,' Jocasta said. 'He's gone.'

Kedos means sorrow.

Gazing across the plain, where waves washed a sandy, shelving shoreline fringed by pines, Iliona pictured seventeen hired archers breaking their fast that fateful morning. Not daring to risk

276

a fire, they would have spent a cold night in the caves, and, closing her eyes, she saw them knotting up their long, dark hair in that distinctive Cretan style. Gathering up bows made from staves of yew in silence. Taking up their stations, quivers on their backs. Perhaps the herdsmen were already stirring when the first volley hissed out death. The archers were trained professionals, who killed without question, without compassion, certainly without interest. It would not have taken them long to mow down the pride of the Syracusian cavalry, whether prize stallions, pregnant mares or newborn foals and yearlings. Theirs was systematic slaughter in return for silver.

With no idea that they would be repaid in kind.

On this bright spring morning, with the first wave of the replacement herds grazing peacefully, the plain bore no resemblance to a killing field.

But Kedos means sorrow...

'And you thought it would be hard to find Manetho,' Jocasta said.

'I did,' Iliona admitted, and wished with all her heart it had been.

Because in the end, all they'd had to do was follow the vultures.

Jocasta's thoughts were also on a blaze of arrows raining down. But instead of open pastureland where horses grazed and frolicked, her mind saw a canyon wrapped in cliffs, where sulphur bubbled through the hot springs of Thermopylae that

277

gave the Pass its nickname.

The Gates of Fire.

The men inside the canyon knew they'd been betrayed. This Pass, so crucial in defence against the Persians, was secure enough – until a local tribesman told the enemy about a secret back route through the gorge. The three hundred Spartan warriors trapped inside were not afraid. They had faced the Persian army many times before in victory. Now they would face it one last time in certain death.

They had no illusions. Their spears were snapped, their swords were blunt, the Persians outnumbered them forty to one. But providing they still had hands to throw rocks, teeth to bite with, breath to breathe, it would buy time. Time for the allied army to catch up. So when the Persian Emperor begged them to throw down their arms and was told to come and fucking get them, three hundred cheers rose up.

Even when the first volley of arrows came, they jeered. 'What manner of warfare is this,' they called out, 'where cowards stand out of range and call it battle?'

Ah, but what was dishonour compared to victory? The Persians' only thought was winning, and the battered shields that had been the mainstay of the Spartan defence were no defence at all against the volleys. Within minutes, every man lay dead. Picked off like fish inside a barrel, and it was said the arrows rained down so hard, they blocked the sun.

Jocasta stared across the open pastures and

thought, Kedos means sorrow.

It was right that the memory of three hundred brave, betrayed warriors should live on. That their story be engraved in bronze inside the temple of Athene in Sparta for all to see. But what of the hundred *helots* who fought alongside them? Who cheered and jeered every bit as hard?

And died without a mention?

'Single stab wound to the heart.' Jocasta withdrew the metal spike with which she'd probed the corpse. 'Quick and clean.'

Iliona turned away. 'It couldn't have been an accident? Or suicide?'

'A careless man might slip and fall on his dagger. A man with an intimate knowledge of anatomy might even be able to kill himself with one strike.' Jocasta wiped the probe on the grass. 'But neither's going to be in a position to clean and sheathe his own knife afterwards, no matter how houseproud or tidy they feel about it.'

You mock, little flea, but there's an entrance to Hades on this cursed island. Just make sure you don't take the wrong turn.

Did shades give one another affectionate clips round the ear?

One more word about blood-sucking fiends that haunt those bloody caves, and it'll be you riding side-saddle to Hades, my young friend.

This time Iliona could not control her stomach. Retching up her breakfast, she thought about the tracker and the thief on the same Ferry to the Underworld. The tragedy was, she'd bought

279

both their tickets.

It's a sad fact that we lose half a dozen men each year to ravines and bad weather. This time it was Lysander's voice that echoed. *And their bodies are not always found.*

Sad fact be damned. He'd walked away, leaving Manetho to be torn apart by scavengers, but then the *Krypteia* had no ethics. He had no friends, no conscience, only this absurd fixation with power. What was one more paltry tracker when you can rule the world?

'No attempt to hide the body.' Jocasta watched dispassionately as Iliona was sick a second time. 'No attempt to make it look like an accident.' She took a long swig from her goatskin. 'Unlike Phillip and Drakon.'

Iliona swung round. 'What do you mean?'

'As a colleague and a friend, I felt obliged to lay them out.'

'Bollocks.'

It was customary for the deceased to be washed and anointed with oils before being garlanded with poplar to lend what dignity one could to the indignity of death. It wasn't customary for physicians to be involved in the process, though.

'You didn't even like them.'

'I'll start warming to the Secret Police when they stop wanting me dead.' She tossed Iliona the goatskin and made her drink. 'But right from the start I was suspicious. Who raised the alarm that the horses had been slaughtered? Who told the City Council where and when the archers were making their escape? And why were there

280

no survivors, when at least one mercenary is usually kept alive to interrogate afterwards?'

Together the two women began to cheat the vultures of their dinner.

'Drakon might have been a gifted singer and musician, but first and foremost he was part of the *Krypteia*.' Jocasta's words came out in jerks from the effort of heaving rocks. 'Only the most reckless of warriors stands with his back to danger, and whatever else you can say about them, you can't accuse a Spartan of being reckless. Accident, my arse.'

Any response Iliona might have wanted to make remained locked inside. The vultures had pecked out Manetho's eyes.

'But there was no proof that Drakon was anything other than misguided. Whereas Phillip...' Jocasta tucked a coin on what was left of his tongue to pay the Ferryman. 'Phillip's neck was broken, but not, you may be interested to note, as a result of the fall. I also found bruising on his body that suggested he fought with his attacker.'

'So you can *prove* it was murder?'

'Do you know what lividity is?' Jocasta placed two more coins in each of the empty sockets. 'It's the blotching where the blood pools after death.'

Iliona forced herself to follow this conversation. 'In other words, if I'm lying on my back when I die, that's where the blood drains, so my back will turn purple.'

'Exactly so. And given that dead people cannot move, it also follows that they cannot lie. Cimon found Phillip lying face down in the cellar, but instead of his chest showing signs of lividity as I'd expect, my examination revealed it ran the full length of his side. Do you follow?'

'Phillip was dead before he was thrown in the vault?'

'Which is why I took a long, hard look around that little shrine.'

'And?'

'I found traces of blood on Arethusa's foot. Not a lot, because being gilt, the statue was easy to clean up, but the toe is the same shape and size as the indentation in Phillip's skull. And considering lividity takes a while to establish, it seems his killer spent a lot of time figuring out a way to make it look like an accident. Hence the time lapse.'

Phillip's neck was broken, but not as a result of the fall.

'Guess again.' Perhaps it was reaction after throwing up, but Iliona suddenly felt very, very cold. 'This bastard gets pleasure out of suffering.'

With an expert twist, he'd paralysed his victim, then sat there, drinking in Phillip's terror. And even when he'd smashed his head against the stone, he remained beside the body. His trophy. His triumph—

Jocasta's eyes narrowed. 'You do know it's Lysander?'

She thought she ought to feel surprise, but didn't. Only numb. 'And you do know he is not my lover?'

Jocasta threw down the rock that she'd been holding. 'You just can't stop, can you? First, you betray my trust by stealing seeds from my medicine box, now you abuse my loyalty by lying through your teeth. It's just been one lie after a bloody other—'

'How dare you! How dare you lecture me about loyalty and trust? You suspected Drakon's death was murder and you knew damn well Phillip's was, but did you think to share this information? No, you were looking for a way to use it against Sparta. And please don't insult my intelligence by denying it, because I'm bloody sure you didn't trek up here to make sure Theo had a good night's sleep.'

'I deny nothing and apologize for nothing.'

'Bigots never do.'

'This is a question of allegiance, not bigotry, you self-righteous, lying bitch. And if you think my commitment to freedom is extreme, you try living without it for a while.'

'Is this where you give me that we-have-no-homeland speech? Where you start talking about that dreamy, pear-shaped valley, where your parents carved their names? Because if so, it's high time you grew up.' She gave her no time to interrupt. 'Where do you know a valley that shape cradled by hills, where orchards and wheat fields stretch to infinity? Where chestnut trees grow in abundance?'

'Are you saying that was *Sparta*?'

'Where the stream of Limnos joins Eurotas, if you want to be exact. You've been there many

283

times.'

'No way!' Jocasta's eyes blazed with fury. 'That was their homeland they described to me—'

'Exactly. They'd never been to Messenia, any more than you. How could they, for heaven's sake? But that doesn't mean a person can't love the land where they were born, and if you can't see that, Jocasta, you're not the woman I thought you were.' Iliona released a weary breath. 'You don't help deserters because it's one conscript less for the *Krypteia*. You help them for the same reason you helped Hyblon, you're helping Myron and you treat the worshippers at Eurotas. You want them to get well. You want them to enjoy the best quality of life they possibly can—'

'Damn right, and the best quality of life is freedom, Iliona. You take it for granted, so you don't understand. The way you eat, the way you sleep, the way you breathe, everything's so different when you're answerable to no one.'

'Everybody's answerable to someone.'

Like Silas said, we're all slaves, one way or another.

'Then stop pretending Lysander was not your master.' Jocasta tossed her hair over her shoulders. 'When you said he blackmailed you into coming on this mission, I never doubted you. Not until I saw him climbing from your window, blowing kisses on his fingers—'

'Precisely my point.' He blew a *kiss*? 'He's the *Krypteia* and I assure you, he saw you long

284

before you'd spotted him. That man does nothing without thought or calculation, and on balance I'd say his plan to drive a wedge between us worked out rather well, don't you? Now I don't know about you, but I'm seriously tired of arguing and we're running out of time. For gods' sakes, let's stop hissing like a pair of cats and see if we can't salvage something out of this bloody awful mess.'

She'd forgotten that combat was Jocasta's chief form of entertainment. 'Not until you tell me what he was doing in your bedroom.'

'Baiting me, humiliating me ... The list is as long as you've got ears to listen.' The sadist wanted to make sure she felt every barb. 'But what his ego is too big to see is that the more I meet with him, the more we fence and flirt and hedge, the better I'm able to get the measure of my opponent.'

The bat, my friend, is learning from the weasel. Iliona paused from humping stones. 'How did *you* know Lysander was a traitor?'

Jocasta, too, had underestimated just how big Manetho was. 'Because after examining Phillip's corpse, I stood in the precinct and took a good, long look around.'

She had to wait an hour, she added, maybe more, before the gods finally smiled upon her and she heard the distinctive sound a baby makes when it's troubled with the colic.

'It seemed rather mean-minded, don't you think, not to offer my services as a physician? Its mother, whose window happened to overlook

285

the precinct by the way, was embarrassingly grateful. But you know the thing about the colic, Iliona? It doesn't confine its torture to the daytime, and while I fed her babe an infusion of dill and aniseed, a simple remedy but astonishingly efficacious, its mother and I, well, we got to chatting. And guess what? Three hours after sunset on the night Phillip was killed, she'd been comforting the child and happened to notice someone slip into the temple.' She paused. 'A man with long hair tied back in a thong, dressed in the tunic of a warrior.'

They placed a marker for the grave. A run of pebbles in a vee to form the *lambda*. In time, his bones would be dug up and carried back to Sparta on his shield. Assuming anyone was left alive to know where he was buried.

'Pity you hadn't taken Lysander to your bed.' Jocasta brushed the red dust off her hands. 'If he'd screwed you half as well as he's screwed his country, you'd have been a very happy woman.'

All that teasing, toying, tasting, testing? That slow deliberation and contrived sensuality steadily edging its way to ecstasy? Oh yes. Had he been able to resist the ultimate in humiliation.

'If he'd screwed me, Jocasta, I'd be dead.'

'You are anyway, we all are, Iliona. Without Theo, there's no way of exposing Lysander's treachery.' She threw her hands up in the air. 'What the hell got into him? Did he run off in panic? Did the Athenians get to him? Croesus, for all we know he could be stalking us right

286

now, because I tell you, it gave me the creeps the way he couldn't take his eyes off you.'

'You're right, we can't expose Lysander and we can't clear Sparta's name.' Iliona pushed her hair back from her eyes with weary hands. 'But what I can do is what I should have done right at the beginning.'

Kill him.

The homestead looked no different from any other day when Helice's father walked back up the track. Same low, windowless walls. Same thatch on the roof. Same polished step with a cat asleep on it. Had he been less preoccupied, perhaps he would have noticed that there was no straw mattress airing against the wall today. No coil of smoke rising from the fire over which the cauldron bubbled night and day. No little squab of a woman bustling about with leather pails to fetch water or sitting cross-legged on the doorstep, shelling peas.

A wiser man would have realized that the heart had gone out of his cottage. As it was...

See? Told you nothing bad'd happened to the girl. If there was, Kyniska wouldn't still be at her bloody sister's, would she? She'd be here, wailing, howling and raising the bloody roof, running down the path to see what he had found. Helice's father slung his empty goatskin on the floor. Well, he'd found bloody nothing, had he? Hollered till his throat was hoarse, searched every rock and boulder, but his gut was right. His gut was always bloody right. Nothing wrong

287

with Helice, except that fever in her loins. Never could control the itch, the little whore.

'Bugger.'

No bread in the bloody oven, either. No cheese for his bloody lunch. The stew hanging on the cauldron was even bloody cold, because the lazy bitch had let the fire go out.

'Kyniska!' His roar carried on the wind. 'Kyniska, you come home this instant, d'you hear?'

He'd half a mind to go over to that bloody sister's and drag the fat bitch home by her bloody hair. Well, to hell with her, that's what he said, he was bloody starving. With a snap of his dagger, down fell one of the hams curing for the winter. Well, to hell with that too. Something had to stop his belly rumbling, he was a working man, for pity's sake. Several slices disappeared before he wiped his mouth and thought, bloody women. Now if Esmon was here ... His son, his brave, brave fisher son ... Aye, he thought, belching. They never messed about, them two, when he were still alive.

Thirty-One

News is a funny thing. No matter how dangerous the fire eater's act, how exciting the rope walker who juggled terracotta plates while he balanced, gossip still took precedence. The disappearance of another girl swept through the city like a forest fire. Iliona and Jocasta couldn't miss it, not above the crash of cymbals, the banging of drums and the blare of gleaming trumpets as they led their horses through the crush.

'Vanished without trace, milady, what d'you make of that?'

'Ooh, it were dreadful. Sucked into the tomb, she was, the lid snapped shut behind her, so they reckon.'

'Now we know what tempted Theo from his cave,' Jocasta muttered. 'The urge for butchery apparently overriding the urge for freedom.'

It always did, Iliona thought, that was half the trouble. And, dammit, she knew that. She knew that, when she left him alone up there in the hills. She knew he'd kill again. That he couldn't help himself. Instead, she gambled that the drive to kill would be staved off a little longer, and that the blood of thousands was worth the blood of a few.

She was wrong.

'There's nothing we can do about it now.' Except live with it. Somehow. 'Tomorrow I'll go back up there. He's bound to have returned to the safety of his little sanctuary by then, pretending nothing's happened, and after that, there'll be no more weeping parents, no need to fear the dark.'

Only her conscience to fear, and the slow realization that she was indeed her father's daughter. A thought occurred to her.

'Is that why you went up there this morning? To put an end to Theo's carnage?'

She'd been so busy trying to find Theo, then Manetho, that she hadn't stopped to ask herself why Jocasta was already at the cave.

'As it happens,' Jocasta had never shied from the truth, no matter how uncomfortable, 'yes, it was.' There has to be a first time. She swiftly changed the subject. 'How do you know that slippery bastard will be at the festival tonight?'

'Lysander? He's been on the fringes of everything else, why wouldn't he?' His ego wouldn't allow him to miss a single second. 'But I'm taking no chances,' Iliona said. 'I'm relying on Roxana to draw him to me.'

The *Krypteia* was as elusive as the wind, but there were ways and means of trapping winds. And if you cannot then contain them, you can still harness their powers and use their own forces against them.

'If I tell Roxana that I suspect a traitor in the camp, she'll run straight to her brother with the information.'

One eyebrow rose in scepticism. 'Suppose he decides to eliminate her, too? Before she tells someone else?'

'Too risky.'

For one thing, a third 'accident' would arouse too many suspicions, even for the superstitious Sicilians, and Periander and the City Council were not stupid. For another, if Lysander told his sister to keep it to herself, she'd die before revealing her secret. But mainly, of course, because once it came to Lysander's ears that Iliona smelled a rat, he'd need to establish exactly how much she knew and who else she might have told.

'While I'm going through the motions at the temple, he'll be keeping an eye on his investment.'

Without any inkling that the bat had the weasel exactly where she wanted him.

'You be careful,' Jocasta warned. 'He sets traps and so far you've fallen into every single one.'

As it happened, Lysander enjoyed setting traps. Cracking his knuckles and tying back his long, dark, warrior hair, he satisfied himself that this latest one was baited adequately.

She would walk straight into it, the silly bitch.

'Evil spirits stalk them tombs at night.'

Another scandal monger!

'Aye, that Helice wouldn't have stood a

291

chance, poor cow.'

'What?' Iliona grabbed the gossip by his sleeve. 'Did you say Helice?'

'That's the one. Daughter of a hill farmer – Here, are you all right?'

All right? Of course she wasn't all bloody right! Helice had risked her own life and her family's for what? Her baby son—

'Hey!' Jocasta jumped into the saddle and rode after her. 'Where the hell do you think you're going?'

'Kyniska's place. I need to tell her I'm so very, very sorry.'

Jocasta grabbed the reins, nearly jerking Iliona off her horse. 'You're going nowhere,' she snapped. 'For one thing, there's barely two hours of daylight left, and for another, you didn't force Helice to visit the City of the Dead at night. The choice was hers, and it's not as though the silly cow didn't know the danger.'

'She said the smith looked lonely, but I should have warned her. I should have put her right.'

'And that's your problem, Iliona, you can't put the whole world right. Theo *did* look lonely. You and I felt sorry for him, for Croesus' sake. It's just that his idea of companionship differs from the rest of us.'

Too much compassion, that was Iliona's trouble. As a physician, Jocasta knew you had to stay detached. It was the only way that one can be objective, because once you let your heart start ruling your head, mistakes are made and patients die.

All the same, both women could smell defeat drifting on the breeze.

'Come on.' Jocasta turned their horses back towards the city. 'You can't afford to miss the start of the procession.' It started at sundown.

Iliona understood that, really, she had little choice. Peace was held by only the thinnest of threads, and if the *Krypteia* so much as sensed blood in the water, everything was lost. Sparta. Syracuse. Even the chance for retribution. She turned her eyes towards the sinking sun.

Time was running out.

And so were options.

As far as the grooms in Niobe's stables were concerned, the Festival of the Fountains was better than a holiday. People came flooding. They handed over their horses. And they stayed. There was none of the usual bustling turnover in the yard, because no one was heading out, and once the customary feeding, cleaning and brushing down was out of the way, they settled down to a good old-fashioned game of knucklebones as the sun began to set.

'Mind if I join you, gentlemen?'

'Feel free, sir.' The head groom made room for the cultured stranger. A fringe fell over his left eye, giving him an air of shiftiness, but this was cancelled out by his boyish grin. 'Copper a point all right with you?'

The bones clacked and rolled, clacked and rolled, four dice in the cup.

'You've brought me good fortune, that you

have, sir.' The head groom scooped his winnings off the step. 'I win again.'

'There's something wrong with them dice, that's what,' his colleague sneered, scratching at a flea bite. 'No one can throw an Aphrodite as often at that.'

'Don't you believe it,' another player said. 'I've attracted more Vultures than a carcass rotting in the desert.'

'At least Vultures count for something on the scoreboard,' the stranger murmured. 'I have thrown nothing but Dogs.'

'Aye, talking of dogs, my Daphne's taken a right old shine to you.'

'Ah, well.' Talos ruffled the ears of the bitch nuzzled up against his side, its tongue lolling proudly from one side of its mouth. 'Everybody loves me, don't you know.'

The head groom chuckled and he patted Daphne's side. 'Everybody loves her little puppies, I know that. All going to good homes, aren't they, my sweet lass?'

'Is that all you lot can find to talk about?' asked the harness man, breezing into the yard. 'A dozen ugly pups?'

'Don't listen, Daphne, my love.' The head groom covered the dog's ears with his hands. 'They're beautiful babies with beautiful natures, my darling.'

'They'd bloody better have,' the harness man retorted. 'You talked me into taking home a pair, and my wife can't stand dogs!'

Everyone was still laughing when two horses

cantered through the gates.

'Off you go, lad.' The head groom nudged a pock-faced youth in the ribs. 'Help the ladies dismount.'

'Why me?' the boy grumbled.

'Because you're the only one not playing. And step on it. That's Lady Niobe's honoured guests just ridden in, the High Priestess and her attendant. Now you keep them waiting any longer, lad, and my boot'll be so far up your arse you won't sit down for a month.'

During the course of the upheaval, no one noticed that the stranger had slipped away from the game. Or that he did not return until the women had disappeared inside the palace.

'The horses look tired,' he observed, leaning his weight against the stall while the stable boy unbuckled the saddles and removed the foam-flecked bridles.

'And thirsty,' the boy said, leading them to the trough. 'First time the two ladies have ridden in together, mind.'

'Really?' In his arms, the stranger fondled one of the puppies.

'Previously they'd gone off and come home separately. The dark-haired one took off, don't laugh, on a donkey on one occasion.'

'I don't suppose you know where each of them was headed?'

'Neither of them said...'

The suggestiveness in his tone brought a slow smile to Talos's lips. 'But you can make an educated guess?'

At the chink of silver, the youth stopped what he was doing. 'Aye, sir, reckon I can.' The coins changed hands. 'See this?' He pointed to the red dust in the horses' sweat. 'This is from the scrubland over yonder. The soil's red and thin and crumbly up there, nothing grows, it's only fit for sheep. But!' He straightened up. 'You take a look at this.'

He licked his finger and ran it down the horse's withers. When he held it up for Talos to see, it was stained a much brighter reddish orange.

'No amount of riding gets it out, sir, only brushing, 'cos it gets right down deep inside. But the point is, this here's fertile soil.' He shot his benefactor a broad and knowing wink. 'There's only one place within riding distance from here that's got orange soil. The Kedos Plain.'

The severity of the stranger's oath made him blink.

'Right,' the head groom said, rattling the dice. 'Let's see who Aphrodite smiles on this time round.'

Thirty-Two

Illuminated by a thousand shimmering flambeaux, acrobats tumbled and dancers swirled, magicians turned tricks and conjurors juggled, bards recited poetry to the strum of their lyre. Around the fountain house that mirrored the Shrine of Arethusa, the line of soldiers still maintained the picket line, but though their metal cheek plates gleamed with menace in the lamplight, their shields seemed more for resting on than for protection. It appeared the pitcher girls hadn't exactly given up their fight, but they were starting to sense that the hillsfolk hadn't left their lambs at risk just to watch a foul-mouthed slanging match. The lure of cockfights, mime and puppeteers was winning. Fame, they were discovering, was sadly short and fickle.

Pushing between a masked actor lacing a fake hunch on back and a satyr dressed in goatskins, Iliona was conscious of a weariness that went far beyond the physical. Everything was slipping through her fingers, hope fastest of all. She ached. She ached for Helice, and the manner of the death to which she had consigned her. She ached for Kyniska, heartbroken and grieving, as only mothers can. But most of all, she ached for baby Jason, growing up without a mother. A mother who had loved him far too well.

Beside the shrine, the little tent selling replicas of the city's patron goddess stood deserted. *Who wants a Lucky Arethusa now?* Who indeed? Thanks to Lysander, Syracuse believed it had been abandoned by its patron goddess – thrown to the wolves in every sense. A wolf with grey eyes and a smile that was colder than the Styx. Out beyond the marble portico, an old crone in stencilled robes offered spells and incantations in exchange for a full skin of wine (or even half), and a small boy abandoned his catch of turtles to watch a Nubian, his thick curls held in place by a yellow headband, juggling painted wooden globes.

I will not let you down, my lady. Roxana had all but saluted. *Sparta will not be disgraced, sir.*

His own sister. Even his own sister would think him a hero, when Sparta fell under the shadow of Athens...

Iliona felt a sadness in the boy's excitement. He was so engrossed with the juggler that he didn't see his turtles slithering back into the sea. And the crowds. So happy, so complete, so secure in their newly won democracy, yet so un-aware that change was round the corner. It would not be sudden, as it had been under Gelon the Tyrant. But day by day, season by season, they would gradually notice that prosperity was being sucked out. That control was sliding into the night, like those turtles. Athens was perfectly sincere in its belief that Greece would be better off under its Empire's control, and in financial terms, in terms of progress, science, even quality of life, maybe they were right. But it was like Jocasta said. Until you lose your freedom, you don't appreciate what you used to have.

'My lady? My lady, is that you?'

The golden hair, the big wide smile, the baby in her arms, they looked familiar and yet—

'Helice?'

'Oh, not you as well!' Blue eyes rolled. 'Why is it everybody looks at me as though they've seen a ghost?'

Iliona was speechless. 'We thought – I thought—'

'What? The Cyclops had gulped me down for supper?' Laughter bunched her cheeks into tight red apples. 'Did he kill Hyblon?'

'Of course not.'

'Then why should he kill anybody else?'

Time to shake some common sense into the girl. 'Helice, several young women have disappeared lately—'

'No disrespect, but this is a really busy port, in case you hadn't noticed. Girls go missing every year when the seas are open. Some run away, some elope with sailor boys, and some I'm sure come to sticky ends, but it's got nothing to do with Theo. Theo!' Her laughter echoed round the portico. 'Nice name for a cannibal, don't you think?'

This was no joke. 'The other night they found a large pool of blood beside the grotto—'

'It's them big hands, milady.' She didn't seem the least perturbed. 'He went up to shave, it

299

drives him mad, that stubble, once it starts to itch, and when he clenched his fist, he forgot the blade were in it. Nasty gash, it was, too. But he knows herbs to make it heal up fast and—'

'Helice, for heaven's sake—'

The laughter died from the young girl's eyes. 'Don't you dare to patronize me. I told you before, I ain't educated, but I ain't stupid either.' She transferred the sleeping infant to her other arm. 'You're the one who's a fool, and I told you that as well, because you can't see what's under your nose. It's small men who fight,' she snapped. 'Big men don't need to prove themselves, and you ask yourself how many big men have ever started wars.'

'I think you'll find that's more a question of proving superiority than strength.'

'Small bodies, small minds, what's the difference? Big men are rarely aggressive for the sake of it. And you've met him. Did he strike you as a monster?' She didn't wait for an answer. 'Did he strike you as the sort of bloke who goes round gutting women like a herring? Of course he bloody didn't.'

A storm had capsized her brother's fishing boat, she explained, so she chose a stone among the sepulchres where she could lay flowers and talk to his shade.

'And that's how I came to see him. He was hiding in the shadows, trying desperately not to be seen, but the moon was bright and that's how I could make him out. Just as I could see it wasn't no third eye in his forehead. And you know the odd thing?' Her lips pursed tight. 'Big as he was, he looked scared. Scared, and lost, and just ever so lonely.'

Having been betrayed every bit as deeply as the Cretan archers, Iliona was not surprised.

'So I retraced my steps, real quiet like, then came back up the path, singing and waving my flowers so he'd think well, if a mere girl weren't frightened of ghoulies and ghosties, he'd have nothing to worry about either.'

'That was a very brave thing to do.' Or stupid.

'What? I'm supposed to let my son grow up, knowing his mother has no compassion? Oh, no.' When she snapped her fingers, the baby woke up. She placed a kiss on his eyelid. Jason blew two bubbles then drifted straight off to sleep. 'I went up the next night, and again the big fella stepped back in the shadows, only this time I left sweet cakes for him on the stone. Honey, walnut, even wine cakes once.' The softness returned to her eyes. 'He has quite an appetite, does Theo.'

But not for blood, apparently. Iliona felt sick and stupid, tired and confused, as it all made terrible sense. The fact that every sign pointed to his guilt didn't mean he was responsible. Just as all the signs pointing at her own treachery did not make her a traitor. In not looking beyond the obvious, she had done Theo a terrible injustice, and there but for the grace of the gods a good man might have died. Because, she realized dully, orphaned, penniless, misunderstood and feared, this big mountain man truly had been the

301

loneliest person in the world. But above all her feelings of guilt and regret, Iliona felt the stirrings of hope.

'Where is he?' she asked.

'Safe from them dogs, that's for bloody sure!' Rocking the baby in her arms, her hair shone like corn silk in the flickering light. 'First, I took a skin of sheep-dip and poured that over him, to destroy any spoor, then I hid him somewhere safe—'

'Yes, but where?'

'It used to be a shepherd's hut before the gales tore the roof off, but trust me, my lady, no place is safer. It's where I used to tryst with Jason's father.'

'Can you take Jocasta there?'

'Not you?'

'I'm needed here. But Theo trusts her, and when she tells him it's safe to come into Syracuse, he'll believe her.' Finally, the gods had removed the blindfold from the eyes of Justice! Finally, Iliona could clear Sparta's name! 'One more thing. Does anyone else know Theo's hiding place?'

'My mother, but she won't tell a soul.'

Iliona breathed a sigh of relief.

'Oh, and that other Spartan, of course.' She smiled with the confidence only the youth can have. 'The one they call Lysander.'

'From the Great Burning Mountain
To the plains that spit mud
To the hills that fall into the sea.'

Helice's song floated softer than gossamer through Theo's brain. He thought of how her corn silk hair would gleam long and shiny in the moonlight. How her sweet, clear voice cut through the silence of the night, bringing life to that grim, dark metropolis of rotting flesh.

'Oh, isle of the gods,
Sweet isle of the Sicels,
I devote my whole being to thee.'

Even now, he thought he must be dreaming. Certainly, he hadn't meant to scare her last night among the tombs, but he had ached so long, so very long, for this lovely, fragile creature who brought flowers every night. He knew he had to stop. For his own sake, he must forget the sound of her light, bouncy step on the path. The memory of her singing. He was ugly. Mutilated. A freak. While she was everything he was not, and if she saw him, she would scream in terror, and honestly, who could blame her. All he'd wanted last night was to come close enough to smell the perfume of sweet lilies on skin. After that, aye, after that he would leave the City of the Dead and not come back. He owed it to himself.

'From the Great Burning Mountain
To the pastures and streams
Where the oxen of the sun god would graze.'

He must have made a noise, because suddenly
303

Helice spun round and there he was. Standing right behind her. But the weird thing was, she smiled. Smiled like she'd known him all her life.

Like he was a child, she fed him almond cakes and honeyed buns. Like he was a child, she sat beside him, her long hair sprawled across his lap so he could stroke it, even though he daren't. Some things were just too painful. But they had talked. Oh, how they had talked, and when dawn finally began to break, once more like a child she led him to this abandoned shepherd's hut, which she'd brightened up with herbs and flowers, and made a bed of straw for him in the corner.

'Oh, isle of the gods,
Sweet isle of the Sicels,
Let it be here where I end my days.'

Burying his head in his hands, Theo marvelled that such a depressing, empty world of dead bones and lifeless statues could bring such joy to a grown man's heart. And to his shame he'd allowed himself to be treated as a child, because he'd ached for her so long and to be this close to her was the best thing he'd ever known.

For it was Helice who made him put down the knife he'd held to his throat. Helice who convinced him that life was worth the living.

It was, he knew, as long as she was with him. So he came with her to this roofless hut, helped her clear away the stinking rat droppings and fill it with yellow pine ajuga, purple hyacinth and the soft, feathery leaves of wild fennel. When

304

she kissed his blue tattoo, he accepted it as the kiss a mother gives her child. But when she pressed her lips to his, there was nothing maternal in the gesture, and even less of the child in his response.

And in their union, a pact was sealed. Whatever hardship life may bring, they would see it through together. All the way. Which is why he'd sent her to search out the High Priestess who walked the winds of knowledge and tell her that he was ready, now, to make amends. With Helice by his side, Theo would never hide again.

The Cyclops was a smith. And proud of it.

Thirty-Three

With the sun dipping fast, Iliona needed to change into her ceremonial robes, if she was to command the respect of the crowd, Niobe and the City Council. As for what was required of her at the ceremony itself, Roxana had spent so much time with the attendants that Iliona only needed to follow her cue. Any anomalies she could dismiss as nerves, the newness of the job. So as she approached her bedroom, it flashed through her mind that maybe it was the festiveness of the full moon, or perhaps simply another of Tyche's whims, but the ball of fortune suddenly seemed to have been thrown for her to

305

catch. With Helice and Jocasta on their way to fetch Theo from the hills, things were looking up, she thought. And weren't they just.

Because there, standing right beside the window, was Lysander.

'I was getting worried about you,' he drawled. She believed him.

'No need.' She closed the door behind her with a flourish. 'I simply got carried away with the latest musical instruments. Have you seen them?'

She tossed her veil on to the chair and noticed that his long warrior's hair was no longer tied back in a queue. In his hand was a goblet of wine.

'There's something called a *barbitos* which is similar to the lyre but has longer strings and thus a lower pitch.'

'How interesting.'

'Isn't it? And a man from the orient had us totally enthralled with his row of stones set between a pair of metal bars. When he taps them with a copper rod, each resonates with a different note.'

'Hm.'

And with each sip that he took, the fatigue washed away until no trace of it remained in her body. 'Now, might I ask what this visit's in aid of?' she asked briskly. 'Or are the vultures simply starting to circle?'

'Never underestimate the value of vultures, Iliona. They're pacifists who clean the battlefield but never kill, although I'm not quite sure what carcass you expect me to be circling.'

'Well, for one thing, the King wishes to appoint his sister in my place and I'm assuming you don't disapprove of the substitution?'

Lysander refilled the goblet from the jug on the table and offered it across. She declined.

'Sparta's a wonderful paradox, don't you agree?' He rested his hip against the edge of the bed frame. 'It controls the balance of power over a thousand city states, yet confiscates silver and gold from its citizens and forcibly exchanges it for lead. But then,' he rubbed his temple as though it ached, 'it's not nations that are greedy, is it. Only individuals.'

'I gather you don't approve of the luxury within the King's palaces?'

'Don't I?' He moved to the window and leaned out. 'Our army stands by itself and the whole world knows our strength.' The breaths he drew were deep. 'But surely luxury is vital when it comes to entertaining foreign dignitaries? It promotes an aura of peace and prosperity, which I'd have thought was equally essential for maintaining the balance.'

Balance. The very core of Sparta's soul.

'Temples, on the other hand, now they're another matter,' he said. 'You've seen yourself the rich depositories at Delphi.'

'Every year they build another one to house the new donations, and every year a fortune is locked away inside that could have been used to help those who need it most.'

'Unlike Eurotas, where I'm told the High

307

Priestess turns the shrine yellow with gorse during the spring equinox and throws sumptuous feasts for any worshippers who wish to partake without charge.'

'Not any worshippers,' she reminded him sweetly. '*Helots* and *perioikoi*, if you please. The lowest, I think you called them, of the low.'

He winced, though whether from having his own words tossed back at him or from gulping down the last of the wine without thought to the dregs she didn't know.

'So the poorer they are, the more people need the reassurance of pomp and ceremony?'

Something glittered at the back of his mountain wolf eyes. She held his gaze. 'People are people, Lysander.'

'Which is why you promote yourself as the mouthpiece of Eurotas, of course. So you can interpret their dreams, set them riddles, read their auspices and generally put their troubled minds at ease, while all the time they believe you've brought their god close to them.'

'Sorry, are you now telling me that you think I serve Eurotas well?'

Hooking a stool across the floor, he rested his foot on it and leaned his weight on his knee. Just like he had when he'd been waiting for her that first day. 'Better than the High Priestess of Arethusa, who enjoys female emancipation so much that she refuses to share it with her fellow Syracusians.' When he ran his hands through his hair, she smelled leather and woodsmoke. The distinctive scent of treachery. 'And the pitcher

308

women would not have spoken to you the way they did to Niobe.'

'Ah, but I wouldn't have let the situation build up in the first place.'

'My point exactly. You walk the winds and look down on the actions of mortals.'

Iliona didn't realize she was chewing her nail until it snapped. 'What's your point, Lysander?'

The side of his face twisted as though in spasm. 'Well, it all goes back to people seeing what they're expected to see. That we're conditioned to believe the evidence laid before our eyes, particularly where sabotage is concerned – I say, is it hot in here?'

'A little.'

He moved to replace the empty goblet. It missed the table by several inches. 'Damn.' As he leaned down to retrieve it, his leg buckled. She watched comprehension dawn too late in his eyes.

'You're not the only one who can set a trap, Lysander.'

'C-can't kill m-me...'

He dropped to his knees, his bronzed hands clawing at the coverlet.

'Only the gods are immortal, but don't worry. This is just a little sedative.' She smiled. 'I had a feeling you'd drop by, so I took the precaution of drugging the wine. And my, my, weren't you the greedy boy.'

Glazed eyes turned on her as he slid towards the floor. 'B-bitch,' he rasped. 'B-b-b—'

Iliona waited until she was certain that he'd

309

lapsed into unconsciousness, then changed into her robes and secured her headdress with ivory pins.

The game wasn't over yet.

Thirty-Four

She could not have timed it better. As Iliona swept into the precinct from the left, so Niobe entered from the right, the procession accompanied by the beat of tambourines and enlivened by the clack of castanets.

'My dear, you look ravishing.' Niobe had not forgotten her earlier diatribe, but she had no intention of airing her dirty linen openly. 'Why, you look so radiant and happy that if I didn't know better, I'd say you'd had a man in your bedroom.'

For the first time in god knows how long, Iliona laughed. 'And here's me, thinking it was part of the hospitality.'

She was still smiling when she took her seat on the dais. Looking round, she saw that everything was silver and whereas before it stood for evil and betrayal, she now found herself revelling in its softness and generosity. From the flagstones shimmering in the moonlight to the bowls from which the lustrations were being poured, from the ceremonial robes that encased the celebrants to the froth of costumed children at her feet, she drew strength from it, and as the watery pair plunged into each other's arms, knew the circle that was broken trust was close to being whole.

'*The tributes Arethusa promised as a maid,*' Alys recited proudly, '*are by Alphaeus duly paid.*'

Iliona smiled. The flowers in her hair might have kinked over her eyes and her little robe might be caught up in her knicker cloth, but Alys was as proud as a petrel when she set her tribute of myrrh on the altar. Watching her scamper back down the steps, Iliona knew that the pair of puppies from the stable would go some way to compensate for the lack of human playmates. And who knows? Perhaps in time they might even rout poor Zygia!

'I'm going to call them Raven and Puddles,' Alys said, when Iliona took her down to pick them from the litter.

Raven, well, that was pretty obvious, the puppy was jet black. But: 'Don't you mean Cuddles?'

'Uh-uh.' A stubby finger jabbed in the direction of an ominous yellow pool. 'I mean *Puddles.*'

Watching Niobe straighten Alys's chaplet and tug the hem out of her knicker cloth, she thought, that's the beauty of this gift. No one, not even Niobe, scowling away at her with a face like thunder when she thought no one was looking, could confiscate another High Priestess's gift. Alys and her dogs would be together until she

311

cut her hair and put away her toys, and even then Fortune might bestow her husband with a soft spot for dogs.

Meanwhile, dancers wove meanders round the precinct to represent the lovers' chase. Torches of hawthorn were lit, symbolizing devotion and fertility. Virgins showered the altar with fruits, nuts and sweetmeats.

Jocasta hadn't said how long the drug would render Lysander unconscious, but he was strong and very fit. Would that affect its efficiency? By Iliona's calculations, Helice and the physician would be halfway to the abandoned hut by now. Was the drug strong enough to keep him out until they returned with Theo?

'...by the love that binds our deities,' Niobe shot her counterpart another acid glance, 'let us light candles that peace may come between them, that they may put their differences aside and heal their anger and their hurt—'

Iliona saw her opportunity. The instant Niobe wound up her speech, she swept from the dais, her robes billowing like a silver cloud behind her as she beckoned everyone to follow.

'I need a distraction,' she hissed to Silas, leading the way towards a tiny open shrine beyond the spring. 'And I need it to be a long one.'

As befitted the king of the gods, the shrine was carved from marble and wreathed with sacred oak into which gilded acorns had been set. Beads of frankincense crackled in the bowl, releasing intoxicating vapours into the night.

'Arethusa has just delivered a sermon about

312

love and emotion, so Alphaeus is going for the practical.' She poured a libation from the sacred phial while she whispered. 'I want you to recite stories about the elements. Anything you can think of that concerns earth, air, fire and water, only for gods' sake, draw it out.'

'Oh.' He gulped, blinked and bobbed simultaneously. 'Oh, Lady Iliona, what an honour.' He cleared his throat and faced the crowd. 'As a tree springs from the darkness of the soil and stretches up towards the sky—'

The change was astonishing. The nervousness vanished. His gestures became polished. His voice took on the tone of an orator's, and within seconds Silas had his audience spellbound. When she pulled Roxana behind the shrine, the crowd didn't even notice.

'What's the matter, my lady?'

In her ceremonial robes and spangled headdress, the girl had never looked more lovely. Iliona wished with all her heart there had been a better place and gentler way to break the news.

'Roxana, I'm sorry, but someone, someone within our group, is an Athenian agent.'

'With all due respect, my lady, I very much doubt it.'

'I didn't want to believe it, either, but Ly— the traitor doesn't see it as betraying his country. In his eyes, he's simply making the inevitable work to Sparta's advantage, once Athens has toppled the Confederacy and the King is out of the way.'

'Nonsense. Whatever happens politically, Sparta is still a democracy and the King and his

Council are elected members. Until their term is up, nothing on this earth can bring them down.'

'Unless I'm proved guilty of treason.'

Green eyes narrowed to hostile slits. 'You?'

'No, no, no. Someone just wants it to look that way.' This was harder than she thought. 'He undoubtedly murdered Chloris—'

'When you say undoubtedly, you mean you're not sure?'

'Well, no, but then there was Drakon—'

'That was an accident. In fact, my brother took great pains to reassure me on that score.'

'Which means you were suspicious.'

'Surprised,' Roxana corrected firmly. 'Drakon was a good soldier. Indeed, a careful soldier. But I assure you, Lysander wouldn't lie to me.'

'Then what about Phillip? His neck was broken, but not from the fall, and you don't need to take my word for it. Ask Jocasta, ask the temple mortician. Ask anyone with an ounce of medical knowledge to explain the technicalities of lividity.'

'Oh, for heaven's sake, the boy was looking to pocket a few trinkets and he slipped.'

'No, he didn't. Both those deaths were designed to appear accidental for the benefit of the Syracusians, but once we returned to Sparta, I can assure you that all this would be laid out as evidence of my treachery.'

'My lady, it's been a long day and you're tired—'

'Roxana, listen to me! Your brother already has proof that I'm a traitor because I've been helping deserters to escape.'

She all but recoiled. 'You? You helped deserters?'

'There isn't time to explain, you'll have to trust me that I've been set up. The point is, I'd be seen as the King's puppet on this mission, so you can forget democracy. The King and his entire Council would be swept aside, and Sparta would fall right into the pit alongside them.' She drew a deep breath and braced herself. 'That's why your brother watched me for so long. That's why he waited before calling in his debt. So he could—'

'That's a lie! That's a spiteful, wicked lie!'

'Is it? Lysander didn't pick this team for any individual skill sets. He chose you because you trusted him. So that Drakon would be standing in the wrong place at the wrong time and die in a hail of arrows. Because Phillip could pick any lock in the world, but he couldn't pick a traitor. Because Manetho—'

'*Manetho?*'

Croesus, it was like driving nails into the poor girl. 'Yes, Manetho. And he died because he couldn't believe that someone as honourable, as feared, and dare I say it as charming as your brother could be the seat of such immeasurable evil, either.'

'I don't believe you.' But her face was bloodless and her chin was wobbling. 'Lysander loves me, I'm his kin. He wouldn't kill me.'

'No, he wouldn't, but think about it for a minute. Has he ever asked you to do something on

315

this mission that struck you as odd? Out of character, perhaps?' Roxana's hesitation was proof enough. 'He's using that loyalty and love as weapons in his quest for personal power—'

'You're wrong.' She was blinking back the tears. 'You—'

'I have proof,' Iliona said. 'The smith who minted the coins that were planted on the archers. He's coming here to testify tonight.'

'If there was a witness, Lysander would have killed him.'

'He assumed his Athenian contacts already had, only they weren't smart enough to think of it. Look, I'm really sorry. I know how hard this has hit you, and I know how much you believe in him, but you must see that the only way I can clear my name and Sparta's is to expose Lysander, here, in front of everyone, tonight.' She paused. 'But for that I need your help.'

'You go to hell,' she sobbed.

Her face was so white, and she was shaking so badly, that Iliona's fears for her emotional recovery resurfaced with a vengeance. When you believe in a cause so unreservedly, when you've dedicated everything that's precious to it, the hole can often be too great to fill. She could only pray that Roxana would find salvation through abandoning that ridiculous idea of keeping her virginity to produce the babies she was so obviously longing for. In the meantime, though, there was a job to be done.

'You know I'm right,' she said quietly. If salt had to be rubbed into the wound, so be it. 'Deep

316

in your heart, you know everything I've said is true. The very fact you asked yourself those questions proves it.'

Tears were streaming down Roxana's face, and she'd bitten into her lower lip so deep that she'd drawn blood. And now that she'd broken the poor bitch, Iliona still needed to kick her while she was down.

'Right now, your brother is unconscious, but I can't be certain that the drug was strong enough to keep him out until the smith arrives. And since I'm required here, I need someone to guard him.'

'Why me? Why not Talos there? Why not—'

'Because he's in the women's quarters, for one thing, and because you swore an oath to serve your country for another.' She paused. 'Now will you do it?'

She waited for what seemed like eternity before Roxana's bowed head finally nodded. 'Yes,' she sniffed, 'I'll do it, but only until I've heard this coinsmith's testimony for myself. After that, I'm not making any promises.'

Nothing could be fairer, Iliona supposed, but could she trust her? This girl had looked up to Lysander all her life. She'd held him up as her example. The hero to end all heroes in her eyes. Could she honestly be trusted to stand beside her idol and not be taken in by his lies when he awoke? Could she hell.

'Whereabouts in the women's quarters will I find him?' Roxana asked.

Iliona glanced round the shrine. Silas was

reciting the story of the North Wind, imprisoned in a sack. Beside him, Talos tried without success to stifle a yawn. No one would miss her for a while.

'Come with me, I'll show you.'

She'd set aside a second phial for just such a contingency. No lies could sway Roxana while he slept.

'If there are any problems, wave a lamp across the window.' She lifted the latch on her bedroom door. 'I'll be able to see your signal from the precinct—'

Suddenly, an arm grabbed her and she was flying through the air. She landed face down on the floor. Turned. Just in time to see a vase come crashing down.

Thirty-Five

Light. There was nothing but light. White, bright, blinding, dazzling, there was nothing but the light. Then slowly, very slowly, its brilliance began to dim and was replaced by a throbbing deep inside her head. Through the mist, she saw Lysander, slumped on the floor where she had left him, a steady pulse beating in his throat. Not him, then, so who?

Other senses clawed their way towards the surface. She was seated. But when she tried to

318

lift her arm, it wouldn't move. Glancing down, she saw that her ceremonial gown had been cut into strips that bound her to the chair. Silver. Funny, she thought, how everything came back to bloody silver.

'Scream if you want.' Roxana's voice floated through the miasma of confusion. 'No one outside can hear above the trumpets and the drums, and there's no one in the palace to come running.'

Of course. Even the slaves were given the night off for the Festival. The kitchens were deserted, the corridors, the courtyards, even the stairwells and the stables. And what on earth made her think Roxana would blindly take Iliona's word?

'This really isn't necessary, you know.'

'Actually...' The redhead heaved her brother on to the bed and slapped his face to bring him round. Nothing. Not a stir. 'Actually, it is.'

With a sigh of resignation, she plumped the pillows beneath his head, then made herself comfortable beside him. In her hand was the dagger that Iliona kept strapped to her calf.

'You see, I love Sparta,' Roxana said dreamily. 'I love its hills, its valleys, its rivers, its cliffs. I love every inch of its soil. But,' she stared at a spider crawling down the wall, 'there's a wind of change blowing across my beloved snow-capped peaks, and in the same way that the act of love renders a strong man weak in its aftermath, so Sparta has grown weak under the harlot who masquerades as Peace.'

319

Oh, for goodness sake, what rubbish had he been feeding her!

'Our army is the strongest in the world,' Iliona pointed out. 'Our economy has gone from strength to strength.'

She might as well have saved her breath.

'Athens, now. Athens hasn't been seduced by peace. It swings its broadsword across the map, and any who stand in its way fall like trees in a tempest. Incidentally, I don't know why you bother carrying this puny little thing.' She tossed Iliona's dagger in the air and caught it. 'Hardly better than a toy.'

Bending down with the grace and agility that Iliona so admired, she wedged its blade between the floorboards and snapped it clean in half.

'See? Useless. Absolutely useless.' She un-sheathed a jagged hunting knife from beneath her robe. 'Whereas this. This knife means business.'

When she placed her lips against it, something slithered in Iliona's stomach. Too late, she realized it was Truth. That Roxana hadn't been shedding tears of pain, they were tears of laughter. That she'd bitten into her lower lip to stop it breaking out.

'Not that Manetho had his mind on business, I might add. Too busy gawping at my naked breasts, but what fools men are, eh? One pert little nipple and — ' She clicked her fingers. 'Dis-tract them, despatch them, so painfully simple. Where was I?'

She tossed the broken dagger through the window. Iliona heard it clatter on the cobbles a thousand miles away.

'Oh, yes, while Greece remains divided, it remains deadlocked, with neither side moving forward. War is not an option, which really only leaves stealth as the battering ram to break down the wall.'

'Hardly breaking it down. You're opening the gates so the enemy can walk right in!'

Not a warrior with long hair that an anxious mother saw entering the temple on the night that Phillip died. A woman in a warrior's kilt.

'Once we're working together, they cease to be the enemy, because don't you see? Between us, the whole world is ripe for the taking. Carthage, Judea, Assyria, Egypt, nothing can stand in our way.' Roxana gave her brother's arm an affectionate squeeze. 'And what finer man to lead Sparta in this brand new order.'

Oh, yes. With the King disgraced, the Council fallen, a hero in the mould of Leonidas would be called for. Step forward the Head of the *Krypteia*.

'You make a wonderful team,' she said bitterly.

'Indeed. I mean, that wife of his?' Roxana snorted. 'Lifted her skirts for every man who so much as smiled at her.'

Iliona tried to remember what he'd said. 'He didn't divorce her, though.'

'No, but it's easy enough to find drugs that induce an after-birth haemorrhage, because who ever questions a child's curiosity—'

'*You* murdered her?'

'I prefer to think of it as matrimonial assistance, and anyway it's not as though the spawn was his. It was no worse than—' She leaned up and pressed the spider to the plaster with her thumb – 'squashing a bug.'

Iliona blinked. 'Had you no compassion when the boy died?'

'Well, obviously I did. For Lysander.' She waited for the impact to sink in. 'The little bastard was starting to look more like his real father every day, and I couldn't have people sniggering, now could I? Snakes are such *pliable* weapons.'

An expression flickered over Roxana's face that was almost serpent-like itself.

'I have discovered something, Iliona. I have discovered the excruciating pleasure of watching a person trapped between life and death ... Now can you begin to imagine what goes through their head?'

She slid off the bed and advanced across the room.

'First, bewilderment. *Why me, why me, oh why poor little me?* Followed by disbelief. *There's a way out of this, I just have to find it.* Which there isn't, of course. I am nothing if not thorough.'

How true, and no wonder the colour had drained from her face and her strong chin had wobbled. She feared she'd been found out and was about to be exposed. But who was there to know? Even in the pitiless world of politics, where strategy is played out like a board game and people are merely chess pieces, where

322

deception is the norm and double standards are expected, who would question the honour of this solemn young woman who had sacrificed any prospect of motherhood to the State?

'You know, Drakon was speechless when I told him I wanted to give my precious virginity to him. Too excited, even, to question our meeting place. And Manetho was no better. So transfixed by his penis, poor lamb, he didn't see the knife that punctured his heart – well, not until it came out. Which was this knife, incidentally. If you're interested.'

She levelled its point at Iliona's eye.

'It's the same with you, my beautiful priestess. Surprise, shock, that exquisite moment when you realize how stupid you've been. And let's face it. You have been very stupid.'

She began to stroke Iliona's eyelashes with its tip.

'Which brings us to what you're feeling right this minute. Weighing up what you could have done, what you should have done, but, um ... didn't.' She let out a long and satisfied sigh. 'Our boys, the smith, that charlatan physician. Quite a pile of corpses to your credit.'

'Theo and Jocasta are still alive.'

'Only until they reach the bridge, where I'll be waiting for them. So when Lysander eventually stirs, he'll need no further proof that you were indeed the traitor in our midst.'

'You mean he doesn't *know*? You ... you're not in this together?'

'Ah yes, that's the next stage. Fear. The

unadulterated terror as realization finally dawns. Any minute now, you'll burst into tears, plead for your life, wet yourself, and oh, it's humiliating, isn't it? Though, if it's any consolation, you won't be the first, only for goodness sake, please don't start on that we-can-be-friends routine. If I've heard that speech once, I've—'

She could barely concentrate. Nothing mattered, except that steel point stroking her eyelashes. 'Lysander knows I'm not the traitor.'

'But you are! You lured Drakon into the clearing. You showed Phillip where to find a few pretty trinkets. For pity's sake, you even brought your *helot* along. The bitch who brews death for a living.' Roxana clucked her tongue in sympathy. 'Now agreed, Lysander might not have *expected* you to be behind the betrayal, but he *does* know you tried to poison him.'

'He'll wake up.'

'Indeed he will, and guess what? The first sound he hears will be my scream, as I discover you trying to kill him after the first dose didn't work. The second sound, of course, will be your death rattle.'

'Quite the heroine, aren't you?'

'A man of Lysander's standing needs a wife he can be proud of.'

'Wife?' Iliona flinched at the coldness of the blade against her eyelid. 'For gods' sake, you're his sister.'

'Zeus married Hera and together they rule heaven. Tell me that's a bad alliance.'

'Lysander won't want anything to do with you.

324

Not now you've lied to him.'

The knife retreated faster than a whiplash. 'I've never lied to him.'

'You told him Sparta wouldn't be disgraced.'

'Thanks to me, it will be bigger, stronger, better than before.'

She struggled to break free, but the more ferocious her fight, the tighter the knots. 'What about that business of dedicating your virginity to the State?'

'What's your point? Lysander is the State, and there's no point in squirming, by the way. I learned that knot from the helmsman of the *Tyche*. It works on the same principle as a noose.'

'Has it occurred to you that Lysander might not want the job?'

'A country in chaos is in need of a champion. My brother will rise to the occasion.' Roxana looked across to where his chest rose and fell on the bed. 'But not for a little while, I fear, so in the meantime, I think I'll do what I always do when I have people powerless and totally under my control.' Her fingers began to stroke Iliona's throat. 'I'm going to have some fun.'

Watching despair cloud those big, blue eyes, the Serpent writhed in pleasure. Women. Such perfidious creatures. From the dawn of time they'd set out to deceive. Medea, betraying her father for her lover, then killing her own children. Queen Helen, abandoning Sparta and her husband for a pretty Trojan boy. Even the beautiful

325

Pandora, who opened the box and released every known evil into the world.

Lysander had had first-hand experience of perfidy. His wife made him wear the cuckold's horns, but, luckily for him, his baby sister was on hand. While he was risking his life to serve his country, she was settling scores at home, and now, with her at his side, Lysander would never know deceit again. She pictured him riding shoulder-high through the crowd. A hero. Sparta's saviour in its darkest hour. She saw the brood of children she and he would raise together.

Oh, how happy they'd all be.

'How does it feel, Iliona?' Roxana watched the knots on her struggling victim bite into her skin. 'Knowing no one's going to come looking for you, least of all Niobe, since you've already set a precedent for swanning off. And here you are, without a knife. In fact, without as much as a hairpin to stab in your defence, while all the time the straws you're clutching are slipping through your fingers one by one.'

'Why don't you crawl back underneath the stone you came from?'

She laughed. 'That's a Spartan for you. Always goes down fighting. But you don't fool me, my lady. For all the force of your struggle, there's an emptiness behind your eyes. Phillip, Manetho, that ugly mutant smith, it's all there for me to read. You've let your country down and, oh dear me, you even think you've failed my brother.'

'No, Roxana, you've done that.'

'And you're wishing, why couldn't this bitch have resorted to physical torture? Why this awful gloating? Well, I'll tell you, Iliona. You'd have probably withstood pain, but this. This is where it hurts the most. Inside. Corroding you like acid, knowing everything's been washed away. Hope, faith, optimism, call it what you like, they amount to the same thing, don't they? Which is nothing.'

By heaven, this *was* fun. Maybe a point to bear in mind next time, although not with the smith or that sour *helot*. Speed would be of the essence with those two. But afterwards, once the team was safely back in Sparta, she could work on her technique. After all, no warrior goes into battle without practice.

'Oh, my, what's this?' She wiped the tear from Iliona's cheek and tasted its salt on her tongue. 'A sign of weakness at long last. How sweet.'

Across the room, Lysander fought his way to consciousness with a groan. Pity, because she was enjoying this, but then all good things come to an end, she supposed. And in Iliona's end there was a new beginning.

'He's coming round,' she said, picking Iliona up, chair and all, and depositing her beside the stirring figure. 'Time for milady's death rattle, I believe.'

'Indeed it is,' a cultured voice murmured from behind.

Roxana felt her head jerked back. Metal flashed. There was a gurgle. Then a hiss...

Talos stepped over Roxana's twitching body as though it wasn't there. On his tunic, Iliona noticed rose petals from where he'd scrambled up through the window. Except the rose was white, she thought, whereas these were red and dripping. She wanted to say something – no, actually she wanted to burst out laughing, but her teeth were chattering, so she cried instead.

'I hope you've got a good excuse for missing the Festival finale,' Talos said, slicing gently through the knots. 'It's already a national scandal, the amount of time you spend in this bed with Lysander.'

Thirty-Six

In the courtyard scented by pomegranates and where fig trees scrambled against the white-washed walls, the High Priestess of the river god Eurotas stared up at the night sky.

A month had passed. The full moon over Syracuse slowly ebbed away into nothingness, taking with it secrets, lies and any hopes that Athens might have for world domination. At least for the time being.

In the end, there was no dramatic, public exposure. Only a long and sometimes bitter conference between the members of the City

Council and Sparta's gravel-voiced envoy, backed up by the evidence of a lumbering mountain man, who looked like he needed a razor over the rest of his body, not just his face. During this debate, apologies were both offered and accepted, even though it fooled no one. Both sides knew the rhetoric was nothing but a superficial dressing to patch over a wound that ran deep, would take a long time to heal and even then would leave scars.

All the same, as the old moon faded, a new one took its place. A diplomatic mission headed by none other than the King himself had set off only yesterday to win back the Confederacy's trust. It didn't hurt, of course, that he had shipped two boatloads of horses to graze the Kedos Plain, since from Macedonia to the Cyclades, no self-respecting charioteer would drive a team of four that hadn't been raised in Spartan paddocks.

But that moon, too, had reached its peak. The Pleiades were rising, the signal for the soil around the vines to be forked over and the first hay to be cut. Right across the Peloponnese, there was rejoicing. Men dressed up in goatskins to ride the May Queen Moon. More wine was drunk than was good for anyone, and no doubt the cloak-maker's wife would be at death's door again tomorrow. Indeed, Iliona had already set the riddle. Such festivals were a necessary release after weeks of backbreaking labour, and she watched the pinpricks that were their bonfires flickering along the banks of the river in the distance, or up in the hills around the edges of the woods. But none of the laughter and singing carried down to the shrine. Here, the night was warm and still. Only the occasional white swoop of a barn owl cut across the blackness, or maybe the ghost of a deer, come down to drink. Yet, as Iliona picked her way towards the deep, dark pool that was the haunt of the demon, she swore she could smell woodsmoke. And yes, the faintest hint of leather.

'Well, well. If it isn't the Lady of the Lake.'

He rose from where he'd been sitting, cross-legged, on the Rock of Contemplation and bowed. She wondered how long he'd had to wait.

'What do you want?' she asked.

'And they say the art of small talk is dying out,' Lysander murmured.

Watching his oiled skin reflected in the pool, the way his warrior's hair fell around his shoulders and the tunic that was embroidered with the *lambda*, she mused that the Head of the *Krypteia* wore no armour, but was dressed for war just the same.

'I'm perfectly capable of making polite conversation. For instance, I felt sure you'd be halfway to Syracuse by now.'

Lysander's nose wrinkled and twisted. 'It seems we have a King who not only feels my skills in the diplomacy department need refining, but who also hasn't quite forgiven me for talking him out of meeting with Periander when this business blew up.'

'Talk him out of it be damned!' Sparta had

330

treasury officials, civil servants, documents and records coming out of its ears, all proving without question that it hadn't minted that bloody silver. 'What did you do, suggest you knew where the bodies were buried?'

'Oh, Iliona. Surely you must realize by now that I always know where the bodies are buried.'

'So where did you bury Roxana's?'

Something crossed those measureless eyes. And as quickly, it was gone. 'Providing it's not contaminating Spartan soil, who cares.'

You do, she thought. That day in her bedroom, when she put on that ridiculous pretence about more members of the team dying unless he abandoned the mission, she'd told him the gods would hold him personally responsible.

You, he'd whispered, leaning close. *You have no idea.*

Every time we confront death, no matter how often, a piece of ourselves dies as well.

She thought he was passing it off as words of comfort meant for her.

The Krypteia *will be poorer without Phillip*, he had added with what she realized now was grief. *That boy could steal a shadow.*

'You knew, didn't you? You knew it was Roxana all along?'

In the moonlight, she saw his jaw clamp. 'Suspected is a better word, and like I told you on board the *Tyche*. No side ever really trusts the other.'

'Pity you forgot to mention that I was the bait.'

She thought he'd set Roxana to guard her,

331

when in fact Iliona was the live goat in his nasty little trap.

'I'd rather hoped it wouldn't come to that.' He stared up at the constellations twinkling above. The Great Bear. The Little Bear. The Dragon. 'In fact, I went to great lengths to inveigle myself with an Athenian double-agent, who promised to deliver me my traitor for a price. Unfortunately, he got greedy. He turned back again and ... Well.' He clucked his tongue. 'She disembowelled him, would you believe. Very messy. Very slow.'

At the beginning, with no one to confide in and nobody to help her, Iliona had believed herself the loneliest person on the planet. Then Theo came along. Feared, misunderstood and a pariah, he'd stolen that dubious honour. But now, listening to the croak of frogs around the margins and the rasp of night crickets in the trees, she began to see that, in a game where every player was either king-maker or dissenter, enemy or ally, Lysander would always walk alone.

'Which is where Talos came in,' he added slowly. 'Remember I told you he had special skills that would come in handy, should the cheese fight turn dirty.'

Iliona thought back to when Talos was cutting through the last of her bonds. How on earth did he know where to find her? she had asked. Or know she was in danger? A single eye had glittered through his fringe as he drew her broken dagger from his belt. He'd been following Roxana, he explained, only it seemed the *Krypteia* had trained her far too well. She'd proved amazingly effective at giving him the slip, and at the Festival, among so many people, it was even easier. But then he saw a light in Iliona's window. A broken knife lying on the flagstones. Classic *Krypteia* tactic, to render your opponent's weapon useless.

'So his job was to shadow Roxana and confirm your suspicions?'

'No.' Lysander lobbed a boulder into the pool and watched long after its ripples had disappeared. 'His job was to kill her.'

Big man, strong man, ruthless head of Sparta's feared and hated Secret Police and decorated hero. But also big enough to know he didn't trust himself to kill his baby sister. And strong enough to know it must be done.

Iliona swallowed. 'Roxana was completely misguided in her beliefs, but in her heart she loved you, she really did.'

He stood stiller than a statue, but a pulse beat at the side of his throat, a life-force in its own right.

'My sister had no heart,' he said at length.

Iliona walked across the rock to the pool's edge. Saw her reflection moonlit in its sluggish waters. 'So if you're not here to explain and you're not here to apologize, why did you come?'

'Hm.' He scratched at his jaw. 'As to the first part of your question, you have to ask, what's the point, since you know the answers anyway. And as for the second, apologies are meaningless. Just look at me and Periander.'

333

'So why, then?'

He paced the rock with measured tread and didn't smile. 'The fact remains that you conspire against the laws of your own country.'

Iliona felt the fury rise. 'You gave me your word that the slate would be wiped clean once I fulfilled my obligations. Or doesn't saving the Confederacy and Sparta's reputation count?'

'More than you will ever know, and that's the point. Spartans are proud, Spartans are brave, but most of all, Iliona, Spartans are perfect.' He paused to turn his fathomless grey stare on her. 'There is no place in our society for weak or mis-shapen babies. Or, I regret, anyone who saves them.'

He was bluffing. Other city states exposed their unwanted children on the mountain sides, but here it was the Council of Elders who decided who should live and who should die. They who also served the execution.

'Rejected infants are tossed over a cliff,' she retorted. 'There's no possibility of saving them.'

'Hm.' From inside his tunic he withdrew a piece of webbing. The type commonly used to trap game birds in the woods. 'Someone seems to have rigged up a safety net over the ravine.'

Iliona said nothing.

'While it cannot be a coincidence,' he murmured, 'that a disproportionate number of sickly babies have been born to *helots* and *perioikoi* of late. And to women who were previously believed to have been barren.'

She considered how the State was in no way

334

weakened from the adoption procedures she had instigated. Now contrast that with the blackmailer, feeding off his victim's fears and exploiting their vulnerability while offering no guarantees at the end.

'What do you want?'

'I want you to continue with what you've been doing. Walking the winds and looking down on the actions of mortals – oh, not literally, of course. But like seers and bards who are universally blind, it's not a physical loss of sight that they lack.'

No. Their blindness was a metaphor for the fact that poets and such like looked inwards and were thus blind to what went on around them.

'You see beyond the person and you read what drives them, Iliona. It is not their dreams that you interpret, but their character. You see the real person that is revealed through actions, speech, their mannerisms, even, dare I say it, their lies.'

'I wouldn't say I read Roxana with any great accuracy. Or you, for that matter.'

'For a beginner, though, you show remarkably good promise. You will serve the *Krypteia* well.'

'You really are a bastard.'

'Like Helice's son, some are born that way, but me,' a muscle twitched in his cheek, 'I'm a self-made man.'

She clasped her hands in front of her. 'Lysander—'

'Save your breath. If I'd left you in any position to bargain, I would not have been doing my job.'

335

She unclasped her hands. Ran them down the pleats of her robe.

'So until I can be sure I can trust you,' he whispered, 'or indeed until I am sure that I can't, there isn't anyone in Sparta who will be of better use to me.'

And suddenly he was gone. Swallowed up by the night, invisible, hated, feared and despised, but always, yes always, watching. Watching, and holding her prisoner.

But as she stood before the demon, Iliona saw her father's daughter reflected in the waters. From the folds of her gown, she withdrew a small scarlet seed with a black spot, like an eye. This was her insurance policy. She had stolen it from Jocasta's medicine chest on board the *Tyche* and by chance, Lysander had discovered it by her bedside in her room. Luckily, he didn't recognize it for what it was.

For it was death.

And the beauty of it was, next time, when he came calling, he wouldn't even feel the scratch.